REC'D JUN 1 4 2021

NO TY OF
SE RARY

D0975193

NO
SE

RURAL VOICES

RURAL WORKS

RURAL
VOICES

15 AUTHORS CHALLENGE ASSUMPTIONS ABOUT SMALL-TOWN AMERICA

edited by

NORA SHALAWAY CARPENTER

CANDLEWICK PRESS

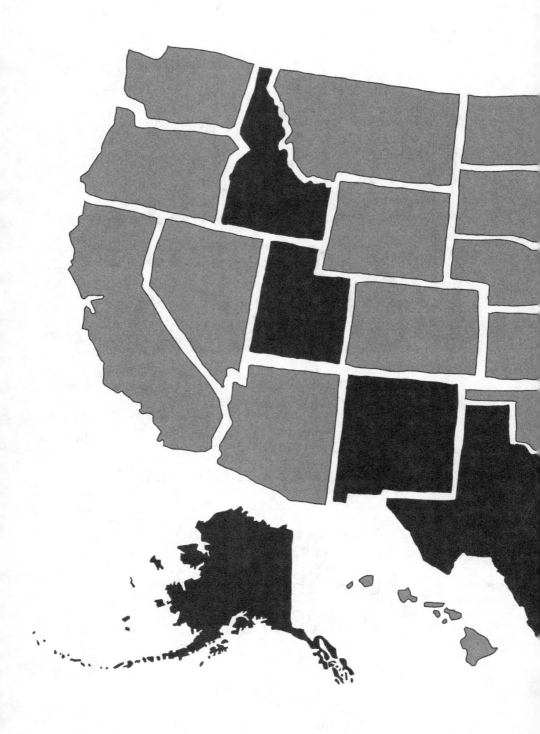

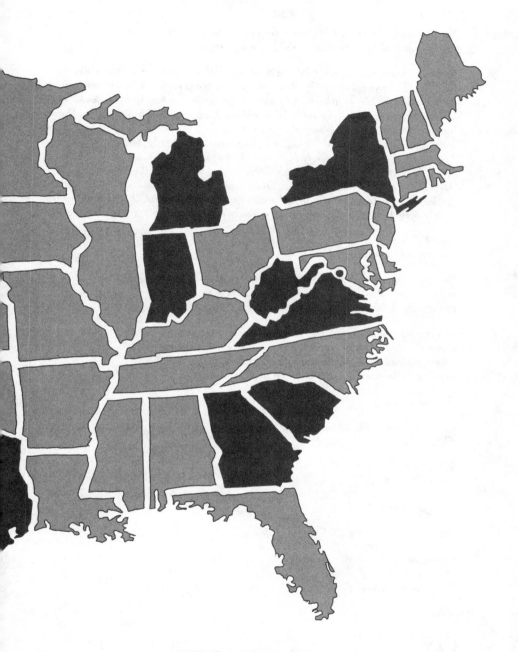

STATES FEATURED

Alaska * Georgia * Idaho * Indiana * Michigan * New Mexico
New York * South Carolina * Texas * Utah * Virginia * West Virginia

Names, characters, places, and incidents in the fictional pieces in this book are either products of the authors' imaginations or, if real, are used fictitiously.

Compilation and introduction copyright © 2020 by Nora Shalaway Carpenter * "The (Unhealthy) Breakfast Club" copyright © 2020 by Monica Roe * "The Hole of Dark Kill Hollow" copyright © 2020 by Rob Costello * "A Border Kid Comes of Age" copyright © 2020 by David Bowles * "Fish and Fences" copyright © 2020 by Veeda Bybee * "Close Enough" copyright © 2020 by Nora Shalaway Carpenter * "Whiskey and Champagne" copyright © 2020 by S. A. Cosby * "What Home Is" copyright © 2020 by Ashley Hope Pérez * "Island Rodeo Queen" copyright © 2020 by Yamile Saied Méndez * "Grandpa" copyright © 2020 by Randy DuBurke * "Best in Show" copyright © 2020 by Tirzah Price * "Praise the Lord and Pass the Little Debbies" copyright © 2020 by David Macinnis Gill * "The Cabin" copyright © 2020 by Nasugraq Rainey Hopson * "Black Nail Polish" copyright © 2020 by Shae Carys * "Secret Menu" copyright © 2020 by Veeda Bybee * "Pull Up a Seat Around the Stove" copyright © 2020 by Joseph Bruchac * "Home Waits" copyright © 2020 by Estelle Laure

Excerpt of letter from Millicent Rogers to her son Paul on page 286 courtesy of Millicent Rogers Museum, Taos, NM.

Every effort has been made to obtain permission from the relevant copyright holders and to ensure that all credits are correct. Any omissions are inadvertent and will be corrected in future editions if notification is given to the publishers in writing.

All rights reserved. No part of this book may be reproduced, transmitted, or stored in an information retrieval system in any form or by any means, graphic, electronic, or mechanical, including photocopying, taping, and recording, without prior written permission from the publisher.

First edition 2020

Library of Congress Catalog Card Number pending
ISBN 978-1-5362-1210-5

SHD 25 24 23 22 21 20
10 9 8 7 6 5 4 3 2 1

Printed in Chelsea, MI, USA

This book was typeset in ITC Esprit and Halewyn.

Candlewick Press
99 Dover Street
Somerville, Massachusetts 02144

www.candlewick.com

A JUNIOR LIBRARY GUILD SELECTION

To anyone who's ever felt "less than"

NSC

INTRODUCTION

Dear Reader,

When I was growing up, my family traveled a lot, a perk of having a parent who took on freelance travel-writing assignments. I was seven years old when, on one such trip, an adult I'd just met cracked a joke about me. In response to learning I was from West Virginia, the person wondered how that could be—because I still had all my teeth.

There was a pause, and young me realized I was supposed to laugh. To join the "fun." I don't remember what the person looked like or whether we were in an airport or a fast-food restaurant. But the smallness that comment instilled in me—the idea that I should feel shame because of where I lived—*that* I remember to this day.

Unfortunately, this was only the first of many ugly West Virginia stereotypes I'd encounter. I spent most of my childhood and young adulthood internalizing shame about where I was from and trying to reconcile my lived experiences with the almost universally negative and simplistic portrayal of rural people on TV and in other popular media. I grew accustomed to casual jabs about my background and learned not to mention it. On the occasional times I did challenge those jabs—when I managed to communicate some version of *What you're saying doesn't match my reality and it also insults many people I love*— my experiences were seen as exceptions to the rule, not proof of its invalidity.

This reaction depressed me, but it didn't surprise me. After all, for most of America's history, rural people and culture have been casually mocked, stereotyped, and, in general, deeply misunderstood. But then 2016 happened. In the months following the presidential election, rural people became something of a media obsession. Derogatory remarks about rural Americans became increasingly prevalent and intense. Over and over again, people outside the rural experience tried to understand and explain the rural narrative. Over and over again, the story of a rural monolith—a uniform, like-minded population that shares the same beliefs, value system, identities, and political leanings—was told and accepted as truth.

Because this is a foreword and not a political-science or economics article, all I'll say here is that yes, I saw the electoral maps like everyone else, but those visuals don't tell anywhere close to the whole story. However, in the eyes of most Americans, it seemed, there was only the monolith.

I was done with the monolith.

Rural Voices emerged as a counterpoint to that harmful narrative and the hurtful idea that accompanies it—that "rural" equates with "less than." Being rural is deeply embedded in many people's identities, but it is definitely not a punch line.

As I began envisioning this anthology and the authors who might want to contribute, the slipperiness of the "rural" label became more and more apparent. Some townships and unincorporated areas are technically (according to mailing address) classified as part of larger towns, but due to the reality of geography, the residents' lifestyles are vastly different from those of the people living in the towns' centers. Some areas, while tiny in population, are nonetheless major tourist attractions and posh vacation hot spots. Does that somehow negate their rural status?

The nature of this project did require some kind of *rural* definition, and so, for the purposes of this collection, it is this: *Rural* refers to belonging to a community consisting of ten thousand people or fewer that is a significant driving distance from an urban area. Contributors either grew up in rural communities or lived in one long enough at some point to self-identify as a rural American.

The fifteen authors whose work you're about to read are diverse in ethnic and cultural background, sexual orientation, rural geographic location, physical ability, and socioeconomic status. You'll find powerful new voices alongside award-winning, established authors. Still, this collection portrays only a fraction of the innumerable experiences and voices that compose rural America. And that, indeed, is the point: *There's not just one type of rural.*

These stories will transport you all over the United States and into the lives and hearts of the characters who inhabit them. In Virginia, you'll solve a mystery and right a wrong.

You'll roam the arctic tundra of Alaska and meet the ghosts of a mountain town in New Mexico. In New York, you'll discover a hollow's powerful, dark secret, and you'll be invited to pull up a seat and learn of real-life experiences that bloomed into poetry. You'll navigate a private school in South Carolina and learn to speak your truth. You'll walk—painfully—down cracked Indiana sidewalks. In Georgia, you'll take a life-altering bus ride in one story; in another, you'll find a forest that makes you remember who you are. In Idaho, you'll discover the secret menu of a small restaurant and, later, how speaking up can shatter barriers. You'll find fear and freedom in East Texas and political—and personal—unrest in a Texas border town. You'll climb trees in West Virginia and visit a county fair in Michigan. In Utah, you'll experience a teen's struggle to bridge two very different parts of her identity. Every one of these places is rural; yet every one is its own unique universe.

Just as there's no one uniform rural place, there's no one kind of rural teen, either. The teenagers in these pieces range from amateur sleuths and academic scholarship winners to marching-band members and rodeo queen hopefuls. They are pig farmers and writers, artists and restaurant servers. They navigate relationships, bigotry, and their own identities. Some are popular. Some are misfits. They love their hometowns and hate them, sometimes both at once.

Rural Voices defies the idea of a rural monolith, over and over, with every story. It seeks to change the conversation. To offer new narratives and ways of viewing the incredible people who make up rural America, the people who are so often misunderstood, made fun of, and maligned, who are overlooked or even outright ignored. The short stories, poetry, graphic short stories, personal essay, and author anecdotes in these pages dive deep into the complexity and diversity of rural America and the people who call it home.

Whether your own experience is rural or not, I hope you find something of yourself in these pages—and more than a few somethings that surprise you.

Thank you for reading,

Nora Shalaway Carpenter

The (Unhealthy) Breakfast Club
MONICA ROE

Interstate 95 slices our state north to south like a crooked scar. Far from cities and college towns and the sprawling beach houses of the coast, I-95 cuts through swampland and cotton country, peanut fields and poultry farms and whistle-stop railroad towns that were poor even before the textile mills all tucked tail and left.

The rural counties clustered along I-95 are nicknamed the Corridor of Shame. I don't know who first called us that, but every few years, some politician visits to make a point about education failures and how "our children deserve a better chance." They bring camera-toting reporters who click dozens of pictures of leaky roofs, busted floor tiles, thirty-year-old textbooks, and desks shored up with a cinder block or two—and maybe a couple of our trophy cases or the framed awards from kids who've placed in the statewide art competition. Once in a while some college research team will come meet with teachers and principals for a couple days. Then a big article comes out, full of terms like "pilot project," or "structural inequality," or "generational poverty."

Then things stay pretty much the same until a few years later, when the whole thing starts all over again.

The internet works best before seven a.m.

But you got to get online first to grab the best bandwidth. I have a video-based assignment due today, so I make Dad leave extra early.

"You trying to kill an old codger, Gracie?" he jokes around a yawn, gulping his coffee as the Golden Arch (half has been burned out forever) appears through the 6:09 a.m. fog. He's just messing—we tried to stream my assignment last night using his phone but gave up after getting kicked off exactly thirteen times.

Broadband, y'all. Some counties just don't know how good they got it.

But the McDonald's at the crossroads of Route 64 and State Highway 125 has a decent signal—if you can get here super-late or super-early. This, plus its location, makes it the logical meet-up for our morning carpool.

"I'll make it up to you," I promise as I gather my stuff and climb out of the pickup. "When I'm rich and famous, we'll get you into the nicest nursing home in the Carolinas."

"With a good bass pond, please," he calls out the window as he leaves.

Inside, I say hi to the morning-shift ladies and order hot cocoa. The only other customers are a pair of loggers too busy scarfing McMuffins to have their phones out. The wi-fi is mine.

It was Ms. Dorothy who clued me in about the back-corner-booth sweet spot. "Router's in the office, sugar," she told me one morning, pointing with one hand and ringing up my order with the other. "Other side of the wall. Sit right there, it's streaming city."

Today, she winks, sticks an apple pie and some hash browns into a bag, and gives it to me. Breakfast in hand, I claim the booth, slide over into the far corner, and get to work. Finals start in less than two weeks, and we've got tons to finish first, so it's not long before the others trickle in. I hear Aquandre' arrive without even looking—his old Ram's needed a new exhaust probably since it was his granddaddy's. Alternator, too, I'd say.

"Morning, G3," he says, and sits down across from me. "See you snagged the sweet spot. Well done."

"Boots," I reply, shoving my books over to make room. "You're looking extra shiny today." I nod at his gold-stitched scarlet-and-cream boots. "Should've brought my sunglasses." We're more what you'd call friendly now than actual friends, but our first-grade nicknames still fit, since all three of my names (Grace Glory Geiger) still start with *G* and he still loves fancy cowboy boots. Boy's big stuff on the local junior rodeo circuit, if you like that sort of thing.

Zeke's next, catching a ride in on his dad's logging truck, which is headed to the pulp mill with a full load. Aquandre' goes over to hold the door, and I bite back a laugh as his fancy-booted feet have to dance a bit to avoid Zeke's fly-by wheels.

"Well met, fellow sojourners!" Zeke sings, like we're meeting at a plank table in some medieval tavern instead of a dingy plastic McDonald's booth.

I grab my cocoa to keep it from spilling as he flies over and lets the table stop his wheelchair for him, but we're used to Zeke's speed factor by now, so I just say hi and keep working. Zeke pulls out one of his thick-as-a-doorstop fantasy novels—he probably finished all his internet assignments from now until finals during his one study hall. I bet Zeke could write a ten-page paper in his sleep and get an A+, which just isn't fair. One day we'll see him on the news for discovering a new planet.

Or for pulling a midnight break-in at Disney World to try and set some magical creatures free.

Either way, I've learned far more than I ever wanted about the Mystical Realms of Wherever since we all started riding together. I half-expect Zeke to come in some morning wearing a cloak and a sword.

Florecita arrives last, which means she had to get her little brothers over to her abuela's first. She says hi to her aunt, who's manning the fryers, and Aunt Inez slips her a bulging bag and a huge coffee before ducking back to get orders up for a crowd of boot-stomping loggers.

Flor comes over and thumps the bag onto our table. "Brain fuel." She sits, pops in her earbuds, and fires up her old tablet. Flor doesn't mess around when it comes to schoolwork.

"Lembas bread and butterbeer!" Zeke crows. "All hail the Unhealthy Breakfast Club!" He upends the greasy bag with a flourish, sending paper-wrapped lumps skittering.

"Dude!" I sigh as we all scuffle for the chicken biscuits. "I don't think it's legal to have this much energy before seven a.m."

Zeke laughs and snags the last chicken biscuit. "Here," he says, handing it to me. "You clearly need this more than me."

"Boy has a point." Aquandre' devours half a breakfast

burrito and scoops up a hash brown. "I haven't eaten this bad since . . . like, ever. No offense, Flor," he adds, loudly so she can hear him. "It sure fills up a hollow."

We all know what he means. The bags of free food from Flor's aunt have been great for keeping us fueled as we head toward finals, less great on our stomachs.

But food is food, so we all keep munching and get back to work.

"Eat hearty, adventurers!" Zeke grins around a bite of biscuit. "For the Capitol awaits!"

Our Zero-Dark-Thirty study group didn't happen by choice. We've known each other forever—hard not to in a county like Barndale—and Flor and I both live in the Cypress Grove mobile home park on the back loop of Daisy Flinch Road. But we're all about as different as you can get, other than being short on internet and long on worries about all those random little expenses our Hammerlin scholarships don't quite hit.

Hammerlin's a private school in the big town two counties west. Mostly for rich kids, but they give a few scholarships to kids in our county through some rural outreach. It's a great opportunity, but over an hour each way and the school doesn't provide a ride. Instead, it put the Barndale kids' parents into contact to "leverage and collectivize your transportation resources."

When Aquandre' turned seventeen last October, our parents decided we should all just carpool with him every day. He's the only one old enough to legally drive a truckful of minors, so we all pay him gas and wear-and-tear money. It's easier on our parents, for sure.

For us, it's been sort of like opening four random pens at the zoo and shooing a bear, an otter, a coyote, and an elephant all into one fake habitat.

Then expecting them to be instant best friends.

The internet gets good at mile marker 32

Two hours later, we get to school, where the parking lot always makes it impossible to forget how much separates us from most other Hammerlin kids. The drop-off line is jam-full with Audis, BMWs, Infinitis. More V-8s and leather seats and understated chrome than I've ever seen outside a dealership. The few pick-ups—huge and new—have clearly never hauled hay.

The student lot's no different. I know it's wrong, but I catch myself judging kids when they casually climb out of cars that cost more than my home. They wear them so *easy*, like the perfect clothes and the trips they talk about like it's no big thing. *Machu Picchu. Vail. Lisbon was okay.*

I've never even been to Dollywood.

Like usual, Aquandre' parks in the farthest corner of the lot that's partly shaded by tall hedges. He'd drop Zeke off closer, but Zeke always says no. Honestly, we all prefer it this way. We know how Aquandre''s truck sticks out.

Also, the long trek over to the school's front entrance gives us time to spread out.

The rest of us shuffle bags and gather cups while Aquandre' lifts Zeke's wheels from the flatbed. I hand Zeke his backpack once he's swung down from the truck. He slings it over his chair's handgrips, then shades his eyes and gazes at the shiny cars inching past the entrance.

"Another day!" he says. "Fare thee well, District Twelves!"

Zeke's jokes about Hammerlin being the Capitol made more sense after he convinced me to watch *The Hunger Games* one afternoon while we waited for Flor's play practice to get out. It was pretty good, but I'll still take Nat Geo or a *Popular Mechanics* podcast—stuff that's real—any day.

As we cross the lot, Flor slips away, earbuds still in, to join a few theater kids. Aquandre' lengthens his stride and heads over to some student government buddies.

Zeke and me go a few more yards together until he starts eyeing the smooth, perfect sidewalk that runs beside the school. He's obviously itching to play a little before the bell—pop curbs, practice that moving wheelie he's been perfecting. Accessible architecture isn't exactly the norm out where we live, and Zeke loves cutting loose when he can.

"Catch you later," I tell him, and he hurtles off with a quick backward wave.

Just like that, it's almost like we didn't arrive together at all.

"Gracie!" someone calls. "You dropped these."

I turn and see John Conover IV holding two purple leather juggling balls that must have fallen out of my pack. I really need to fix that rip.

I stuff the balls back into a different pocket of my bag. "Thanks."

John paces me as I beeline for the doors. "How many you up to these days?" he asks.

"Four, maybe." Lie. I can do five with my eyes closed, six on a great day, but I'm not giving him any reason to ask me to show him a new trick.

"Nice! I just nailed four too," he says, though I didn't ask. "We still need to try duo sometime, yeah?"

Then the bell rings, thank God.

"Maybe," I say. "Sometime."

How about never? I think.

I stride ahead of him and escape into the crowd and through the doors. Once I'm inside, though, that familiar imposter feeling settles over me like spiderwebs—invisible, sticky, impossible to wipe off. Yeah, we got the test scores to earn these scholarships, but that sure doesn't mean we belong.

I never much thought about it before I came to Hammerlin, but maybe *Corridor of Shame* isn't so wrong. Only I didn't know I was supposed to feel ashamed of where I come from until I landed in a school two counties over that might as well be another planet. And it's great, I guess, that someone pays for a few of us Corridor kids to come to a school this good . . . but what about everyone else at my old school? My old friends?

We four know we're insanely lucky to be here. So mostly we keep our mouths shut and work our tails off. And if we sometimes feel poor or dumb or like we've tumbled onto a planet where we're the alien species . . . I guess that's just the price of things.

Other than everything being decorated for Cinco de Mayo, school's nothing special today. Class all morning, homework in study hall. I eat lunch with Riley and Makayla, my friends from robotics club. They're excited about their summer plans.

Riley's going to summer robotics camp at Duke.

Makayla's going to Vanuatu while her mom does some kind of research.

Note to self: Look up where Vanuatu is.

"What about you, Gracie?" Riley asks. "Anything fun?"

I shrug. "Probably do some work for my dad." I don't add that the work will be repairing cars. My friends know I'll probably study engineering, but I'm not sure they'd understand how much I still love getting under a hood. "Maybe hit the beach."

"Cool." Makayla opens a pack of gum, and her new sweet sixteen gift—a tiny diamond-encrusted flip-flop—glitters off her charm bracelet as she passes us each a piece. "Nothing beats the beach, right?"

Flor's got drama club after school and Aquandre' has student government, so I head to the library—where the internet's so jam-up fast it never bogs down no matter how many people are online—to battle my government paper. The library's empty, which is great because writing's not my favorite and the assignment—a big chunk of our grade—is due in three days.

But just as I'm finally getting into the zone, John Conover IV sits down across from me and says something I can't hear through my earbuds.

I bite back a sigh and pull one out. "What?"

"I said, you never stop practicing, do you?" He points to the pen I'm flipping over and around and through my fingers. I always do this when I'm nervous or bored—or trying to concentrate on something tough. It's such a habit I barely notice when I'm doing it.

I clench the pen in my fist to keep it still. "Just trying to finish up some work," I tell him, hoping he'll get the hint. Instead, he pulls out his phone and shows me a juggling video.

"Check it out," he says as two jugglers work three, four, six, and even eight clubs between them. "I'm thinking Winter

Showcase next year—we could totally nail this!"

Then Zeke rolls in. "Gracie!" he calls. "Almost time—Oh hey, John."

"Five minutes," I tell him. "Just wrapping up."

Zeke pulls up and he and John start talking about some role-playing game they're both into while I pop my earbud back in and write a couple more paragraphs, resisting the urge to stop typing and flip my pen every thirty seconds. When I get to a stopping place and close the computer, John tries to get me into the conversation, but I give him one-word answers until he finally gets up and tells us bye.

"Think about it, Gracie," he says on his way out. "Winter Showcase! Duo act! Epic!"

"Not likely," I mutter under my breath.

Zeke gives me a funny look.

"Time to go," I say, "right?"

I gather my stuff and we head out. I know Zeke's wondering why I was so chilly. John's nice to most everybody, always into some volunteer project. Probably hugs his grandmom and flosses his teeth and doesn't kick puppies. He's cute, on the soccer team, and the only other kid at school who loves juggling.

But no way in heck will you catch me fangirling over John Conover IV.

The internet drops off at Horsefeathers Hill

"Okay!" Zeke says as we ride home a few days later. "You know what today is, team! Good Thing / Bad Thing time! Who's got one?"

Crap. It's Friday.

We all groan, but mostly from habit. Only Zeke could have

invented this weekly Good Thing / Bad Thing talk. Everybody felt weird doing it at first.

But today Flor speaks right up. "Tuesday," she says, glancing up from her open biology notebook. "Cinco de Mayo."

Zeke looks confused. "Good Thing?"

"Bad Thing."

"You mean the cafeteria enchiladas?"

Flor snorts and slams her notebook shut. "I mean Mr. Tate asking me to explain the holiday to my whole class," she says. "I've been at this school almost a year and he still thinks I'm Mexican."

Flor's family moved here from Belize.

We all know how Mr. Tate can be. He teaches social studies, he's youngish for a teacher, and he's clearly pretty proud of how much he's traveled and stuff. Once he pulled me aside after school and gave me what I guess was supposed to be an inspiring speech about "rising above my life circumstances." Made me feel like he was trying to hand me a ladder . . . only I wasn't standing in a hole to begin with.

Aquandre' drums the steering wheel and rolls his eyes. "Tate pulled that on me during Black History Month," he says. "Dude tries, but . . . yeah. What'd you say, Flor?"

Flor grins. "That their guess was as good as mine."

We all laugh and then Zeke shares a possibly Good Thing about the guidance counselor recommending him for a summer writing program in Atlanta.

"No way I can go unless there's some sick financial aid available," he adds, shrugging. "But nice to be asked, right? Who's next?"

"Good Thing," Aquandre' says. "My AP Chem and AP

Psych exams are *finally* in the rearview . . . and I don't think I bombed."

Aquandre"'s been stressing about that chem test, so we all congratulate him, and I feel grateful that I won't have to deal with AP classes until next year—all the regular finals starting next week are bad enough.

"What about you, Gracie?" Zeke asks.

"Me? I'm good—maybe I'll sit this week out."

"Then what was up in the library the other day?" he presses.

"Nothing," I protest, but now Aquandre' and Flor look curious. And since they shared, I'll seem like a jerk if I don't.

I give up. "It's no big thing. I just don't like John Conover."

"He likes you," Aquandre' says. "Anyone can see that."

To my surprise, Flor nods. "And you've both got the juggling thing going, right?"

I've never shared with anyone why I feel prickly about John. But home's still forty-five minutes away, and I can't exactly bail out of the truck and grab an Uber.

So, finally, I just tell them.

Last fall, I got invited to a Halloween party up at John's huge house by the university where his mom is some big-name professor. I'd met John in my English class and we'd discovered our mutual goofy love of juggling. Sometimes we'd mess around in the courtyard after lunch, seeing who could get more balls—or cups or crumpled-up papers—flying through the air.

I liked him. He was sweet and fun and funny. I'd only been at Hammerlin a couple months and it seemed like I'd met someone I could connect with, like maybe I was going to fit in okay after all.

As much as I wanted to go to the party, there was no way I could get a ride an hour each way, and I wasn't about to ask John or his friends. They were nice about it, said maybe next time and they'd be sure to post some pictures.

I spent Halloween the same way as usual—at our tiny county library's teen night with all my regular friends, bat and pumpkin cupcakes, and hot apple cider—and tried not to be too bummed about missing the fun at John's house. Next morning, I saw the photos they'd posted. And found out John's Halloween party had a theme.

Trailer Trash.

I'm not stupid. I know how books and TV and movies show people like us. People who live in way-out places and drive old trucks and go hunting and stuff. I've heard all the not-funny jokes about rotten teeth and inbreeding from plenty of people who'd consider themselves nice and woke.

But I got to admit, I never expected a whole party devoted to making fun of just . . . being rural. Or poor. But the pictures didn't lie—rich kids in a perfect house, decked out in sleeveless undershirts, with blacked-out teeth and fake beer bellies, eating cheese-in-a-can on Ritz.

I never practiced juggling with John again. I make a point to never let myself laugh at any of his jokes. And I know it confused him, how quick I ran cold, but how could I ever be honest about who I am or where I'm from after that?

When I finish telling it all, I actually feel better.

Aquandre' shakes his head and drums the wheel a bit harder. Flor looks annoyed but not surprised. Zeke's quiet at first. Then he pulls one of his brick-thick fantasy books from his backpack.

"Behold the Tome of Enlightenment, Grasshoppers," he says, tapping the cover.

We all give him blank looks.

"Why do you think I love reading books like this?" Zeke persists. "And don't you dare say *Because you can magic away a wheelchair*," he adds, rolling his eyes.

We wouldn't—we've all seen how it irks Zeke when people say stuff like that.

"Help me out," I beg. "Or you know I'll just point out all the things that are mechanically impossible in those books of yours."

"Philistine." Zeke rolls his eyes good-naturedly, like he's trapped in a truck full of endearing amoebas.

"What are fantasy books about? Kids from the sticks who become heroes. And when they get picked on or pitied for being from some District Twelve backwater, you root for them even harder. You know everyone who gives them crap will get karma in the end."

I'm no fantasy expert, but I have to admit that makes sense. Flor, who does read some fantasy, nods.

"Then, when the quest is over," Zeke says, "a lot of them go back to their villages, or districts, or wherever. And they've succeeded. How often do you see that in non-fantasy stories?"

We all try and figure out what he's getting at. Aquandre' gets there first.

"You don't. Rural kids are supposed to want to get out . . . and never come back."

"Or 'rise above our circumstances,'" I add, as my lightbulb finally goes on.

"Exactly!" Zeke looks satisfied. "That's what John and

his friends probably don't get—I bet it never occurred to them someone could live in a trailer, or be poor, and just be . . . a regular person."

"Or that we might actually like where we live," Flor says.

"Right!" Zeke says. "But if characters like Katniss and Peeta, or Frodo, or Eragon were real, they'd probably have lived in trailers, too. It's okay—cool, even—if it's just fantasy. And if they come home after the adventure's over, nobody thinks they're a failure."

Flor looks at Zeke like she's just seen him for the first time.

Even to a gearhead like me, his theory makes a weird sort of sense. But why is *this* what makes me angry about Hammerlin sometimes? The kids and teachers are mostly nice. We've all made some friends, gotten involved in cool things.

Sure, all four of us struggle to catch all the cues, to afford things the other kids don't think twice about. And the rest of the group deals with even more stuff—Zeke gets the same awkward wheelchair comments he gets anywhere else; Aquandre''s one of just a few black Hammerlin students; I've heard other kids' parents tell Flor how good her English is like it's some big surprise. So why's this what's getting under my skin?

Then it hits me.

Even if they don't always get it right, most people at Hammerlin *know*—or say they know—it's uncool to say crummy things about wheelchairs. Or immigration. Or to act racist.

But being from the sticks and not having much money?

They don't even try to pretend. It's just the butt-end of a trailer trash joke.

Come to think of it, Mr. Tate was basically saying the same

thing with his "rise above" crap. Just dressing it up in earnest, well-meaning teacher words.

And that makes me mad, because now I see how we play right into that nonsense—parking far away, staying apart at school, not wearing certain clothes. Always holding back, watching that we don't say or do something to call ourselves out as hicks, as backwoods, as poor.

It's like we believe we're not as good as them, too.

Things are feeling a little heavy, so Flor breaks the silence.

"All right, Zeke," she says. "You're officially banned from my book club."

"You have a book club?" Zeke says.

"My *future* book club, then," she clarifies. "I don't care if it's when we're all in nursing homes—you can't come!" It's not a super-funny joke, but it cuts the cloudy mood a bit.

Then Aquandre' tells us a funny story about drawing his nemesis bronc at his last rodeo practice and getting bucked off into a watering trough. I show Flor how to flip a pen, she helps me proof my government paper, and we all take turns choosing music on Zeke's phone until the internet drops off halfway down Horsefeathers Hill. By then, I feel pretty good again.

Maybe I shouldn't gripe so much about Good Thing / Bad Thing. Turns out I sort of like it.

Sometimes the internet's just an excuse

A week later, we're all back in the corner booth. But it's Saturday morning, and we're tying up loose ends and studying before finals start next week. Even Zeke has swapped his fun books for schoolbooks, and Aunt Inez has kept us stocked with food since seven a.m.

It's lucky we're mostly done needing internet, because the weather's warmed up and things are getting busy. Route 125 is a direct route to the beach about an hour east of here, and people use it to avoid interstate traffic, adding a scattering of fancy cars to the pickups and logging rigs in the lot. The extra people have slowed the wi-fi way down.

The beautiful weather makes it tough to study, and the trickle of flip-flop- and sunglasses-wearing beachgoers doesn't help.

"Honestly," Flor says as a group of college-age kids leave with their food and pile into a brand-new Wrangler. "Doesn't anyone else have finals?" She rolls up a hotcake from the plate she and Zeke are sharing, sighs, and tears off a bite.

Aquandre"'s boots—black and silver today—start *tap-tap-tap*ping under the table. "It's a beach day for sure," he says, looking wistfully out the window. "Or a barrels day," he adds, clearly thinking rodeo. Then he grins. "Hang in there, Unhealthy Breakfast Club. We'll make it to that beach."

"We just have to surmount the Grand Final Finals Trial first," Zeke goofs, pretending to brandish a sword. Then he points out the window. "Looks like a tourist's got car trouble."

We all turn and see a red Mini Cooper with a roof rack full of boogie boards stutter into the lot. I can tell the engine's misfiring from the jerky way it rides.

"Spark plugs," I say without thinking.

The car parks and three kids from Hammerlin get out, all wearing shorts and flip-flops. It's Nate, Spence, and Makayla. Then John climbs out of the driver's seat. My stomach does a little twist as they come inside. John's got his phone out.

"I know Dad renewed my Triple A," he says. "But I can't catch a signal."

Makayla sees us. "Gracie!" she says, coming over. "You all headed to the beach, too?"

Before I can think of an answer, everyone else follows her. Flor says hi to Spence, who she knows from theater.

"Car trouble?" Aquandre' nods toward the lot.

"Yeah," John says. "It's like it's got no power. Looks like no beach for us today—you think I can get a tow way out here?"

"Yep," Aquandre' says. "But you may not need one."

"Yeah? You know cars?"

"Nope. Cars aren't my thing. But it's your lucky day—there's an expert right here."

The guys look to Zeke, who shakes his head and points at me.

Part of me wants to let them call a tow and miss the beach. Clearly, none of them need to worry about doing well on finals to keep a scholarship. But then I notice a look I've never seen on John Conover IV's face before.

Uncertainty. He's in a situation where he doesn't have all the answers, a place he doesn't wear easy and loose. Spence and Nate and Makayla sort of have the same look.

It's surprising to see. But I know how it feels.

Besides, I can't let them call a tow for such an easy fix.

I shrug. "I could take a look. Meet you out there in a sec."

"You still got that toolbox in your truck?" I ask Aquandre' when they've gone outside.

He does, and he walks out with me to get it. He winks as he props the Cooper's shiny hood when I pop it and then hands over tools as I ask for them.

John and Nate hover, trying to quarterback as I rummage through hoses and wires. Finally, Aquandre' shoos them off with a blunt "She's the expert; maybe let her get to it?"

It's the spark plugs, like I thought, and they're not even broken—just dirty. Super simple. I brush out the crud, then retighten them and let the hood slam just a tiny bit harder than necessary. "Crank it up."

John turns the key, and when the engine roars to life, I feel like I'm secretly roaring, too.

Makayla high-fives me. "That was badass, girl."

John looks surprised. "Thanks, Gracie. That was impressive."

"Not bad for trailer trash?"

Aquandre"s eyebrows go up. Everyone goes quiet.

John looks confused. "What?"

My heart's thudding in my ears, but suddenly I don't care. These guys are on our turf now. They'll get to the beach today because I fixed their car when none of them could.

I think I've earned the right to say a thing or two.

I take a deep breath. "Living in a trailer means someone doesn't have as much money as you," I say. "It doesn't make someone *trash*."

"What do you mean? I never said—"

"Your Halloween party was not cool. Trailer Trash? Remember?"

Now everyone looks a little embarrassed. John blushes. "It was just a joke." His voice is way less confident than usual.

"Not a funny one. Besides," I add, because now I might as well go big or go home, "*I* live in a trailer. Am I trash?"

John blushes redder. "I . . . didn't mean you."

Aquandre' steps up beside me. "I live in a trailer, too," he says, calm and friendly. "Did you mean me?"

John glances though the window at Flor and Zeke watching

us. I can practically hear gears clicking as he puts together the pieces. It probably never occurred to him that anyone who lived in a trailer on a red dirt road could be in class beside him at Hammerlin, let alone be a girl he wants to juggle duo with or ask to his parties.

Maybe he remembers how I stopped being friendly with him right after Halloween. Well, now he knows why.

"You all . . . aren't headed to the beach," he says slowly.

"Nope." Now I'm not a bit afraid to be honest. "Studying for finals—there's good internet here. And unhealthy-breakfast clubs. And we've all got scholarships to keep."

John looks at me, and I think maybe he actually gets it. Sort of. "I'm . . . sorry," he finally says. "I guess I never thought . . ."

I decide to cut him a break. "We're cool. Maybe we'll try duo this fall. Enjoy the beach."

"Maybe we could all go sometime," Makayla says. "Mom and I don't leave for a few weeks." Then she adds, "When I get back, I totally want to learn how you fixed the car!"

"Sure," I tell her. Then Aquandre' and me tell them bye and head back inside.

"Dang, G3," he says. "You're full of surprises, aren't you?"

The sun's higher now, and I let myself enjoy the way his dark eyes sparkle in the midmorning sun. "Always, Boots."

"You should come watch me bronc ride sometime."

"I should show you how to fix that sorry alternator of yours, too."

"Y'all won't believe this!" Aquandre' bursts out when we get back to the booth. He tells Flor and Zeke what happened, and Flor pretend-punches him for letting them miss it. Zeke looks like a cat who got the cream.

"Thus the nimble-fingered village girl holds the Mirror of Truth before the young princeling," he says. "Excellent tale!"

I roll my eyes. "That's a hot mess even for you. And so not even a real story."

Aquandre' chimes in. "Maybe Zeke should write it," he says, "and put us all in there."

"That might be one I'd actually read," I say, and we all laugh.

Then Flor points outside. "Check it out." The Cooper's idling right outside the window, and John, Nate, Spence, and Makayla are waving at us.

I hesitate a second, then wave back before they pull away.

I trade glances with the rest of my friends, and it hits me that—yeah. We really *are* friends, aren't we? They all look as happy as I feel.

And yeah, it'll take us a bit longer to get to the beach this summer—and to all those other places we're working our tails off to get to after that. But we're sure as heck going to do it.

And maybe—just maybe—Zeke is right and we'll do it without turning our backs on who we are or where we're from. Just like those spell-slinging village girls and heroic farm boys from his books. Then I think how funny it is that we're all sitting right here, at this beat-up old McDonald's smack-dab in the middle of the so-called Corridor of Shame . . .

And I feel anything but ashamed.

The Hole of Dark Kill Hollow
ROB COSTELLO

About the only thing the hole wouldn't fix was death.

Jesse had already tried that once, with Matilda, when he and Tyler were still little kids. Bleary-eyed from tears and the glare of flashlight beams, the two best friends had carried her scabrous, flea-infested body through the looming woods to the bottom of the Hollow, where the hole's maw belched its sulfurous breath into the moonlit air. The old tabby was riddled with cancer and covered in the filth Jesse had found her in beneath the porch, where she'd crawled to die, and as Dark Kill gurgled nervously nearby, he'd leaned over the hole and dropped her corpse down its throat.

His heart had screwed up with irrational hope as he'd watched Matilda plummet into the darkness. Maybe this one time the hole might bend the rules. Tyler had squeezed his shoulder and tried to reassure him that it was going to work, it *had* to work, but when Matilda reappeared the next morning on the rug beside Jesse's bed, though she'd been as clean, unscarred, and fresh-smelling as a kitten, she had still been quite dead.

He'd realized sometime later that he was hardly the first brokenhearted kid in the village to have sneaked down to the Hollow to try (and fail) to bring back a beloved pet. But while Jesse could've recited the hole's rule about death as if reading it from the pages of a Stephen King paperback, even at that age he'd understood that certain lessons needed to be learned the hard way: Home and family didn't automatically mean safety and love; unlike Santa Claus, real magic came with a stiff price; and no matter how much you begged and pleaded for it, the hole of Dark Kill Hollow just wouldn't fix death.

Good thing that's not what he aimed to ask it for today.

The late-afternoon sun blazed hotly through the skeletonized branches of white oak and hemlock, raising droplets of sweat on the back of Jesse's neck despite the November chill. The leaves had dropped early this year. A nor'easter had torn through the week before Halloween, with rain and wind so fierce they'd raked the trees bare clear across the Catskills, leaving most of the color browning on the ground. Parts of the trail were ankle deep with leaves now, and as he and Tyler shuffled their way in silence through the crackling carpet, they kicked up plumes of mildewy humus that coaxed allergic tears to his eyes.

He hadn't come this way in years, not since he'd helped Tyler lug a crushed and bleeding Ace to the hole on what turned out to be another fool's errand. But even on that crisp April morning it'd felt more like descending into the bowels of a stinking crypt than an emergency dash through the woods to save his friend's run-over bluetick. Something heavy hung in the air here, something more than just the rotten-egg stench wafting up from the hole. Though there was nothing particularly remarkable about this lonely stretch of wilderness to distinguish it from the thousands of acres of forest that surrounded it, the moment he crossed into the Hollow itself, a slippery kind of foreboding prickled his skin, sending shivers skittering down his spine. It was a sensation as hard to pin down as a chill in a graveyard, and it was just as unnerving.

On the plus side, he knew this worked better than a thousand No Trespassing signs to keep strangers away from the hole, which had managed to remain a secret known only to the villagers for as long as anyone could remember. While hordes of day-trippers from New York City and the Hudson Valley swarmed the area each summer and fall, they always skipped the Hollow, with its reputation for strange vibes and unpleasant smells, favoring the less objectionable hikes offered by the Mohonk Preserve or the ice caves of Verkeerder Kill Falls. The few sightseers who sometimes wandered in found themselves quickly turning back, if unable to put a finger on exactly why, and while deer season would open soon, no rifle reports would be heard echoing through these woods: Even the villagers gave the Hollow a wide berth unless they had a damn good reason not to.

Yet as he and Tyler approached the hulk of Preacher's Rock glaring in the sunlight like the crown of a half-buried skull, Jesse came to a halt, unsure whether he could go through with this after all. His mother's words buzzed in his head: *Never bet your soul when the devil's dealing.* This was the mantra he'd spent the past few days quietly trying to shoo from his thoughts. Now that he was here, the words stung like a riled wasp.

The hole was hungry. The hole was unpredictable. The hole could take everything you loved and everything you *were*.

"Why'd you stop?" Tyler asked, coming to a halt beside him. His slim, pale face glowed ruddy with the cold, his soft brown eyes wide and trepidatious behind the thick lenses of his glasses. He tugged absently at the red-and-black hem of his granddad's hunting jacket, so large it practically hung to his knees. In a hopeful voice, he said, "You change your mind?"

"Naw," Jesse replied weakly, and feigned a wince. "Just my ribs, you know? I need a minute."

"Oh, yeah . . . Sorry."

Tyler averted his gaze and his cheeks grew redder, and Jesse felt a stab of guilt for rubbing more salt on that particular wound. It was a stupid, clumsy lie. His ribs were all right. The pain had begun to fade a little with the bruises, and besides, he sure as hell didn't need to dredge up the beating again. Tyler was shaken up enough already.

"You know, you can go back and wait for me," Jesse said gently. "I'll be all right."

Tyler's back stiffened, and he met Jesse's eyes. "Don't be an asshole, man," he said with forced bravado. "I go where you go. Always. I'm not letting you do this alone."

But Jesse detected the fear behind his friend's words because, well, he felt it, too.

Everybody knew that the hole wouldn't—or maybe couldn't—fix death. That was the main rule, the one Jesse had needed to learn for himself with Matilda, and Tyler with Ace, who'd stopped breathing mere minutes before they'd reached the hole and whose body had materialized hours later in Tyler's backyard, pristine as a puppy yet stiff as a board.

But while death was off the table, the hole *would* fix other things, within certain limitations—the kinds of things that were broken or flawed or diseased about you. For example, it couldn't turn you rich, but it would make you content enough to live with your poverty. It couldn't force somebody else to love you, but it would ease your heartbreak at their rejection. It might not peel years off your age, but it would cure your diabetes or make that terminal heart condition go away. And although it flat-out refused to transform you into a dead ringer for your favorite movie star, it would obligingly erase your acne scars or replace that finger you lost to the chainsaw.

Though neither of the boys had taken the leap before, half the village had jumped at least once to fix something or other—insomnia, melanoma, addiction, guilt, envy, despair—and each one had come back more or less "cured" of what ailed them. The trick to being successful was to follow the rules by tempering your wish to what was within the hole's power to grant.

But even so, that didn't mean a jump was without peril.

For one thing, everyone knew to be damn sure to keep your eyes shut tight. There were horror stories about those who hadn't heeded this warning, either out of obstinacy or an involuntary response to leaping blindly into a bottomless stinking pit in the woods. While none of them had ever dared to speak about what they'd seen down there, they each returned drenched in sweat and trembling, their eyes wide with fear, their clothes soiled with their own piss and excrement. Soon, their sleep became plagued by night terrors, and it would invariably take another jump—this time with eyes taped shut and a Bible clutched firmly in hand—to fix the damage and forget.

But for those who heeded this warning and kept their eyes

closed, a jump was said to be a piece of cake, little more than a rush of foul air in darkness, and then you were deposited safely back home—albeit hours later—lying comfortably in your bed, standing at your kitchen counter, or plopped down on your living room sofa in front of the TV.

That was one thing about the hole at least: It sent you back to where you belonged.

Too bad a little time was the least of what it took in payment.

Tyler pushed his glasses up the bridge of his nose and announced, "We should get going if we're gonna do this."

Jesse gave a slight nod. A kind of numbing resignation had crept over him. What other options did he have? Mom was dead. School was nothing but a dropout factory; with nearly half the county at or near the poverty line, there was no point getting your diploma when the few jobs around didn't even require a degree. Any future around here was a sucking black void, especially now that the Old Man had finally kicked him out. After Jamie had run off to Florida without him, Jesse had managed to weather the hurricane force of the Old Man's drunken rages on his own for a while, but all it'd taken was one stupid mistake, one browser history left unerased, and that'd all blown to smithereens.

It hadn't always been like this. Back before Mom died, the Old Man had just been Dad.

Dad, who'd toss flies with him and Jamie down to Roundout Creek. Dad, who'd let him help tune the big V-8 under the hood of the F-150 by passing wrenches and cleaning the plugs. Dad, who'd let him ride shotgun as they delivered cords of firewood to the professors' houses out in New Paltz. It was Dad who'd showed him how to aim his .22 so squarely he could hit the neck of a beer bottle at fifty yards, Dad who'd climbed onto the roof with a broom handle to make sleigh tracks in the snow each Christmas Eve, Dad who'd held him all through the night she died and gave him private time alone to cry at the funeral parlor before they buried her.

But it was the Old Man, not Dad, who'd left him doubled over and bleeding in the backyard with Tyler looking on in horror; the Old Man who squeezed his fists and shouted, "Don't let me catch you back here, you little faggot, until you learn how to be a man!"

What a pathetic joke that was. At six-foot-one and two hundred and fifteen pounds of meat and muscle, Jesse was even bigger now than Jamie. He was a star fullback, nicknamed "The Hammer" by his Blue Devils teammates, yet he'd toppled at the Old Man's feet like a sapling felled by a hatchet. At least Tyler had been there to help him up off the ground. He'd bandaged him up, given him a place to sleep, to lick his wounds and figure things out, until Jesse finally accepted the fact that there was no going home again. Home was gone. Just like Dad and Jamie. Just like Mom. Nothing would change that now. The only thing left to change was himself.

That was the moment he decided to jump.

Tyler had already gone on ahead, so Jesse sucked in his breath and trudged slowly after him. Beyond Preacher's Rock, the Hollow steepened into a gorge and the trail zigzagged down a narrow ledge along the sheer wall to where Dark Kill had gouged its way through the bedrock a couple of hundred feet below. You needed to watch every step on the loose shale path to avoid tumbling headlong to a nasty end. You couldn't see the hole until you reached the trail's bottom. A ring of deformed white cypresses had grown up around the hole, twisting inward at their tops to form a kind of towering arbor that kept it hidden from the trail. In fact, the trees were so good at obscuring the hole from above that even on satellite maps it was impossible to spot, despite being as wide as a backhoe.

But while he might not be able to see it yet, Jesse could sure as hell smell it. The stench was as putrid as zombie farts—the funk of a millennium's worth of rot belched up from the earth's innards. So strong were the fumes here, they kept even the birds away, and he wondered how anyone had ever endured this god-awful stench long enough to stumble upon the hole in the first place.

Nobody knew who that first person actually was. There were the typically ignorant legends of ancient Indian burial grounds and a supposed slaughter of Dutch settlers by a tribe of local Lenape defending their sacred site. But Jesse had heard a like-lier story about an itinerant preacher and his flock who'd passed through the area during a burst of religious fervor in the 1840s and tried unsuccessfully to fill in "the Devil's accursed pit" with rocks and boulders chiseled from the walls of the gorge.

When those very same rocks and boulders began to reappear in the exact locations from which they'd been quarried, the Bible-thumpers had fled in terror, taking with them the Hollow's unholy secret.

It wasn't until the village was founded another forty years later—by, some said, a handful of descendants of that very same preacher's flock—that the hole was rediscovered and its powers tested and explored.

Jesse couldn't begin to imagine what half-mad process of trial and error had led to the current understanding of the hole's peculiar gifts, although the villagers now took those gifts for granted, much as the folks of another town might take for granted the prognostications of the local psychic or the restorative powers of their delicious spring water. Yet his neighbors were far more zealous about keeping their prize a secret from the outside world. Nobody wanted a media circus here, and God forbid the crooks in Albany ever got wind of what the hole could do and tried to tax it. It was theirs, it belonged to them, and besides, while no one would say so aloud, the entire village was quietly petrified of what it might do to them if they ever let word get out.

A dozen paces ahead of him, the trail briefly leveled off in a kind of plateau that overlooked a bend in the creek below. Tyler had come to a halt there, seemingly to clean his glasses, though Jesse knew he was just waiting for him to catch up. The sun had dipped below the ridge, casting them both in murky gray shadow, and it occurred to him just how wrong it felt letting Tyler take the lead when he shouldn't even be here. This wasn't about fixing his crap eyesight, no matter what he might claim, and Jesse hated himself for that, hated himself more than he even hated the Old Man for beating him senseless right in front of his best friend.

"I was just thinking," Tyler said as Jesse came to a stop behind him, "at least we won't have to climb back out of here." He gave an awkward laugh, as if he knew this wasn't funny but wanted it to be anyway, and Jesse noticed his face was drained of color. Tyler peered over the edge to where the hole lay concealed in its gnarled berth of cypress. In a hushed tone, almost as if he feared being overheard, he asked, "You think I'll end up like Huffaker?"

"Shit, no," Jesse said, although the thought had crossed his mind too.

Tyler glanced at him. "Why not?"

"Because you're no dumbass, that's why." He cleared his throat and tried to lighten the mood. "You seen him without that ball cap yet? He looks like Professor X."

"Seriously?"

"Seriously." He smirked, then added, "It's kind of hot, though."

Tyler gawped at him a moment, and then they both busted out laughing, even though they knew it really wasn't funny.

Not in the slightest.

When Roy Huffaker had jumped on Labor Day weekend, he'd asked the hole to add a few inches to his manhood so he could try to win back some girl from Wallkill who'd dumped him over the summer. But when the hole returned him to his bedroom later on that same night, his delight with his hefty new member soon turned to horror when he realized he couldn't get it up, no matter how hard he tried. A thousand hours of fruitless porn and ungodly chafing later, and he ended up taking a second jump, only this one cost him all of his hair, though at least he could throw a boner again.

This was the other thing about the hole, the thing that kept most folks from jumping to fix every minor ache and complaint in their lives: While it gave you what you asked for, it extracted whatever price it wanted for the miracle it provided. Sometimes this was little more than a fingernail; other times, a ruinous hunk of your soul. Both Matilda and Ace had returned missing their entire tails in return for what amounted to little more than a bath and brushing, yet Willow Blake's spinster aunt

Grace had been healed of an incurable neurological disease, and all it cost her was her singing voice, which Willow said she only ever used in church or the shower anyway.

Everyone knew you took your chances when you jumped, and there was usually no predicting the outcome. The hole's appetite could be sadistic one day and downright magnanimous the next, and over the years folks had developed their own theories to explain why: The hole choked on the pious, didn't like the taste of drunks, swallowed men's woes easier than women's or vice versa. Some said it was safe to jump only on the Sabbath, and others warned against ever jumping at night, but everyone seemed to agree that the hole's sinister nature fed best on human frailties like vanity and spite, and that only those with a true Christian heart and a clear conscience were safe from real harm.

But Jesse knew better than all that. His family had a deeper history with the hole than most, and if nothing else, this had taught him that the only thing it truly fed upon was desperation. After all these years and all the stupid theories, desperation was the only thing that kept folks coming back.

"Have you seen it yet?" Tyler asked when he'd finally stopped laughing.

"What?" Jesse blinked. "Huffaker's junk?"

"Yeah. Like in the showers after practice or whatever."

"Naw. I try not to look, you know?"

"Fair enough," Tyler said. "I just hope it was worth going bald."

Jesse frowned. "He was lucky the hole was feeling playful that day instead of cruel," he said earnestly, and then gave voice to a theory of his own he'd been mulling over since he first heard the news. "It could've taken an arm or a leg. I mean, it had to do something visible to make a lesson out of him, right? Otherwise every kid in town would be jumping for stupid shit like bigger junk or clearer skin. He should have asked it to make him forget that girl if she broke his heart, not add inches to his tiny pecker. It doesn't like to be trifled with." He said this with certainty, echoing Mom's warning from all those years ago.

Never bet your soul when the devil's dealing.

Or your dick, as it turned out.

"I hope you're right," Tyler said, all seriousness again. "What do you think it'll take from me?"

Jesse held him in a steady gaze and said, "Depends on what you're asking for."

Tyler looked away. "I told you what I'm asking for," he said, and touched the frame of his glasses. "No more four eyes."

Though it would have been easy enough to call Tyler out on his bullshit, he didn't want to add more humiliation to his friend's already heavy burden. "Why don't you go home, man? I'll meet you back at your place when this is done and over, okay?"

"You don't think I have the balls, do you? You think I'm scared."

"We're both scared." Jesse kicked at the path with the toe of his boot, sending a hunk of shale careening over the ledge. It landed a moment later with a feeble splash in the water of Dark Kill. "But I'm the only one who needs to do this. You don't have anything to prove to me. You really don't."

He reached out and squeezed his friend's shoulder, but Tyler pulled away.

"Who says I'm proving anything to you?" he muttered, and

then turned back to the trail and started walking again. "Let's just get this over with."

Jesse's heart pinched with dread, but he said nothing more. Witnessing the self-loathing etched into Tyler's face after the beating had struck him deeper than any of the Old Man's blows. He knew damn well Tyler had *wanted* to intervene. Tyler had *wanted* to shield him, to pull him out of harm's way, to strike back at the Old Man with all the outrage and disgust he felt being forced to watch Jesse whipped like a dog right in front of him. But the truth was, Tyler couldn't bring himself to do anything like that. He didn't have it in him to fight back, whatever it was, backbone or bravery, that instinctual response that made a guy stand up and shout "No more!" when his limits had finally been reached. Tyler had never had it in him, not since they'd first met in Cub Scouts, and that'd always made him an easy target for every bully and mouth-breather they knew.

At least until Jesse kicked their asses.

But that was just Tyler. Even now, he was small and slightly built. While he loved sports, he was the least athletic kid Jesse had ever met and could find a way to hurt himself just tossing around a pigskin in the backyard. At seventeen, he was still just as quiet and skittish as he'd been in third grade, with an abiding fear of the dark and an aching shyness around the girls he liked that was downright painful to behold. Yet he was also loyal and trustworthy, generous, and as smart as a whip, and Jesse had never been afraid to be just exactly who he was around him. It was as easy to talk to Tyler about his secrets and desires as it was to rehash the plays from the latest Jets game, and Jesse loved him for that as purely and effortlessly as breathing. He didn't want Tyler to change. He didn't want him fixed.

He didn't want to risk losing whatever magical quality it was that made Tyler *Tyler*, even if it was the very thing Tyler hated most about himself.

Yet what could he say to stop him? Tyler knew the risks, same as anybody else. Besides, it was Jesse's fault they both felt like cowards, and any argument he might use against his friend, Tyler could just as easily flip around and use against him.

He briefly debated turning back, but he figured it was probably too late for that anyway. The seed of longing had already been planted. The hole's relentless patience was its greatest danger; once you were set on the path, it could wait as long as it took for you to wrestle with the consequences, minimize the risks, and finally convince yourself there was no other way but to jump. He'd seen it happen before, to the Old Man, to Jamie. Now it was happening to Tyler and him. None of the men in his life had ever been strong enough to resist the temptation. The only one who ever had was Mom, and it had cost her her life.

By the time they reached the base of the gorge, the stench of sulfur had grown so thick Jesse's eyes began to water. The ribbon of sky overhead had darkened to a shade just above twilight, but he knew that outside the Hollow the sun wouldn't set for hours yet. An otherworldly calm enveloped them, as if the hole had sucked all the sound straight out of the air.

The hole lay at the center of a raised altar of bedrock not far from the creek bank. It was surrounded by the ring of cypresses twisted into such agonized poses they called to mind a coven of witches hunched over a bubbling caldron. Yet the hole itself was stillness incarnate, a perfect circle of black, a void so pristinely empty it didn't seem to swallow the light so much as defy its existence. Peering inside it revealed no details. It gave back no echoes, and no walls or shadows could be discerned within its depths, almost as if a giant eraser had rubbed through the surface of reality to reveal the nothingness that lay behind. It was as mesmerizing to behold as it was unsettling, and Jesse felt himself drawn toward it, tugged inexorably forward by its mysterious psychic gravity. So strong was the pull, in fact, that he might well have tumbled straight into the hole had Tyler not grabbed him by the wrist to stop him.

"Don't get so close," Tyler warned, and Jesse, startled, stumbled backward and nearly toppled into him.

"God, I hate this place," Jesse muttered, suddenly dizzy, his head throbbing dully. "It messes with your mind."

Tyler blinked at him in surprise. "I'm not the only one who doesn't need to go through with this, you know? Nobody but him is gonna care that you're gay, man."

"Tell that to the locker room," Jesse said drily. "Tell it to Coach."

"Look, there's nothing wrong with you. I wish you'd believe me that you're not the one who needs fixing."

Though Jesse muttered a halfhearted "Whatever," he squirmed inside. He didn't like lying to Tyler about this any more than he imagined Tyler liked lying to him, but he hadn't found the right words to explain himself. Not without revealing too much.

Not without having to dredge up Mom.

As far as Jesse was concerned, while there were a shit ton of things wrong with his life, liking dudes was not one of them. It was who he was, who he'd been for as long as he could remember. And yeah, he'd always been careful about sharing the truth, telling no one other than Tyler and Jamie until the Old Man had stumbled onto his browser history. But that didn't mean he was ashamed of it. He was still deciding what being gay meant for his life and for the future. Mostly it felt like possibility. The possibility of getting out from beneath the macho posing of small-town expectations, of getting away from the Old Man's fists and misery to a better, kinder place where he could slip out of the closet and into his own skin. A place where the air practically vibrated with the prospects of sex and freedom and falling in love. Maybe even with somebody like Tyler.

He sure as hell wasn't giving up on all that just to appease the Old Man.

Tyler was watching him, and Jesse felt the blood rise to his cheeks.

"What?" he said sharply.

Tyler held his gaze. "What about Jamie?"

"What about him?"

"Have you told him what you're doing?"

Jesse bristled. "Jamie doesn't give a shit about me anymore, okay? He made his choice. It's just you and me now." He turned away and edged up to the smooth rim of the hole, trying not to let the hurt bleed through to his face.

It wasn't like he could be angry with Jamie. After all, Dad had turned into a monster. His jump had swallowed the light that kept him sober, that made him human, and that enabled him to still hope and feel and care about his boys through all the pain of her loss. With that gone, he had nothing left to embrace but the darkness inside himself. It was at least something to hold on to during those long, lonely nights without her.

But poor Jamie had been stuck cleaning up the mess the Old

Man had left behind when he checked out on them. He'd only been a teenager himself at the time, and it'd been too much to ask. Working whatever shit jobs he could rustle up in this backwater with no hope for anything better. Raising a kid brother while propping up a broken-down miserable drunk who'd handed over his heart to the hole in exchange for relief from his grief.

So when the time came, and Jesse finally turned old enough to look after himself, who could blame Jamie for what he'd done? Though they'd never discussed it, Jesse knew that Jamie had asked the hole to set him free of his burdens, to cut him loose from his sense of duty and family ties. No guilt. No regrets. No looking back. Too bad the price for his freedom had turned out to be whatever affection he felt for his kid brother, who hadn't heard a word from him since he left.

Jesse doubted he ever would again.

He leaned forward to peer into the hole's bottomless black heart, and he could sense it peering back, judging him, taking stock. A small voice inside his head repeated his mom's stupid mantra again. *Never bet your soul when the devil's dealing.* He knew he should be scared right now, petrified even, but he suddenly felt too pissed off to care. He hated this damn thing with every fiber of his being. He hated even more that he needed it, and so he hawked up a wad of sulfur-flavored phlegm from the back of his throat and spat it into the hole's gaping maw with all the contempt he could muster.

This thing had cost him his family. The least it could do in return was to make the hurt stop. That's all he wanted. To stop giving a shit. To cop out like Jamie had and go numb. To no longer miss the people they'd been before she died. A father who'd loved him no matter if he was gay, straight, or whatever. A brother who'd been there through thick and thin. A mother who'd always put family first, until she'd made one epically selfish choice, which in turn had forced the rest of them into making selfish choices of their own.

He knew he couldn't ask the hole to turn back the clock and set things right between him and Jamie and Dad, but he could ask it to stop his pain. He wanted to move on like Jamie had. The hole owed him that much, at least. And it could take whatever it wanted in return: his hands, his feet, his strength and speed. It could even have his gayness and the hope that it gave him. Anything he had to offer. After all, there wasn't a damn thing left in his life worth enduring this burden another day longer, was there?

He heard Tyler clear his throat and felt him close in behind him.

"Before we do this," Tyler said carefully, "I need you to level with me about something."

"Shoot."

"Why didn't your mom jump when she had the chance?"

The question hit Jesse like a hard pass to the gut. He whirled around to face his friend.

"I'm sorry, man," Tyler said, averting his gaze. "I know you don't like to talk about her. Maybe it's none of my business, and it's a shitty thing to sandbag you with now." He shrugged. "But I'd really like to know before we jump. People talk. People wonder. *I've* wondered. I mean, it's cured cancer for other folks before, so why didn't she just, you know, come here and let it cure her?"

"It doesn't matter," Jesse said too quickly.

"Maybe it doesn't," Tyler persisted. "But I'd still like to know."

Jesse rubbed his eyes and turned back to the hole. Leave it to Tyler to see right through him. There was no use holding back anymore. It was time Tyler understood the private burden he'd been carrying these past five years.

"She did come here," he began, so quietly he wasn't sure if Tyler even heard him. "The night of her diagnosis. Before she even told Dad what the doctors said, she hiked down here after we went to bed and stood where I'm standing now."

His voice trailed off and he kicked at the dirt, sending a small shower of pebbles scattering into the mouth of the hole as he tried to imagine what that must have felt like for her. Alone. Scared. Desperate. It wasn't too hard to picture.

"And?" Tyler gently prodded.

"And so she asked herself, What's the worst I've got to lose here? What's the most this hole can take from me? Only, as soon as she'd answered that question for herself, she said she knew, instantly and for certain, that that would be the price, the thing it would keep. The very worst she could imagine. And so she turned around and marched straight home and refused to come back, no matter how much we begged and pleaded with her."

"Jesus." Tyler sucked in a breath. "What the hell was worth her life?'

Jesse's chest squeezed up like a fist.

"Us," he said quietly. "She said the worst thing she could imagine losing was her love for us. And then she knew that's exactly what the hole would take. She said it felt like something had given her a warning. She could go home cured, but the price would be that she wouldn't give a shit whether we lived or died anymore. Any of us. We might as well all be dead to her if she jumped. It was a raw deal, a fool's bet, and so she decided to go all in on the chemo instead, because it was better to risk dying than to lose us. And so that's what she did, and never mind what it would do to us after she was gone. How it would make us feel."

"It's like that saying, right? Never bet your soul when the devil's dealing?"

It was as if Tyler were channeling her ghost.

Jesse flinched but managed to say, "Something like that."

They fell silent.

Jesse focused his attention on the hole, on sussing out its sinister motives and intentions, but they seemed just as cruelly unfathomable now as they must have on the night it let his mom choose to die. He wondered how old the thing really was. Older than the mountains? Maybe even older than the world itself. Not that it mattered. His curiosity about it was as worn out as his endurance. The hole was nothing more than a means to an end now. He would be the last to use it to shut the door on his family, and after today, he would never come back here again.

After today, he wouldn't even think about this place anymore.

"Why are we doing this?" Tyler demanded, his voice suddenly urgent. "Why are we risking it? I mean, the worst I can imagine is some pretty dark shit." Jesse could feel Tyler's eyes on him as Tyler added, almost in a whisper, "What if we end up like your old man? Isn't that the worst you can imagine?"

It was the one question Jesse had refused to contemplate.

"Maybe she was wrong, man," he said, his fists clenching at his sides as he tried to hold back frustrated tears. "Maybe it wasn't a warning at all. Maybe she just got cold feet. Who knows what it would've really taken from her? Maybe she'd have gone bald like Huffaker, or blind, or, I dunno, gotten hooked on painkillers, gained a ton of weight, or forgotten how to ice skate. Christ, even if it'd done what she said it would do, if that was the worst she could think of, it was still better than this." He let out a deep sigh, his shoulders collapsing as exhaustion swept over him. "And besides," he added softly, "I can't keep going on like this. It hurts too much."

He regretted these words as soon as he said them. They sounded too much like a plea, too much like he was trying to guilt Tyler into following through with him.

But before he could take it back, Tyler said simply, "All right, then. Let's get it done," and stepped up to the hole beside him.

Jesse wiped the moisture from his eyes and turned to face his friend, who was now staring into the hole, his eyes fixed and his jaw set. They would go through with this together, he knew, not just because Tyler wanted to be braver, but because he was pissed off on Jesse's behalf. This damned hole owed Jesse for what it'd taken from him, for what it had refused to give, and if they needed to lay the worst they could imagine on the line to make sure Jesse finally got the peace he had coming, then Tyler was willing to roll those dice.

"You don't have to do this," Jesse said one last time.

"Shut up, asshole," Tyler said, and then: "Just so you know, I'm not asking it to fix my eyes."

"I figured." Jesse flashed him a grin. "I'm not asking it to make me straight, either."

Tyler nodded and turned back to face the hole. "On three?" he said.

"On three."

Jesse closed his eyes and tried to picture this being done and over in a way he could live with. Maybe he'd come back a weakling. Maybe he'd come back a drunk. Maybe he'd come back deaf, or stupid, or mean as a junkyard dog. He didn't care. He'd happily give up boners and football and every hair on his body if it meant he could make it through a single day without aching for the way things used to be. Without longing for what might have been.

"One," Tyler said.

Jesse's knees tensed as he pinched his nose and prepared to jump. His mind raced as he tried to envision what it would feel like to have something ripped from inside him. Would it hurt? Would he even notice it was gone when he returned to—to where? To home? To Tyler's bedroom? He had no idea where he'd belong after this, where the hole would choose to deposit him. He hoped that wherever it was, it wouldn't be far from Tyler. He wanted to be there when Tyler returned. After all, Tyler might be scared, even confused. He didn't want him to linger alone for too long with his own sacrifice, whatever that might turn out to be.

"Two."

Jesse's heart fluttered as an icy chill crawled up the nape of his neck. *What would the hole take?* The question filled him with a rush of fresh dread, and as if reading his mind, Tyler suddenly reached out and grabbed hold of his hand. His grip was tight, so tight Jesse could feel the bones of his fingers hard as stone beneath the clenched muscle, Tyler's warm pulse trembling beneath the skin that was too soft for a boy's, and yet—

Nothing about Tyler was soft.

Tyler was strong. Tyler was brave. Brave enough to do this, to be here, *to risk everything.*

And all at once, Jesse knew what this vile, greedy hole was going to take from him. He *knew*, just as Mom had known, just as he'd always known himself, though he'd tried so hard to deny it. And the sheer awfulness of losing Tyler struck him with the megaton force of a nuclear blast, tearing away his breath and scorching him to the marrow.

He jerked open his eyes and whirled around to find Tyler staring straight at him, horror splashed across his face.

It seemed that they'd both been given the same warning.

"To hell with three," Tyler spat, and backed away from the hole, though he didn't let go of Jesse's hand.

"Yeah, dude . . . Hell, no."

Jesse shook his head as if trying to clear his mind of what remained of the hole's dark spell. He frowned and stepped back from the edge, finally appreciating his mother's awful choice.

This hole could save your life.

But in return, it would take away whatever made that life worth living.

He flipped it the bird.

Then, still holding tightly on to Tyler, he winced at the forgotten pain in his ribs, realizing with a swell of something like joy that the long walk home was really going to suck.

A Border Kid Comes of Age
DAVID BOWLES

SUNDAY MORNING AT THE TAQUERÍA

Our family is Catholic. Can't eat before
Sunday mass because of the sacrament.
So we go to the early service,
stomachs rumbling,
and try to stay focused.

By 9:00 a.m., we're hurrying
out of St. Joseph's, piling into
Papá's pickup. He almost peels
out, to Mamá's chagrin,
as he heads to Taquería Morales,
a few blocks away.

Most Sundays the mayor
and his wife are already eating—
they're Baptists, lucky ducks.
They can eat all they want
before church.

Mr. Morales seats us, serves
cinnamon coffee and orange juice
in cups bearing the green logo
of Club León, his favorite
fútbol team.

We order. I get my usual, chorizo
and eggs, which comes with
fried potatoes and beans,
which I spoon into fluffy
flour tortillas along with
salsa verde.

By this time, the other parishioners
come spilling in. Papá greets some,
ignores others, especially
his former boss, the disgraced
police chief fired for corruption.
The stuffy air goes chilly for a sec.

My parents mutter to each other
about new scandals and old gossip.
I lean forward to catch snatches
till Mamá frowns. "Cosas de adultos,"

she says, flicking me back in my seat
with her eyes.

"Do y'all know everyone's secrets?"
I ask. Papá gives a little laugh.
"It's a small town, m'ijo. And the nosiest
folks are packed inside this taquería,
including you. Now finish your almuerzo."

So I take another bite. But my eyes
wander across the crowded tables,
and my ears strain to hear,
past clinking and laughter,
the constant heartbeat
of my community.

MY TOWN IN JUNE

My neighborhood teems,
alive with rambunctious shouts—
summer has begun.

La vecina, phone in hand,
glares out her window at me.

I just shrug, hefting
a cooler full of soft drinks
into our Bronco.

Somehow my little brother
is sleeping through this chaos.

The raspa man comes,
pushing his broken-down cart—
kids flock for snow cones.

Comadres in housecoats chat
beside the sidewalk, brooms poised.

And there's la güera,
walking to the store with an
entourage of boys.

Don Mario stands watching as
El Maistro stuccoes his house.

Doña Petra kneels
amidst her blue mistflowers,
crowned with butterflies.

In the placita, old men
play dominoes, reminisce.

The next street is blocked
to serve the loud World Cup dreams
of young soccer stars.

Smiling priests—one Mexican,
one Chinese—visit widows.

Scolding, Mom hurries
my slow siblings and me
through a quick breakfast.

Amidst shady mesquites,
Sara reads fate in folks' palms.

Mr. Cruz, "el Sir,"
gets to sleep in late today—
no classes, no kids.

Two dueling lawnmowers
get the city park ready.

My family piles thick
into our trusty Bronco—
the ocean beckons.

And the splendor of the sun
will light our way.

QUEER IN A BORDER COLONIA

Not easy, awakening to my identity,
when for men in my culture
the worst insult ever
is joto.

And I saw what happened
to my tío Samuel when he came out—
Where do you hide in a colonia?
Where's the sanctuary
along these pitted
caliche streets?

Aguantó vara. He took his licks.
And when he turned eighteen, he was gone.
Off to a big city. San Antonio? Austin?
Far away.

So when I feel my longing for girls
balanced by a yearning for boys,
I know I'm screwed. Jodido.
My uncles and cousins?
They won't understand "bisexual."
Just joto.

I'll push it down, I guess. Bite my tongue
when I want to flirt with a cute guy.
I hear rumors of clubs and bars
on the outskirts of town,
but I'm too young.

Maybe I'll escape, too. Someday.
I could call my uncle, but what would
I say to Uriel, the only one who
has his number? For everyone else,
he is forgotten. Erased.

They'll do the same to me
someday.

TEJANO KID

Let me tell you a story that's destined to last.
One more border kid from my family's past.

My great-grandpa Jorge's a güero like me.
His dad owns a store. It's 1915.

Revolution in Mexico has everyone scared.
Men keep crossing the river, and folks aren't prepared.

They rob trains and ranches. People get shot.
And soon law enforcement discovers a plot.

"El Plan de San Diego," a document
that asks Mexicanos to kill all white men.

A foolish idea. But Anglos feel fear
with so many brown-skinned Tejanos 'round here.

They get the government to send in the troops:
thousands of soldiers, on horses, in boots.

Even the innocent get pushed around,
from hardworking field hands to leaders of towns.

Though Jorge is light-skinned, with dirty-blond hair,
at school every day, the white boys just stare.

One day they yell as they follow him home:
"Hey, you bandit! Get back to Mexico!"

"I'm Tejano, not Mexican! Can't you fools understand?
For eight generations we've lived on this land!"

But the grown-ups' fear has poisoned the boys.
They pay him no mind. They just make some more noise.

As the weeks go by, things start to sour—
rogue rangers and soldiers abuse their power.

Mexicanos are seized at the slightest suspicion
and beaten or hanged with no jury's decision.

Jorge's father's obliged to close the store
as longtime friends are friends no more.

No more studies, for Tejanos stick with each other.
He learns to depend on just cousins and brothers.

He hears bitter whispers. Old wounds bleed fresh—
our ranches sold cheap, so Anglos grew rich.

Tejanos were pushed well south of the tracks
while the border economy was built on their backs.

Now the new landowners can only assume
that all this mistreatment will lead to their doom.

It's a self-fulfilling prophecy—
Jorge grows bitter even after troops leave.

Thousands of blameless Tejanos are dead,
and the loss thunders loud in Jorge's young head.

When his mother's mistreated, he attacks a white deputy
and spends twenty years in the state penitentiary.

That's why he gets married so late in his life,
passing down to his children these stories of strife.

His son Manuel tells his grandson as well:
And that man, my dad, his words like a spell,

Sits me down to recount the tale with chagrin—
"Never forget, boy. It could happen again."

CHICANO KID

Grandpa Manuel
is off in Vietnam
when his younger brother
Uriel, a high school freshman,
joins the walkout
in our small border town.

The 1960s are
very different times—
Mexican American students
aren't allowed to speak Spanish;
they're kept in basic classes,
taught in the worst rooms,
not encouraged to apply
to colleges.

People are fighting
for civil rights across the US,
so my great-uncle Uriel
calls himself a Chicano,
an activist
like older students
at his school.

They put together
a list of demands
and confront the school board.
They are ignored, dismissed,
even threatened,
so they take their struggle
to the next level.

On a particular day
in the fall of 1968,
when the ten a.m. bell rings,
Uriel and a hundred other students

stand up from their desks
and walk outside,
ignoring shouted warnings
from teachers and principal.

Waiting for them
in the parking lot
stand parents
like my bisabuela Luisa
and community leaders
with signs already made.

As the protest begins,
kids marching and chanting
with supportive adults,
a group of white teachers
gathers outside
and starts to take names.

Before long, the cops arrive,
and for unknown reasons
six of the older teens
are taken into custody.
Nearly every other kid
is suspended or expelled.
A few days later,
Uriel finds himself enrolled
in another high school
in another town.

But the spark has been struck.
Our small border towns
are on the national news.
All over the Southwest
Chicano students raise their fists
as they too stage walkouts
in peaceful protest.

The case goes to court,
and a judge says
these kids have
a constitutional right
to demonstrate.
The next semester,
Uriel is back at the school
with the other Chicanos.

Conditions aren't perfect,
but they get to speak Spanish,
and a new counselor's hired
to guide these border kids
to the colleges and lives
they deserve.

Fifty years later,
Uriel smiles at me
as he tells this story,
lifting a gnarled brown fist.
"¡Sí, se puede!" he exclaims.
"Yes, it can be done!

Together, muchacho,
la gente—our people—
as one."

COMING OUT

Hard to believe,
but our little high school,
obsessed with 2A football,
gives me the tools
to face my family,
say who I am.

An English teacher sponsors
a GSA club: *gay-straight* or
gender-sexuality alliance.
Some parents object, but
the principal supports it.
They meet twice a week
during lunch.

It takes me a while
to find the courage.
I show up one day.
Everyone's so good to me.
It feels incredible
to be myself,
accepted.

Of course, word spreads,
and I lose some friends
who never really were.
All these new allies
make it worthwhile.
After a few months,
I've figured out
what I must do.

I start with my great-uncle Uriel.
I tell him my truth.
I tell him my plan.
"You've got guts," he says
with an admiring smile.
He gives me the number
I've been too afraid to ask him for.

Then Uriel convenes the family
for a New Year's Eve pachanga.
Everyone's there, streaming
between the barbecue pit
and his huge kitchen,
spilling all over his yard
in the gentle cool air of a
border winter evening.

Then Samuel arrives, his partner,
Genaro, in tow. There's a little
alboroto, a mix of joyful and

scandalized shouts. Grandpa Manuel
just stands there in shock,
looking at the son he's not seen
in so many years.

"Everyone, cállesen," Uriel calls.
He puts his arm around Samuel
and gestures my way.
"Our güero has something to say."
All eyes are on me. I gulp air.

"Este, y'all have all heard our
stories, how our family has fought
for decades—centuries—to hang on
to our land, to be respected,
standing up against oppression
and erasure."

They all nod and mutter, proud.
"But this family has also become
a source of oppression. Brainwashed
by the folks that tried to hold us down.
Mi tío Samuel, he's not like y'all
in some ways. So you reject him
even though he's familia."

I clear my throat. My heart is racing.
"It's not right. He's just as strong a man
as any of the rest of you. He's put up

with more than most. You should stand
with him. And . . . with me. I'm queer, too.
Bisexual. I know, I can see some of you
shaking your heads. You don't understand.
Right now, you don't have to.
All you have to do is love me. And Samuel."

My father walks toward me, abandoning
the barbecue pit. There's something
strange in his eyes. His fingers clench
and unclench in spasms. I don't know if
he's going to hit me or storm out the gate.
Instead, he gathers me in his arms
and hugs me tight. Mom joins us.

No one says anything else. Words
aren't needed. Uriel turns to his brother.
Manuel's stern face softens.
Samuel reaches out his arm.
The two men shake hands.

I'm no fool. I know this is just the beginning.
I see disgust in some cousins' eyes,
Catholic disapproval on some tías' faces.
But I've broken past my fear,
taken the first step.

If there's one thing my family has taught me,
it's that our struggles are difficult and
never-ending, full of ups and downs,
but we fight for what is right
no matter what.

That's just who we are.

Fish and Fences
VEEDA BYBEE

At exactly seven a.m., a knock rattles our kitchen door.

"Right on time," I say, spooning the last bite of cornflakes to my mouth.

Mom sighs. Every Monday, Mr. Dean, our backyard neighbor, crosses the patch of grass between our houses to bring Mom a fish from his early-morning fishing trip. There is the occasional time when he doesn't come, like when nothing bites, or when the rivers freeze over. Ever since his wife died six months ago, our elderly friend has made it his life's mission to supply my mother with fish.

She hates it.

"Whatever happened to the shortbread cookies he used to bring?" I say. "I miss those."

"Yeah, those were so much better than *fish*!" my older brother, Tom, says. He's seventeen, two years older than me, but the way he's eating right now, he's no more couth than a toddler. Dribbles of milk run down his chin.

Mom is already out of her seat, ready to greet our neighbor

at the door. "He made those cookies with Judy. I don't think he's made them since."

Mom has her hand on the doorknob. "Tom, stop talking with food in your mouth. And brush your hair before you leave." Just before she opens the door, she shoots Tom a look that says *Be quiet or else*.

"Wally!" Mom holds a manicured hand to her cheek. "So nice to see you this morning."

Mr. Dean's smile lights up his wrinkled, weathered face like an Idaho sunrise.

"I caught a beauty today." He holds up a fish. The skin of his hand is pale, almost translucent. "Just for you." His voice is soft, like the gentle wind that blows through our little valley in the spring. "It would make for a good stir-fry or whatever you eat with rice."

Mom clasps her hands together in gratitude. I have to give it to her. As much as she says she hates fish, her thank-you feels sincere.

She places her arm around Mr. Dean, who is just as short as she is. "You are so kind to think of me."

They chat for a few minutes, covering topics like the upcoming Latter-day Saints church picnic, the size of Mrs. Martin's roses down the street, and the shenanigans of the troublesome elder Woo boy, who everyone knows is breaking into the hot springs at night but no one can catch. Finally, Mom says goodbye.

She looks at the clock on the stove: 7:20 a.m.

"Good golly," she says, and I giggle. Mr. Dean's gosh-darn language is rubbing off on her.

Mom holds the fish out at arm's length. "I do hate fish."

I gather up my books and realize I've never asked the reason. "Why is that, exactly?"

Mom places the fish in a plastic grocery bag. "When I was young, one of my jobs was to help Cook. My chore was cleaning the fish." She glances out the window, her eyes looking past the row of homes on our street in Mineral Springs, Idaho. She seems to look past the Rocky Mountains, across the Pacific Ocean, and into her childhood in Laos.

I sink back into the kitchen chair. Mom doesn't often talk about her childhood. Here's what I know: Her father owned a successful engineering company. They had a cook, a maid, and enough money to sneak the entire family across the Mekong River when Communism took over after the country collapsed. And I know that Mom's family spent time in a refugee camp. But she's never talked about helping in the kitchen before. This fish brought something to the surface. I want to dive in and find out more.

"Mom," I press, leaning forward. "So cleaning the fish made you hate fish—cooking it *and* eating it?"

Mom nods. "I used to like fish, until I started having to clean it. I hated the smell." She frowns. "I hated the eyes. They looked so round, so surprised."

She holds out Mr. Dean's gift. "Kind of like this one. Their eyes seem to say, 'What's going on? Am I dead? Where is the water?'"

She waves her hand as if brushing away this recollection. "It was my most hated chore." Her eyes are far away again when she adds, "If I hadn't already hated fish, that night on the little fishing boat would have been enough to do the job."

Tom and I look at each other. "What fishing boat?" I say. "The one you escaped on?"

Mom's brown eyes are dark and sad. "Another boat didn't make it. It capsized. I still think of all those people trying to escape. Only to swim with the fish."

Tom's mouth pops open and a soggy cornflake falls on the table.

"Gross," I tell him.

Mom picks up a black-and-white-checkered kitchen towel and wipes the table. "Mr. Dean thinks we are all the same," she says. "That all Asians like fish." She lifts her head. "Well, we don't."

Tom wipes his chin with the back of his hand. "Why don't you just tell Mr. Dean?"

Mom crumples the towel and places it on the counter. "I tried to, once. When he first brought one over, I wanted to run away. I thought of being in that little fishing boat in the middle of the night." She shudders, then picks up Tom's homework folder and hands it to him. "How could I tell Mr. Dean this? Judy had just died. I remembered how much he liked to bring her fish. How could I take that away from him?"

Tom shoves his folder in his bag. "Yeah, Mom. That's a really sad story. I don't think I can eat fish now."

Mom blinks. "You just don't want to eat fish." She smacks him on the arm. "We are lucky to have it."

Tom shrugs. "Fine, just don't make me clean that thing."

"I should," Mom says. "You kids are becoming too American. Why can't you be more like the Woos? Those kids help out with their family business."

I groan. The Woos are the only other Asian family in our town, so of course people expect us to know each other. And we do, kind of. Mom and Mrs. Woo are good friends. But Mr. Woo and Dad don't have that much in common. Mr. Woo owns the mechanic shop and Dad teaches high school math. They make small talk for the sake of their wives. Even though Tom and I are close in age to the Woo boys, we don't hang out.

Steven, the Woos' older son, is a senior and perpetually in trouble. He skips school, is the cause of a few missing garden gnomes around town, and drives loud and fast down Main Street. Everyone knows it's Steven Woo, out blaring his hip-hop. He's great with cars, though. He and his younger brother, Jon, help their dad out in the shop. And in my mom's eyes, this more than makes up for any "mischief" he gets into.

Jon is my age. He is without a doubt the town's favorite Asian. Jon is the high school quarterback, an honor roll student, and destined for greatness. He knows it, too. He hasn't talked to me since sixth grade, when his family first moved to Mineral Springs and I was assigned to be his new-student buddy. Even back then, Jon was too good for me. After we spent the morning together, he ditched me right before lunch.

"The Woos aren't that wonderful." I sling the straps of my backpack on my shoulders and pick up my clarinet case. "Steven smokes weed."

"Maybe it's for medicine," Mom says. "You can be so judgmental, Sarah."

Tom chokes back a laugh. "Yeah, Sarah. Stop judging."

I swing my clarinet at him, and Mom notices. "You have marching-band practice today?"

"Yeah."

She frowns. "I told you to wear a hat. The sun is so bad for your skin." She grabs her straw gardening hat by the back door. "Here, take this."

"Mom." My voice is stern. "I am not going to wear that. I'll look like an Asian rice paddy farmer."

She folds her arms. "What's wrong with that? Farmers work hard. That should be a compliment. Wear it. You'll thank me when you're forty and you don't have age spots."

I grab the hat by its strings and rush out the door before she offers me a long-sleeved shirt, too. Tom scoots by her as well. He already has a change of clothes for his after-school practice, but that doesn't mean Mom won't find something to bug him about. He still hasn't brushed his hair.

School goes by in a blur. When the last bell rings, I gather with the rest of our small marching band on the practice field of Marsh River High. We are tiny in number, just like the rest of the school.

I love it.

My cousins in California don't know how I can take being one of the few people of color in a mostly all-white community. They ask me if all I eat is potatoes and all I listen to is country music.

They don't know what they are missing. Sure, I actually do eat more potatoes than rice, but that's because potatoes are great. You can mash them, scallop them, bake them, and fry them. Mom puts fresh potatoes from the garden in our curry, and Mrs. Alton down the road even makes them into potato rolls. She shares them every year at Christmas. She always gushes over the plate of fried wontons Mom delivers, but I love her rolls like candy.

I don't particularly like Western tunes, but when Mr. Dean plays his Hank Williams, it nearly softens my country-hating heart. Hank Williams isn't like the new stuff, though. His songs are almost bluesy, sad and sentimental. When Mr. Dean puts on his old records, the sweet twang of guitar strings and bittersweet lyrics float through his open kitchen window into our own. Even Tom will take out his earbuds to listen.

Also, living in a small town gives me more opportunities than my cousins have living in the city. They have to try out for everything. Dance teams. Soccer. Debate. It's a huge deal if they make something. Here, most everyone gets a spot. Not to say there isn't amazing talent—just not as much.

If I'm being honest, I know I'm not that good at the clarinet. I'd only been playing for a year when Mom informed me I needed to either get a job or find an after-school activity. I chose marching band. I'm still kind of terrible at it. Marching in time to music is harder than I'd imagined. Luckily, everybody makes the band. If I had to go against people who could actually play, I'd probably be working at the town's solo gas station right now.

Mr. Goodwin, our band director, calls us to attention. As we come into formation, he looks at me.

"Sarah," he says. "Your mom emailed me this afternoon. She asked me to remind you to wear your hat."

The entire band looks at me.

"Are you serious?" I say.

"Yes. She linked to five articles about skin cancer. Go put your hat on."

I huff a little as I walk off the field to where my backpack is. On top of it sits my stupid hat. Its brim flutters in the wind, mocking me.

I place my hat on my head, tucking the strings inside. I hate having them tied under my chin. Once my hat is on, we resume practice. I haven't memorized my part yet, so attached to my clarinet is a tiny flip folder of sheet music. We go over our drills, and I try to remember to keep time with my feet. Ideally, the heels of my shoes should hit the ground with the downbeat of the song. This requires both coordination and a sense of rhythm, two things I severely lack. My feet are up when they should be down, and my counts are off. I really am quite terrible.

Suddenly, a strong gust of wind sweeps across the field, sending sheet music flapping, water bottles falling off benches, and my straw hat sailing through the sky, soaring like an air-borne alien spaceship. When it hits Abbi Mason in the head, she drops her piccolo on the ground. The half-sized flute bounces once on the grass and lands by her feet.

"What the—?!" she says, the rest of her expletive swallowed up by the loud trumpet chorus.

Heat rises to my face, like a sunburn already forming.

"I'm so sorry!" I say. Holding my clarinet with one hand, I rush over to retrieve my runaway hat.

Students are still playing, their marching feet moving in unison. I dodge the line of approaching saxophones, weave between the thumping bass drums, and make my way to the high-pitched notes of the piccolos straight ahead. I turn just in time to catch a flash of gold before *thwack*! My head throbs, and I crumple to the ground.

"Oh gosh, Sarah!"

I look up to see Nathan Smith's stunned face. His trombone hangs from his hands.

"I'm so sorry," he says, like it's his fault I'm in the wrong place on the field. "I can't believe I just hit you."

I'm not sure if it's actual cymbals crashing, but my ears are ringing. I might be the most terrible marching-band member in the world.

I touch the tender spot on my forehead and grimace. There's no blood, but I'm pretty sure I'm feeling the beginning of a welt. Tom is going to love this story.

The music stops, and Mr. Goodwin approaches me. "Are you okay?"

I manage to sit up, sliding my legs in front. "Yeah, I think so."

I glance around the field. Everyone in the band is watching. My hat is nowhere to be seen, and I don't even care. I can tell Mom what her hat did to me.

"There's some ice in the cooler," Mr. Goodwin says as I push up. "Get some for your head. And maybe, um, sit out the rest of practice."

I follow his instructions while the rest of the band resumes practice. The ice is cool against my skin and melts immediately against my sticky forehead.

"Hey, is this yours?" a voice calls.

Across the field where the football team is gathering stands Jon Woo. Even though he's yards away from me, I can make out his features clearly: athletic build, dressed in a T-shirt and workout shorts, dark hair long and shaggy like a K-pop star's. He holds a football tucked under one arm, my straw hat in his other hand.

"Yes," I shout back.

As I start toward him, Henry Nelson jogs up to Jon. "Hey, man," he says, clapping Jon on the back. "Practice is starting." Then he notices my hat in Jon's hands. His gaze turns to me before swinging back to Jon. "Is that your sister?"

I freeze. Marsh River High has a population of 350 kids. True, I never talk to Henry Nelson. But I'm annoyed that after all this time, he thinks Jon and I are related. I've been mistaken for Jon's sister for years. No matter how much I hear it, it always sets me on edge. We don't even share the same last name or social groups.

Jon drops his hand. Then raises it to the height of his head. With a pass worthy of his star quarterback status, he hurls my hat in the air. It spirals toward me, a spinning straw Frisbee.

Miraculously, it lands in my hands, but Jon is already walking away.

"She's not my sister," he says, his voice flat.

I crumple the rim of the hat with my fingers. Then, thinking of what Mom might make me wear instead, I smooth it out again and place it back on my head.

Band practice ends after a few more runs. As we pack up, I chat with friends and assure everyone that I'm okay. It's just a minor bump, but I can only imagine Tom's commentary about this at dinner.

After saying goodbye, I throw on my backpack. With my clarinet case in hand, I start the short walk home.

When I approach the chain-link fence of the school grounds, the pounding in my head intensifies. The gate is shut, cutting off my usual way home.

I walk over to the gate and shake it. Sure enough, it's locked. I could walk around to the front of the school, but that takes forever, and Tom might beat me home from soccer practice. When he does, he gets first dibs at the television and I'm stuck watching ESPN till dinnertime.

"Seriously?" I say out loud. No one hears me. I'm the only person in sight.

I place my clarinet case on the ground and look up. The fence isn't *that* high. I've seen kids scale it before. How hard can it be?

Shrugging my backpack off my shoulders, I count backward in my head, and in three-two-one—

The bag flies over the fence.

It makes a satisfying *thud* on the other side.

I place the straw hat on my head and grab hold of the fence with my hands. I wedge my feet into the holes of the metal links and begin to climb. My sneakered toes barely fit, but I make it up. So far, so good. I glance down at the ground to see how far I've come. Then I see it.

My clarinet case.

I completely forgot about my instrument. How am I supposed to climb a fence holding my clarinet case? Throwing my clarinet over the fence is also out the question. I can't imagine the punishment Mom and Dad will give me if I break it. Mom would probably make me clean Mr. Dean's weekly fish deliveries.

Through the fence, I see the outline of my cell phone in the front pocket of my backpack. So much for calling for help.

I jump down, and it's disappointing how close to the ground I really was. My hat slides over my eyes and I push it back, letting it dangle from the hat strings around my neck.

I stare at the fence. At my book bag on the other side.

Picking up my clarinet case, I take a deep breath and try my ascent again. My balance is not the same. My fingers slip, and sharp metal rings bite into my palm. I wobble and jump back down. When I land, my ankle twists. For the second time today, I fall.

I feel so sorry for myself at this moment, I simply lie in the grass.

It's like Mr. Dean's windows are open and I can hear a Hank Williams song in my head. I'm so lonesome I could cry.

I turn my head just in time to see Jon Woo walking on the other side of the street, duffel bag slung over his shoulder and head bent over a book.

Ugh. Of course the one person who happened by would be him.

"Hey!" I call, sitting up. "Jon Woo!"

He doesn't look up. He is either ignoring me or super engrossed in his reading. What book could capture Jon Woo's attention like this?

I am happy to discover that while my ankle is sore, it doesn't hurt that bad. I reach over and grab my clarinet case, waving it in the air. "Over here!"

Jon starts to turn up the road.

His silence breaks past any awkwardness I feel toward him. He's not going to ignore me anymore.

"You big-headed, second-string B-grade quarterback!" I'm shouting as loud as I can. "I need *help!*"

Jon stops. He looks around . . . *Finally,* he notices me.

Then, like the good boy he is, Jon looks both ways before he crosses the road. Mrs. Woo would be so proud.

Jon walks up to the other side of the fence. "Did you just call me a B-grade quarterback?"

I swallow. I know I'm not in the best position to be hurling insults, but I can't find it in me to apologize. Today is the first time we've talked in years. All my frustrations with him are leaking out in my words. Plus, my head and ankle *hurt*.

"It got your attention, didn't it?"

He takes a step closer, weaving his fingers through the chain-link fence. "Football isn't ranked that way. I'm first-string, which means I'm part of the team that starts every game."

"Well, aren't you perfect?" I wince and touch my ankle. "Ouch."

"Oh," Jon says. "Do you need help?"

"Excellent deduction." For someone who gets good grades, he's pretty slow on the uptake.

Jon laughs. "Wow, I can't believe you fell down again."

My foot is throbbing now. "Wait, did you see me at practice?"

He grins. "The whole team did. It was hilarious."

I want to cry or scream or both, but instead I feign bravery. Using the chain-link for support, I pull myself up and balance on one foot. "Listen, I just need help getting over the fence." There's disdain in my voice. I try to pull it back. "I hurt my ankle, but it's not that bad. I think I can still make it over. Can I hand you my clarinet?"

Jon squints. He looks at the fence like he's studying it. "I bet if I gave you a boost, you could for sure make it over."

"What do you mean?"

"I'll come over and you can stand on my hands."

"That will work?"

"Sure," he says. "We hop the hot springs fence all the time."

"I thought it was Steven doing that!"

Jon crosses his arms. "Who do you think taught me?"

I look up at the top of the fence. It seems higher than before. I'm not sure. "Maybe I should call someone."

"Sure, do you have a phone? I don't have mine with me."

I nod to my backpack on his side of the fence. "Front pocket."

As Jon opens my bag, a tampon falls out.

I'm so over this day, I don't even care that he picks up my feminine-hygiene product like it's an ordinary object. He places it back in my bag.

Jon lightly tosses my phone over the fence. It lands in the grass next to my feet. I'm impressed by his aim and can see that the guy is quarterback for a reason.

He watches me type on my phone. "Did you just do one-two-three-four?" He leans in close. "You know, that's a horrible passcode."

"Whatever."

It is a horrible passcode, but it's the only one my mom will remember, and she makes me keep it that way.

I try my parents. My calls go to voicemail.

Tom doesn't answer either. I almost consider calling Mr. Dean, but I have no idea how he could help me.

I'm about to try a friend when Jon grabs the fence with both hands.

He pulls himself up with ease, and I bet he could probably climb the fence with one hand. Before I can push the green call button on my phone again, he's standing next to me.

Jon is closer to me than he's ever been.

"That was . . ." I struggle to find the words. "Kind of amazing."

"No big deal," he says. "I climb fences all the time."

"So I'm hearing."

Jon looks me over. "While I have you here, I've got a question for you."

I scan my brain to think of what he could possibly want to know.

"Okay," I say. "What?"

Jon shifts his weight from side to side and actually looks a little uncomfortable. "So, why do you hate me?"

I blink. Maybe that trombone hit me harder than I thought.

"I don't hate you," I say slowly. "You're the one who hates me."

Jon's eyes are on mine. At that moment, I can't believe people think we look alike. I mean, he's Korean American. My family has Southeast Asian roots. Sure, we both have black hair. His eyes are brown like mine but so different. They are dark and intense, and it's like he's looking straight into my soul.

Jon shakes his head. "You hate me because I'm Asian."

I almost fall over. "What?"

"In sixth grade, Mrs. Jordan assigned you to be my new-student helper, and you ditched me the first chance you got. You had Billy Mason show me to the bathroom, and I got stuck listening to him talk about how we should bring cricket over to America. I had to eat lunch by myself."

I try to think back to that day. "No! I remember asking Billy to show you to the restroom because I didn't want to show a boy where to pee. It was so embarrassing. Then you didn't come back."

"I kept away because I thought you didn't want me around." Jon leans back on the chain-link fence. "You were supposed to be my friend during lunch and recess. Instead, you stuck me with cricket-loving Billy Mason."

I'm actually speechless.

"I'm sorry you've felt this way for so long," I finally say. My one good leg feels weak, and I give in, sinking to the ground. "I asked Billy to help you because he seemed so excited to have a new kid in the class. I just didn't want to be stuck talking to a boy."

"So you were avoiding me because I was a boy and not because I was another Asian?"

I brush the grass with my fingers. "Turns out I was just sexist. Not racist."

"Come on, boys aren't that bad."

"Try living with Tom!"

We both laugh.

It's like an invisible wall between us has come down. I give Jon a smile, as if seeing him for the first time. "So Billy Mason was that into cricket?"

Jon sits down next to me. "He kept telling me I should help him start a club because cricket is similar to baseball. He said baseball was huge in Japan, and since I was Asian I probably liked it."

"Yikes," I say.

He nods. "Not all Asians like baseball."

I think of Mom. "Or fish."

"What?" Jon says.

"Never mind," I say. "Just something I talked about with my mom this morning."

Jon doesn't push the question. He lets out a breath, long and deep, like he's been holding it in for years. "You know, I admit it. Back then I thought girls were a little gross, too." He looks over at my crumpled T-shirt and sweat-soaked hat. "Maybe they still are."

"Hey!"

We are laughing again, and it feels so natural, like we haven't spent the past few years avoiding each other.

He stands. "Okay, let's do this." He clasps his hands and holds them out in front of him. "Step on my hands," he says. "Then my shoulders. I'll give you a boost."

He looks strong but not that strong. "Are you sure about this?"

"If I can help a lineman over a fence, I can certainly get a marching-band nerd over."

I also rise. "I have no idea what a lineman is, but enough with the band geek, okay?"

Jon holds his hands out in apology. "You're right. I take it back. Now, let's get you over this fence."

He laces his fingers again, and I stick my good foot in his hands. Then my sore one. I step on his shoulders, and when I start to wobble, I grab the fence, smacking Jon in the face in the process.

"Sorry!"

Jon grunts but doesn't reply.

When I reach the top of the fence, I sling one leg over and sit on the rail. It's so high up here. This was a bad, bad idea.

I close my eyes. I can't seem to go any farther. The wind blows, sending my blasted hat over my eyes.

"I can't do this."

"You're halfway there," Jon calls from below. His voice is casual, friendly. Like we've been pals for years. Strangely enough, it's reassuring. "Hold on, I'm coming up."

Jon climbs the fence. He's next to me again, this time some-where between the earth and the sky.

He passes me and jumps down on the other side of the fence. He holds his arms out. "Okay, now step on my shoulders."

We repeat the process in reverse. I reach for his hand and climb backward. My feet are in his hands. Then on the earth.

I nuzzle my face in sweet, sweet grass. I want to kiss each green blade. I don't care if it's sticking to my sweaty skin. The ground never looked so good.

Jon hops back up and goes over the fence. He gets my clari-net and looks up. "I'm going to have to throw it to you," he says. "I don't think I can climb with one hand."

I nod. Guess I was wrong about another assumption.

"Ready?" Jon says.

"Ready!"

Jon pulls his arms back and throws high.

My little black case turns cartwheels in the air, clearing the fence and heading my way. Miraculously, it falls into my hands.

Jon whoops, and I smile. This time, someone was here to see my catch.

He climbs again, and when he jumps over, he slings one of my arms around his shoulders and we walk down the road. Him carrying two bags and a clarinet and supporting me. I'm suddenly aware of how close we are. I say a silent prayer that I don't stink. I look over at Jon. "Does it bug you that everyone thinks we're related?"

He is watching the sky. With the setting sun, faint shades of pink and purple mingle with the bright blue.

"Yeah," he says, keeping his face tipped upward. "Especially, you know . . . since you're in marching band."

"You said you'd stop your band trash talk!"

Jon laughs. "I'm not trying to make excuses," he says. "But a lot of people just don't know any better. They aren't mean. They haven't been around that many people who don't look like them." He glances at me. "I think they're trying their best."

I think about Mr. Dean and his fish. He made an assumption, and instead of correcting him, my mom chose to love him.

We walk in silence, my arm slung over Jon's shoulders. I study his face. He's supporting most of my weight and doesn't flinch once. Even with his boy-band hair and football player arrogance, he actually seems like a pretty great human. "I don't hate you, Jon."

Jon smiles. It looks really good on him. "I don't hate you either."

Before I can ask about the book he was reading, I notice Mr. Dean waving at me from his front porch.

"Sarah!" he says. "Come here, come here!"

Jon nods to Mr. Dean. "I'll put your stuff by your front door," he says to me.

"Oh, okay. Thanks," I say.

He walks away, and I try to push down the fluttering feelings in my chest. "Hey!" I call. "What book were you reading?"

Jon turns around to face me, walking backward. It's so cute, and I can't believe I'm thinking about Jon this way. But then again, why not? It's not like we're related.

"It's a good one!" he shouts back. "I'll tell you all about it when I'm done."

At the promise of another conversation, I watch Jon Woo leave. Mr. Dean is waiting for me on his front porch.

I slowly walk up his steps.

"Are you hurt?" Mr. Dean asks.

"I'm fine," I say. I look to where Jon is placing my clarinet and backpack on my front porch. "A friend helped."

Mr. Dean nods. He points to a chair. "Well, come sit."

On a table is a plate of cookies.

"Shortbread!" I say, and take a cookie. "My favorite."

"Judy's recipe," Mr. Dean says. He smiles as I take a bite. Mr. Dean shields his eyes from the glaring sun. "I wanted to ask you a question. Your mom seemed a little sad this morning when I came by. Was something wrong?"

I keep chewing. I think of my old neighbor, his long days without his wife. I think of Mom and the faraway look in her eyes when she remembers the trauma of escaping Laos. I think about what it means to live in a town where most everyone knows one another, at least by sight. There's so much going on beneath the surface; do we really know everyone's story unless we talk to people? I went for years thinking Jon Woo hated me. Until today, he thought I hated him. I think about how fish can be a generous gesture to one and something triggering for another. I think about assumptions and ignorance, what happens when we speak up and what happens when we don't.

I decide to speak up.

"Mr. Dean, I really don't like fish," I say.

Mr. Dean sits back in surprise. "What?"

"I hate cleaning them," I say. I've never cleaned a fish, but I bet it would be horrible. "They smell. And, uh, look dead. Do you think . . . maybe you can stop bringing us fish?"

Mr. Dean scratches his hand. A Hank Williams song wafts through his open kitchen window. Then he chuckles. "Well, I'll be. I don't really like to fish all that much, either."

My eyes widen. "You don't?"

"I hate waking up that early! That darn river took my hat this morning, and I only got up to go fishing because I knew your Mom'd be expecting something." Mr. Dean rubs the top of his head. "She's always reminding me to wear a hat, and I done gone and lost it."

I take off the floppy hat hanging from my neck and hold it out in front of me. "Mr. Dean, on behalf my family, I want you to have this hat. In exchange for all the fish you've given us these past few months."

Mr. Dean runs his finger over the brim. He places the hat on his head. It blocks out the sun, and he smiles. "What do you know? It fits!"

As his face lights up, I'm certain Mom won't mind having one less hat. "It looks great on you."

I get up to leave. As I turn around to say goodbye, I notice the baked goods on the table. "I'm glad you made Mrs. Dean's shortbread again. It's a good recipe."

Mr. Dean breathes deep, as if the mention of his late wife gives him air. He hands me the plate. "Take the whole thing. For your family."

I pick up the plate of sweet, buttery goodness. If Tom plays nice and shares the TV, he might just get a couple. "Thanks for the cookies, Mr. Dean. We've missed them."

Mr. Dean smiles and tips the hat to me. "See you Monday— with shortbread this time."

Close Enough
NORA SHALAWAY CARPENTER

"I think you might need a break."

Alina heard her best friend, but she swung the ax anyway, her right hand sliding down the handle just like her dad had taught her. The firewood split into two perfect woodstove-sized pieces and fell with a scrape off the tree stump.

"I'm serious," Mori said, grabbing the pieces and tossing them into the growing pile inside the wheelbarrow. "Wanna race to the fork?"

"What I want," said Alina, adding a new chunk of wood to the chopping block, "is to finish that stupid short story." She brought the ax down hard, severing the wood with a satisfying crack. "The deadline's next week."

Mori's eyebrows rose, shrinking the tiny tattooed star above her left one. "So you've mentioned." She hoisted an extra-large piece of wood onto the stump, grunting under its weight. "And that's why you're, um, working on it so hard right now, yeah?"

Alina stared at the hunk of tree Mori had placed before her.

Mori always found a way to call out her bullshit. Alina supposed that was part of what made her a state champion debate team captain, but damn.

"It's percolating," she said.

"Uh-huh."

Alina squared her shoulders. In reality, she'd written and rewritten and scrapped so many stories she had no idea what she even wanted to say anymore. She brought the ax down, but this time the blade didn't cut through, and she strained to raise the whole thing—firewood and ax together—and bang it against the stump to finish the job. The split pieces fell away. "Okay, fine." She wiped her face. "I'm stuck."

"I know." Mori's lips twitched, and she added a smaller piece of wood to the stump. "You've got that look."

"What look?"

"The my-writing's-sucking-so-I'll-chop-wood-until-my-arms-fall-off look."

Alina rested the ax on her shoulder. "I don't do that enough for it to be a look."

Mori glanced at the lean-to Alina's dad had built for firewood, which last month had been empty. Mountains of split wood stood three rows deep. "Haven't you been working on the story since August?"

"Okay," Alina conceded, "so maybe it hasn't been going well for a while. It's just—"

"You need the scholarship; I know." Mori tossed the wood scraps she'd collected from around the stump into a crate with the rest of the kindling. "Believe me, I know."

Alina knew she did. They were both taking out the same number of loans, even though Mori was going in state. And while Alina could definitely use the scholarship money for New York University next year, winning the West Virginia Teen Writers contest was about much more than that. So much more. She didn't quite know how to explain that to Mori, though, or anyone, really. How the winning short stories always featured typical "West Virginian" topics like dried-up coal-mining towns, mountain dulcimer–playing grandparents, or extended families who'd lived on the same land for generations. How trying to find herself in those stories was like seeking her picture in another family's photo album.

"So how 'bout that race?" Mori stole a quick glance at her Fitbit. "We've been out here for, like, an hour. I've heard a change of scenery can do wonders for percolation." She folded her arms, her mouth an orange-lipsticked smirk, and Alina couldn't help but smile. Even when she wore sneakers, jeans, and a West Virginia University hoodie, Mori's art-chic style managed to shine through.

"Unless," Mori added, "You're afraid I'll beat you?"

"Riiight."

They didn't race often, both preferring sports like volleyball to cross-country or track. But occasionally they challenged each other just for the hell of it. And for bragging rights, of course. Mori, whose legs were two inches shorter, had beaten Alina exactly once.

"Okay." Alina sank the ax into the stump—*safety first*— then straightened, her feet already itching to take off. "But ten bucks says you won't win."

"Oooh," Mori said, eyes widening with satisfaction. "Stakes." She cracked her neck. "Deal."

They took off at the same time, the long gravel driveway

crunching beneath their shoes as they shrieked like children and jostled for position. They passed the old logging road that led down to the creek where they used to catch tadpoles and salamanders, and veered instead for the wooded entrance to the hay field trail, the one that led up to the fork and eventually all the way to the highest point on Alina's family's ninety-eight acres.

Mori entered the tree-tunneled trail first, cutting off Alina as she tried to make a pass near the bottom of the drive. Alina wasn't worried. She attacked the uneven leaf- and root-covered ground with the surety that came from traveling it almost every day of her life. Slowly, inevitably, she gained ground.

"Cheetos . . . bad idea . . . *shit*," panted Mori, but Alina didn't waste energy smiling. The fork was just a dozen paces ahead. She dug deep, ignoring the burn in her thighs, and put on a burst of speed that sent her three strides in front of her best friend.

"Victory!" she called, slapping the trunk of the oak that split the trail in two. "That's ten dollars, please and thank you."

Mori collapsed dramatically onto her back, her razor-cut dark hair accented against the orange and red leaves littering the moss-covered path. "You owe me for lunch yesterday, on the field trip. Call it even?"

"Oh, yeah," Alina said. "Dang."

Mori sat up, flicking a leaf from the back of her pixied hair. "Wanna hike to the top?"

Alina eyed the trail, which turned markedly steeper just a few steps away. "Yeah, okay."

She pulled Mori up, and they leaned into the steep incline

as they climbed, their breathing coming too hard for conversation. Then the ground leveled out for a spell, and Mori gestured around them.

"Do you know how lucky you are? Living out here?" She closed her eyes, head tipped back, like she was soaking in everything—the sweet, musty smell of soil and century-old trees; the soft symphony of rustling twigs and swaying branches; the crisp breeze that toyed with the baby hairs around her face.

"Are you kidding?" Alina said. "Dad could have moved anywhere and he picked here." She'd always considered Mori the lucky one, living in town like she did. Even though their town had less than eight hundred people, it was still a town, and unlike her, Mori had next-door neighbors. She was also closer to school and classmates, and only had to drive forty minutes to the nearest movie theater instead of the hour it took Alina. Plus, Mori had central heat.

Mori's eyes opened. "What's wrong with West Virginia?"

"Huh? No, that's not what I meant." Alina tried again. "We have snakes in our cellar."

Mori stuffed her hands inside her sweatshirt's front pocket. "You wouldn't if you sealed it. Your dad knows that." She kept walking.

"I guess."

"And besides, black snakes aren't poisonous."

Alina nodded. "Um, true."

Mori kept silent, her pace quickening. Alina sprinted a few steps to keep up.

"Is, uh, everything okay?"

Mori let out a short breath through her nose, but it was

probably due to the strenuousness of the trail. She nodded. "Yeah, fine."

Alina wasn't sure that was quite true, but Mori clearly didn't want to say more.

"So . . . How's Angela?"

Mori grinned immediately. "She's good. She went with friends to Cincinnati for the game today. Mariah's from there, so they're crashing at her place."

"Nice." Alina thought back to the tailgate Mori's girlfriend had invited them to last weekend, when they'd met a bunch of Angela's college friends. "Mariah was the one with the trident tattoo, right? The art major?"

Mori nodded. "I kind of wanna be her when I grow up. Even though, you know, she's only two years older than me. Apparently she's working to start a campus-led art collective that volunteers at public schools lacking art programs. Also, she skydives." She stopped short. "Oh, *perfect.* Hang on a sec."

They'd reached the sharpest, steepest part of the hill, where the trees gave way to rhododendron and blackberry bushes. Mori wandered over to the ancient black walnut tree that stood on the brink of the woods, and Alina's mind rewound to the tailgate. It was the closest either of them had come to a real college experience. They'd played corn hole and bummed beer from the over-twenty-ones in the group until it was time to enter the stadium, and West Virginia had upset a major rival. And since neither she nor Mori was allowed to stay over, Alina, who'd had exactly three sips of alcohol, had driven them home. All in all, it had been a pretty wonderful day.

Except for the mustard lady.

Alina didn't particularly want to remember the incident, so she started toward where Mori was bent over, stuffing walnuts into her sweatshirt pocket. Too late, though. The memory was already unspooling.

She'd asked to borrow mustard from the middle-aged woman tailgating next to them.

"Sure, honey," the woman had said. "You from West Virginia or just visiting friends?"

Alina knew why she'd asked. There was a bond—intense and immediate—when born-and-bred West Virginians discovered one another. During Alina's beach trip with Mori's family last summer, Mori had scored backstage passes for a sold-out concert because the bouncer had a West Virginia University tattoo, and it turned out he and Mori had been born in the same hospital. Another minute revealed Mori's great-uncle had grown up in the same town as the bouncer's cousin, and they maybe even knew each other.

It was charming, kind of magical, and something that seemed so closely tied to belonging to the state that it made Alina, with no West Virginia relatives or roots of any kind, feel utterly *other*. Of the sixty-three people in her graduating class, she was the only one who didn't have extended family in the area. The only one without built-in friendships of cousins and lifelines of aunts, uncles, and grandparents. The only one whose third-grade family heritage project for West Virginia History Month didn't include a single person born in the state.

And that was fine. She was used to it. But it also marked her as *different*. So when the woman asked, Alina avoided a direct answer by stating the facts: "We moved here when I was three."

The woman *tsk*ed, but there was something indulgent about it. "Oh, well," she'd said. "Close enough."

Alina wanted to think the words were meant to reassure her, but all she heard were the gaps between them, the ways in which she didn't quite count. The lack that made her *close* but not quite *enough*.

"Got you some, too," Mori said, snapping Alina back to the present. "I thought for our mixed-media project." She held out a handful of green golf ball–sized nuts. The bulge in her sweat-shirt pocket said she'd collected at least twenty more.

"Oh." Alina took them, wondering when the walnut-sized knot had formed in her gut. "Thanks."

By the time they reached the top of the hay field, both of them were breathless and Alina had her hands over a stitch in her side. It was worth it, though. It always was. The falling sun rippled gold through the tall hay grasses, which swayed gently. The woods on every side of them erupted with the fiery colors of West Virginia October.

Alina walked to the middle of the mowed clearing and hopped onto one of the thick wood stumps that lined the bon-fire pit she and her dad had built a few years ago. She turned a slow circle, stopping in the direction of the Mackie farm. Asher Mackie's farm.

"So." Mori stepped onto the stump next to her. "When are you going to ask Asher out?"

Alina followed her friend's eyes to the wire fence that sepa-rated her family's property from the Mackie farm, telling herself the stumbles in her heartbeat only came from the steep hike.

"Why would I do that?"

"Please. Did you honestly think I couldn't tell? You've

crushed on him since last year, and now we're seniors. It's your last chance."

"I . . . He's not . . ." Alina clamped her mouth shut, hating how split open she felt. "Is that why you wanted to come up here? To see if we'd run into him?"

"No, but now that you mention it . . ."

Alina groaned.

"I'm kidding!" Mori's laugh was kind, but it prickled. "Seriously, though, I don't understand why you pretend not to be into him."

A gust of wind lifted the hair from Alina's neck. She pulled her shirtsleeves over her hands. "I'm going away next year."

"That's eight whole months away. It's not like you have to marry him."

"Well, I just don't think we'd work, you know?"

"No, I don't know. He's a nice human. He's really smart. I *know* you think he's adorable."

Alina kept her gaze on the fence.

Okay, fine, maybe she had thought that a time or twenty, but who wouldn't? She'd ended up sitting across the aisle from him in Anatomy this semester, and it wasn't a bad view. Asher had long eyelashes and eyes the color of pine trees in shadows and the kind of lean, muscular body that resulted from helping run a full working farm. Plus, Mori wasn't wrong. He was smart. And witty. And there was also that habit he had, when he found something really funny, the way he bit his tongue with his perfect teeth when he laughed.

"You're smiling," Mori teased. "You're thinking about him and you're smiling!"

Alina shook her head. "Let it go, Mori. He's not my type."

Mori's expression changed then. "You mean he's too *West Virginian* for you."

"What?" Alina's breath hitched. "That doesn't even make sense."

"It makes perfect sense." Mori ticked off a list on her fingers: "He's a farmer. He's big into 4-H. He wears camo pants. You've always thought camo was hickish—"

"I do not think camo is hickish!" Alina jumped off the stump, toppling it in the process, and followed the mowed path that led deeper into the field.

"You've told me!" said Mori. She jumped down as Alina whirled to face her.

"Number one: I never used those precise words. Number two: What I meant is that I think people go overboard. Camo's for hunting! For *camouflaging* with the earth. It's just . . . People have the worst stereotypes about West Virginia, and sometimes I think we play into them, that's all."

Mori's face twisted like she smelled something sour, but Alina cut her off before she could speak. "You cannot really be upset about what I think about camo pants, can you? You don't like them, either."

Mori stared at her, a ripple in her expression that Alina couldn't quite read. "No," she said finally. "I'm not upset about that."

"About what, then? What is going on?"

Mori rubbed her forehead. "I've thought this before, but I didn't want to believe it. But then earlier, what you said about your dad moving here. And yesterday, with that Pitt jerk—"

"What Pitt jerk?"

Mori gave her a don't-play-stupid look. "That guy at the

museum? You know, who made a crack about us wearing shoes?"

And then the memory washed over her, like a too-harsh slice of sun. They'd gone on a field trip with their AP Art class to the Andy Warhol Museum in Pittsburgh. She'd started chatting with a cute college freshman, and it was going well. But then he'd made that stupid joke. *I didn't think West Virginians wore shoes.* He'd smiled like it was a pickup line.

She didn't know why she'd let it get to her. It wasn't like being barefoot was an insult in itself. People went barefoot at the beach all the time. And she knew from a biology essay she'd written last year that "earthing" was scientifically proven to be beneficial for both mental and physical health.

But it was the *way* the guy said it, and the implications behind it: West Virginians were poor. Or backward. Or both. And wasn't that something to laugh about?

Mori threw her hands up in air quotes, dissolving the memory. "You said, 'Well, technically, I'm not West Virginian.'" Mori's impression was borderline mockery, but Alina forced herself not to react. "You're embarrassed about it, aren't you? West Virginia *embarrasses* you."

"No!" Alina said automatically. She loved this place and its wild expansiveness. How it gave her space and solitude but also connected her intimately to the natural world. Her favorite people lived here. "The thing is . . . I . . ."

She closed her mouth. She'd never let herself think about it too much, but what if . . . maybe . . .

What if she *was* embarrassed?

Alina crossed her arms, shame radiating from the deepest part of herself. Could that really be true? And if it was, how had it happened? When had her brain stopped registering camo as just another type of clothing and filed it under a label, a way of marking a person? When had the place she lived, the gorgeous land she loved with every piece of her heart, become a place she didn't want to own up to with strangers?

She felt suddenly very, very exposed. It wasn't like she'd never heard West Virginia cracks before. She heard them constantly, in fact, almost every time she traveled with her dad, a retired, well-published economics professor who had traded teaching for a quiet but manageable living touring the country giving keynote speeches and lectures.

She always told herself it was no big deal, that her dad's colleagues were just trying to make conversation. That the barista in Boston was probably actually trying to flirt with her when he quipped about Appalachia and rednecks and hillbillies, trying to make her laugh. And she *had* laughed at jokes like those. The first dozen times or so.

She thought she'd done a good job of letting the cracks slide over her. But maybe she hadn't. What if she'd become like the rocks in the streambed below her house, worn down without even realizing it? What if she'd let them erode her sense of herself? Her sense of her home.

"Alina!" Mori grabbed Alina's arm.

"I'm sorry!" Alina yelped. "I didn't mean—" But then the scared tone of Mori's voice sank in. She took in Mori's wide eyes and their laser focus on something beyond Alina's shoulder.

Slowly, Alina turned.

Not thirty feet from them—on *their* side of the fence—stood an enormous bull, much larger than the Mackies' cows that sometimes grazed at her property line and didn't mind a nose rub. Alina had only seen him from a distance before. She tried to forget that bulls weigh over a thousand pounds. If he'd been able to break the fence . . .

"What do we do?" Mori's voice was low and raspy. "Do we run?"

"No." Alina spread herself in front of Mori protectively, like she could somehow make a difference if the animal decided to charge. "Stay still." For the first time in her life, she regretted not joining 4-H. Some farm animal knowledge would come in super handy at the moment. "I think movement attracts them, and he hasn't—"

As if on cue, the bull lifted his massive head, thick neck muscles rippling beneath his black coat. Huge dark eyes zeroed in on them. Mori let out a terrified whimper.

"Look big!" Alina said. "I think you're supposed to stare them down." She thought she'd heard that somewhere and widened her stance. "Hold your territory."

Behind her, Mori squeaked again. The bull's tail swished. He stamped his foot once, then began walking. Directly toward them.

"Never mind," Alina said, turning and shoving Mori down the hill toward the trees. "Run! Run!"

Mori cursed as they dashed through the waist-high hay grasses and skidded down the hillside, crashing noisily into the prickered underbelly of the forest. Alina forced herself not to look back and veered away from her friend, hoping to buy them a precious moment by confusing the bull with two targets. Thorns ripped pieces of skin from her hands, leaving hot beads of blood.

It took a minute to gain her bearings in the woods, especially as there was no way she was slowing down. Vegetation snapped behind her, and Mori veered back into sight just as Alina spotted the tree she'd been looking for: a thick multi-trunked oak, much closer to Mori than to her.

"There!" she screamed and almost tripped over an exposed root. "Get off the ground!"

With a running leap, Mori pulled herself into the oak's branches and disappeared. Alina pushed herself as hard as she could, cursing as briars snagged her clothes and hair. Somewhere behind her, she heard a loud bellow.

"Alina!" Mori shrieked.

Alina rocketed over a low tangle of briar thicket, catching her jeans and landing awkwardly on her left ankle. But the tree was only a few paces away, and if she could just push through . . .

She launched herself awkwardly at the bottom branch, not quite managing to pull herself up. She started to fall back, but Mori grabbed her shirt, giving her just enough leverage to swing her legs over the bough.

"Do you see him?" Alina asked when they'd both climbed fifteen more feet or so.

Mori braced herself against two branches while she pushed aside a cluster of red leaves. Some of them broke off and fluttered to the ground.

"No," Mori gasped, still out of breath. "What the hell? I thought he was right behind us."

Alina inched forward and used her foot to push a thinner branch out of their sight line. "I don't see him anywhere." In the distance, the low thrum of a four-wheeler covered the sounds of their panting. Too bad they couldn't somehow signal the driver, but the dirt road was all the way below the north side of the field.

Mori slumped back against the trunk. "Well, now that we're not going to die, I just have to tell you: That was the most West Virginia thing that's ever happened to me."

Alina covered her face so Mori couldn't see her laugh, because damn if that wasn't the truth.

"I mean, we almost got murdered by a bull in your backyard," Mori continued. "That shit just don't happen in New York City."

This time Alina couldn't stop the snort that escaped her.

Mori laughed, too, but there was something beneath it.

"I'll come back," Alina promised. "New York's not that far. I'll be back for visits."

"Will you?" Mori asked, and Alina understood for the first time that her best friend honestly wasn't sure.

"Mori—"

Mori kept her eyes trained on the fleshy pad beneath her thumb, where she was trying to dislodge a thorn. "You get all irritated about people playing into stereotypes." Her words came soft and careful, like speaking them too loudly might shatter something. "But do you really think you're helping anyone by pretending those stereotypes can't touch you? By pretending you can't help dismantle them?"

"What are you talking about?"

Mori swore as she dislodged the thorn, specks of blood falling out with it. Alina watched her consider a response, like she was tasting the words before releasing them.

"You have a way with stories," Mori said at last, rubbing the sore left by the thorn. "You always have. You could help change the way people understand this whole state and the people who live here." She met Alina's eyes. "But no one will ever see that if you can't even acknowledge it's where you're from."

A sharpness pierced Alina, like Mori had pushed the thorn she'd just removed all the way into her soul. "That's not fair," she said. Except maybe it was.

Mori watched her, tense and wary. She deserved an explanation, as best as Alina could offer. She deserved the truth.

"Okay," Alina said. "I think . . . maybe you're right. I think I *am* embarrassed, sometimes." The disappointment that crossed Mori's face gutted her, but she didn't let herself slow down. "And it's not an excuse, but it's like, I don't know—like I have to deal with all the stereotype crap without the good parts."

Mori's eyebrows crinkled. "I have no idea what you mean."

How could Alina explain it, the *not-enough* feeling that clung to her constantly, thick and dreary as mountain fog? How could she put into words the feelings she realized she'd been trying to hide her whole life, even from herself?

"You," she began, "and all our friends, you guys were born here. Your families are rooted here, and your stories. You have so many stories. It's awesome, and I . . ." She tried to ignore the hitch in her voice. "I wish I could feel that, sometimes. You're all connected to this place in a way I can never be."

She told Mori about the mustard lady.

"I never realized," Mori said, "how much it bothered you. The family stuff."

"Your own gramps," Alina said, "he's always going on about being *born and bred*." She shrugged. "I don't know. People say it so much that it starts to feel . . ." She struggled for an analogy.

"You know how one piece of paper weighs practically nothing, but a ream of paper weighs a lot?"

Mori nodded. "Microaggressions. I know a lot about them."

Alina squeezed Mori's hand. "Right, exactly. And obviously what I'm talking about isn't anything like that—" Mori squeezed her hand back, as if to acknowledge it wasn't a contest about who had it worse. "But it does hurt, you know?" Alina looked out over the sea of trees. "Sometimes I feel like even though I've lived most of my life here, I don't truly belong. But I don't belong anywhere else, either."

"Oh, Alina—" Mori took a small step on the branch toward her.

"I think I'm maybe embarrassed about being *too* West Virginian and also jealous that I'm not West Virginian *enough*, at the same time." She looked helplessly at Mori. "Does that make any sense at all?"

Mori wedged herself between two branches, her arm encircling Alina in the safest version of a hug she could manage this high above the ground. "You're talking to a queer person, so yeah, I get it. As much as some things are changing, you don't think I ever feel out of place? Or, like, in some weird space between belonging and not?

"I love this state," Mori went on, "but there is so much that can be made better. That's one of the reasons I want to make art *here*, even though it might be easier someplace else. I want to be part of the change." She nudged Alina's elbow with her own. "You can do that, too, you know—make things better for the people living here. Even from New York."

Alina's head dropped to Mori's shoulder. "You're the best

friend in the universe," she said. "And you make me better every day."

"Wow. That's hella corny." But Mori hugged Alina tighter. "When you distance yourself from West Virginia, you know, you distance yourself from me."

The painful truth of it seared into Alina. "I'm sorry, Mori. For what I said to the Pitt guy. And for how I said it. I'm sorry for every time I haven't stuck up for this place. For us."

"Thanks."

They stayed quiet for a moment, heads pressed together, until Mori said solemnly, "You know, I've always hated mustard."

And just like that Alina was laughing. They both were.

"How long you think we'll have to stay up here?" Mori asked, edging a bit farther out on the branch and toeing aside some leaves. "I didn't bring my phone. Did you?"

"It's still by the woodpile."

"Well, I'm sure as hell not going down there with a wild bull on the loose."

They stared at each other, processing the fact they might be stuck in the oak for hours.

"Don't pretend you won't miss this next year." Mori cracked a grin. "City life can't have anything half as exciting as hiding in trees from livestock."

She was joking, of course, but the thing was, Alina *would* miss it. Well, maybe not getting charged by a bull, but *this place.* The rope-thick grapevines that looped among the brambles below them; the mountain air that tasted of honeysuckle and pine; the leaves, everywhere, bright as flames and breathing in the wind.

It was freedom and beauty and so *alive*, this wilderness. It pulsed through her, as much a part of her as her blood.

Mori was right. She could try to outrun the stereotypes her whole life, but then she couldn't fully claim this part, either. Or Mori, and their deep-souled friendship. Or any of the other million pieces of her West Virginian life that made her who she was.

Her eyes flicked back to Mori. Sometimes it was incredibly annoying having a state champion debater for a best friend.

"Hello?" A voice called, startling both of them. "You guys okay?"

Alina blinked, registering the warm lilt. "Is that—?"

"Asher!" Mori called. She dropped to a lower branch with the grace of a squirrel. "Up here!"

Leaves crunched, and then Asher appeared below them.

"Your damn bull is on the loose!" Mori said. "You better get up here quick!"

Asher rubbed the back of his neck. "That's just Barley. He'd never hurt anyone." He smiled, teeth biting his tongue. "He's still up in the field, you know. He probably just wanted to play with you."

"Wanted to *play*?" said Alina, at the same time that Mori said, *"What?!"*

"I tried to get your attention, but you'd already started running."

"Wait," Alina said. "You *saw* us?"

"I was outside when he broke the fence. But I had to go back for the four-wheeler."

Mori dropped to the ground. "Not a word of this to anyone, Mackie," she said, straightening. "Understand? We thought that was a killer bull, not a genuine Ferdinand." She flicked a leaf off her sleeve as Alina jumped down beside her.

"You sure you're okay?" Asher asked.

"A little mortified," Alina admitted. "But fine."

They picked their way back up to the field. "You're positive that bull's not gonna charge?" Mori asked. She had found a large stick and was carrying it at the ready.

"I'm sure." Asher laughed. "He's like a hundred years old."

Mori gripped her stick tighter, but when they crested the hill, they saw Barley grazing near the fence line, completely uninterested in their existence. They walked Asher to the four-wheeler parked in the middle of the field.

"How are you gonna get him home?" Alina asked.

Mori held up the stick. "Do you need this?"

"Uh, no, thanks. I'll guide him with the ATV."

Mori looked doubtful. "So he'll just go with you?"

"Yup." Asher climbed onto the four-wheeler.

"Thanks," Alina said to him, "for telling us we didn't have to stay up in a tree all night."

The sun lit up Asher's hair, golden as the hay field grasses, and how had Alina never noticed that small freckle on his neck? "Glad I could help," he said. The warmth of his grin stirred something in her and the walnut lump returned to her gut. For months, Alina had told herself a story: They didn't have enough in common, and she was leaving next year anyway. But now, after Mori had called her out, she let the truth thrum through her: In her mind, Asher embodied West Virginia, and she'd distanced herself because of it.

"Wait!" she called as he started the ignition. She could feel

Mori's stare, but also her pride and support. They gave her courage.

Asher shut off the engine.

"Would you wanna hang out with me sometime?" she asked in a rush. "You know, when there's not a bull around."

Asher squinted, his hand blocking the sun from his eyes. "You mean, like, a date?"

She couldn't tell from his tone if he was excited by the possibility or giving her an out, a chance to clarify that she meant only as friends. But it was all or nothing now, and she wasn't going back. "Yes," she said. "A date."

Asher's grin grew warm and a little lopsided. "Yeah, okay," he said. "A date."

"Okay." Alina could barely believe what was happening. "I'll call you tonight. To set it up."

Behind them, Barley bellowed, his tail swishing happily. Asher restarted the ignition. "Tonight," he echoed over the engine's hum. "Can't wait."

"Well," Mori said as they watched Asher herd Barley back across the property line. "That could have gone worse." Her tone was triumphant.

"You were right, okay?"

"I'm sorry. I didn't quite catch that. Can you repeat?"

"Don't push it," Alina warned. "I put myself in front of a friendly bull for you." As she said it, an idea pushed its way into her head. "Oh!"

"Oh, no," Mori said, backing away. "I know that look. You may *not* write about this. No, no, no." She set off down the path toward Alina's house.

"I wouldn't use your name! Or any identifying features, I promise."

"It's a hard no, Alina."

"Mori!" Alina was pleading now, the idea rooted and growing fast. "You're the one who said it was the most West Virginia thing that's ever happened to you! I know I could write a good story about this. I'd fictionalize it, I swear. Come on. *Please?*"

Mori tossed her stick into the brush and groaned dramatically. "Fine," she huffed. "Because I am the best friend in the universe, you can write the bull story."

"Seriously?"

Mori threw up her hands. "If you're gonna be all brave and ask Asher out, I guess I can let you write a story where we look like idiots." She stopped suddenly on the cusp of the forested hill, which made Alina stop, too. "It's gonna be real, though, right?" Mori looked at her. "I mean, not real like it has my name in it, but real like, you can write about West Virginia in a real way, a way that's true to you, not turn it into something that someone else wants or expects?"

Alina nodded. "I'll make it real to me. And to the West Virginia we know."

Mori raised her eyebrows. "Because this"—she gestured around them—"*is* where you're from. Right?"

Alina's eyes focused on the forest below. A bluebird sang out somewhere, perhaps the one that had nested last spring above her porch.

What did it mean to be *from* someplace, anyway? So maybe she didn't have family roots that stretched generations, but she'd grown her own here, and they were deep and strong and nurtured by people like Mori. By her teachers and teammates and everyone else in her tiny, ignored mountain town. This place, and the life she'd lived here, had molded her into who she was, and she knew she'd carry it with her wherever she went. Always.

The mustard lady had been wrong. She wasn't *close enough* to being West Virginian. She *was* West Virginian.

"Yes," Alina said. "This is where I'm from."

Whiskey and Champagne
S. A. COSBY

Juke was sure the temperature on the front porch was only slightly less than the surface of the sun. Despite the metal-bladed fan his daddy had rigged up in the corner, the air was still stifling. He turned a page of his book and tried to ignore the heat and the clanging of the fan. He was almost to the end, and he had to return the book to the library tomorrow. Mayflies buzzed near his head, whispering their threats of mastication in his ear. They were harder to ignore than the heat and the fan combined. He waved them away and pushed on, nearing the end of the Bible–sized book he was reading. *The Collected Works of Agatha Christie* weighed slightly less than a brick. The flies, heat, and fan were annoying, but trying to read in the house while his mother cooked Sunday breakfast and his little brother played with his army man action figures was damn near impossible.

He wondered if that was why his daddy had decided to

change the alternator on their truck this morning instead of lying in bed on his day off. Juke turned another page. His father had parked the truck under an old oak tree that looked like it was one good stiff wind from shuffling off its mortal coil. (Juke liked that phrase. "Mortal coil." There was something sleek and deadly about it. His AP English teacher told him he had an ear for language. He didn't know if that was true. He just thought it sounded cool.)

Usually Sunday morning meant church for him, his mama, and his brother, Darrell. But the air conditioner at the church was broken, and this Sunday was the seventh day in a row where the thermometer had hit ninety-nine degrees or higher, so they called off church.

"It's hotter than this in hell," he'd heard his mama say on the phone when one of the trustees had called her about the cancellation.

His daddy had snickered and grabbed his toolbox. His daddy didn't go to church much. Juke had a feeling it wasn't some deep philosophical belief that kept his daddy at home on Sundays. It was purely physical. The man was tired.

His daddy worked three jobs. Monday through Friday he worked at the Walmart as a janitor from six in the morning until three in the afternoon. Then he left Walmart, changed his clothes, and went down to a private estate on the Rappahannock River and worked part-time on a groundskeeping crew. Every other Saturday he cut hair at Joe Tice's barbershop, way out in Colleen County.

"If the Lord could rest on Sundays, so can I," his daddy was fond of saying. Whenever he did, Juke's mama rolled her eyes so hard, he was afraid they were going to pop out and go rolling down the hall. His mama worked at the crab factory, picking and packing crab meat from four in the morning until five in the evening. Monday through Friday it was Juke's job to get him and Darrell from the bus down the lane to their tidy modular home and make them both a meal while they waited for their parents to get home. Juke wondered what his parents were going to do with Darrell next year, after he graduated. Come September he planned on being a freshman at either Virginia State or Virginia Union. His mama and his daddy were always enthusiastic about him going to college, even if they were a little fuzzy on the details.

That was okay; he was working out the details on his own. He'd applied for more than four hundred scholarships and grants. Everything from scholarships for left-handed people to grants for Southeastern Virginia students who cited Edgar Allan Poe as a personal hero. Juke did not want Labor Day to find him still in Mathews County, working at the McDonald's, talking about going to college "next year." Juke had seen enough to know that "next year" never came. Especially for people like him. He was a black kid in a small southern town. Expectations were already being foisted upon him, both high and low, from multiple corners. Church folk and upstanding members of the black community pinned all their hopes and some of their dreams on boys and girls like him—those in advanced classes who didn't have their names in the police blotter every week. Good ol' boys sipping beer in the parking lot of North Star convenience mart thought he was stealing a spot that belonged to one of their sons or daughters. Even though some of their sons and daughters couldn't spell *cat* if you spotted them the *c* and the *t*.

Juke turned another page.

"Dang it!" His daddy stood up straight and tossed his socket wrench to the ground, massaging the knuckles of his right hand. The thick, ropy muscles in his father's back undulated under his ribbed white tank top. After a few seconds, he bent over and picked up the wrench and plunged under the hood of their truck once again.

Juke was ten pages from the end of his book when he heard the high piercing whine of a finely tuned motor. A black sports car was barreling down their lane. It summoned a huge cloud of dust as it flew over the arid clay. Juke's daddy stopped battling his truck and walked over to the porch just as the car came to a stop near their circular concrete pump house.

"What in the world does he want?" Juke heard his father mumble. The bone-dry air caught his words and carried them through the screen door and into the house.

"Jimmy, who is that?" Juke's mama called.

"Theo Jackson," Jimmy said. He crossed his arms and waited for Theo to get out of his car.

Juke knew a few things about Theo Jackson. He was from New York. He owned one of the biggest homes in Mathews. And he was the richest black man this side of the Blue Ridge Mountains. It was Theo's estate his daddy toiled away at when he was done scrubbing toilets at Wally World. He'd ridden with his father to Theo's place once or twice when his dad went to collect his pay. The Jackson estate had more in common with a feudal castle than a home. It had six chimneys for its six fireplaces. His daddy told him the fireplaces were only decoration. The place had a massive HVAC system for heating and cooling. It also contained a movie theater, an indoor basketball court, and a home gym. Juke figured you needed GPS to find a bathroom.

Theo Jackson climbed out of the driver's side of a car so low to the ground Juke wondered if he had to lie down to get in it. Theo was a tall man, taller than Juke's daddy by at least a foot. But he lacked Jimmy Davidson's hard-won muscular physique and broad shoulders. Theo was a reed, while Jimmy was a fire hydrant.

A young man climbed out of the passenger side, noticeably slower than Theo had exited the driver's side. Juke knew the young man. Tyree Jackson, Theo's son, home from college for the summer. Theo and Tyree were more similar in appearance than Juke and Jimmy. They both had a light complexion, with wavy black hair and bright green eyes.

Theo had made his money in stages. First as a lawyer, then an investment banker, and finally as a tech mogul. He'd gotten in on the ground floor of some killer app and had retired at fifty-two to become a country gentleman. He'd traveled from his hometown of St. Louis to Atlanta, then New York, and finally ended up in Virginia. Juke thought he would never enjoy anything in his life the way Theo Jackson seemed to enjoy being a southerner. Skeet shooting at his estate in the summer. Snowmobile rides in the winter. Spring cookouts and autumn bonfires. His daddy had told him that Theo even had a jacked-up truck that was the usual vehicle of choice for daredevils who liked to challenge the factory warnings for their chassis in a foot-deep mud bog.

If Theo's love for the country was the yin, then Tyree's hatred of it was the yang. Juke had seen him once or twice. Down at the basketball park or over at the Hardee's. He rode around town during the fall and summer breaks in his own low-to-the-ground sports car. Contempt and disdain battling for dominance on his face the whole time.

"Jimmy. We need to talk. Do you have a moment?" Theo asked.

Juke was shocked at how deep his voice was. It rumbled out of his thin chest like a thunderstorm.

"I'm just working on my truck. Go ahead. Talk."

Theo sighed and crossed his arms, then thought better of it and put his hands in the pockets of his crisply pressed blue jeans. Overhead, a hawk flew by and cast its wide shadow over Theo and Tyree.

"Jimmy, this is difficult to ask, but it has to be done. One of my watches has gone missing. A watch with great sentimental value for me. A watch you complimented me on a few weeks ago. Now, my son here says he saw you coming downstairs from my bedroom Friday evening when he got home. I told him that was a serious accusation. I also told him if he was making that kind of accusation, he damn well better have his facts straight and be willing to look the man he is accusing in the eye. So, Jimmy, I have to ask, have you seen my watch?"

"He just gonna lie, Dad," Tyree said.

"Shup up, Tyree," Theo said.

Juke closed his book. He wasn't worried about losing his place. There were only nine pages left. His daddy stared at Theo then Tyree then back at Theo. There was a shift in the atmosphere. The merciless heat was now the second most uncomfortable thing in the air. Jimmy clenched then unclenched his hands. Then he chuckled. It was a rueful sound.

"Ain't this just my luck," he muttered.

That phrase triggered a memory for Juke. It took him to a sultry night last summer on the same porch he was sitting on now.

"You know the biggest difference between rich people and poor people?" His daddy had been knee-deep into a second case of beer with a few of his buddies. They'd been interrogating him about what it was like to work for a rich man. Let alone a rich black man.

"Rich people never have to accept bad luck. Their car breaks down, they get a new one. Toilet backs up at four in the morning? Plumber comes out and is happy to step through sewage. 'Yes, sir! Get it fixed for you right away, sir.' They can't never suffer any kind of inconvenience. It ain't in their nature," his daddy had said before killing another beer.

Jimmy slapped the hard-worn calluses of his left hand with the socket wrench. It sounded like a rifle shot. Juke snapped out of his reverie.

"How long have I worked for you, Theo?"

"Jimmy, this isn't about—"

"Four years. Four years I've been working for you. I ain't never even stepped in your living room. The furthest I've been in your house is the kitchen. To get a glass of water. But now I'm supposed to be all upstairs? Really?"

Juke stood up and walked to the edge of the porch. Tyree glanced at him, then studied a pine tree off the left side of the house. Jimmy Davidson was usually quick to laugh and slow to anger. But Juke knew that when he finally got angry, it was like a rock slide. The longer it went on, the more momentum it gained, until it was almost unstoppable.

"Jimmy, I don't want to believe it, but Tyree swears he saw you. If you're saying you didn't go upstairs, then you're saying my son is a liar," Theo said.

"Well, I'm telling you I didn't go upstairs."

"Jimmy, everything all right?" Juke's mama called from the hallway.

"It's all right, Dina," Jimmy said. The words came out his mouth like bullets.

"Oh, so now I'm a liar?" Tyree said.

"Be quiet, Tyree," Theo said.

"Nah, Dad. You letting him call me a liar right in front of you? You asking him if he took the watch. Look at this house. Look at him. You know he took it. You just trying to give him a chance cause he a 'brother,'" Tyree said. His voice rose to an earsplitting pitch.

"You need to watch your mouth, son," Jimmy said. The veins in his forearms stood out in sharp relief under his skin.

"Or what? Touch me if you want. See what happen. My dad will put a lawsuit on you your kids will be paying off," Tyree said. Spittle flew from his lips.

"Tyree! Get in the car," Theo said.

"Sure, whatever. You gonna let him get away with sneaking around your room, tearing through your stuff, treating your room like a scavenger hunt. Ooh, what's under the bed? Ooh, what's in the closet? Ooh, what's in the nightstand? Bingo, a fancy watch! You putting up with all this because you don't want to hold another brother down. He's not your brother, Dad. He just trash," Tyree said.

"What you say?" Jimmy asked.

Juke stepped down off the porch. Tyree heard the threat

in the question and took a step back. Theo stepped forward between his son and Jimmy.

"Jimmy, I just want the watch," Theo said. His voice nearly cracked.

Jimmy glanced toward Tyree. "I'm about check your chin, boy," Jimmy said in a whispery voice. A tremor slithered across his face like a snake. The muscles in his jaw twisted and roiled.

"Mr. Jackson," Juke said.

Theo snapped his head to the right. He seemed to notice Juke for the first time.

"Juke, go in the house," Jimmy said.

"Mr. Jackson, do you always keep your watch in the night-stand?" Juke said.

"Juke, go in the house!" Jimmy roared.

Tyree flinched. Theo lowered his eyes, his lips moving in silent contemplation. The taller man then turned and stared at his son.

"Mr. Jackson, if you didn't always keep it in there, who knew you had moved it from its regular place to the night-stand?" Juke asked.

Now it was Jimmy's turn to stare at his son.

"No one. No one knew where in the bedroom I'd put the watch. It was broken, so I put it in the nightstand instead of Lisa's jewelry box so I wouldn't forget to take it with me to New York next week to get it fixed. No one knew," Theo said.

Juke watched as his daddy's arms and back relaxed. The rock slide had become a waterfall.

"How did you know the watch was in the nightstand, Tyree?" Theo asked.

Tyree laughed.

"You listening to this, Dad?" Tyree asked. He laughed again, but Juke could tell his heart wasn't in it.

"Get your ass in the car," Theo said. His deep voice had dropped an octave. Juke could almost feel the bass from it rattle his chest.

Tyree bit his lip, then got into the car, slamming the door.

Theo turned to face Jimmy. "Jimmy, I'm sorry. I'm very sorry. Tyree is . . . Well, Tyree is my problem," Theo said. He smiled sadly and shook his head. Then he climbed into his car. Theo paused before closing the door. "You know, your son has a real good head on his shoulders. He's a son you can be proud of." Theo closed the door and started the car. They didn't summon as many dust clouds leaving as they had arriving.

Jimmy sat down on the top step of the porch. Juke plopped down next to him. Jimmy gently poked him in the thigh with the socket wrench.

"That was pretty swift," Jimmy said.

"It won't nothing. It just kinda jumped out at me," Juke said.

"Don't do that. Don't sell yourself short. You caught that boy slipping while I was thinking about punching both of them in the face."

"Why would he steal from his own daddy?" Juke asked.

Jimmy let out a sigh. "Some people like to drink whiskey. And some people like to drink champagne. And some people like to drink both, and they can never get enough," he said.

"Daddy, that make no sense at all," Juke said.

Jimmy laughed. "It don't right now, but it might someday. When it do, you remember I said it. All right, help me get this damn alternator off," he said.

Jimmy stood and walked back over to the truck as Juke followed. As they walked, it occurred to Juke that he hadn't given much thought to what he was going to major in when he did indeed get to college. Maybe he'd look into criminal justice.

He felt like he might have a knack for that kind of thing.

What Home Is
ASHLEY HOPE PÉREZ

Home is white sunshine and towering pines; it's a tangle
of wisteria in the highest branches.

Home is your crib, the trundle bed where your older
brother sleeps, and the tiny flowers on the blue cotton
curtains.

Home is the backyard deep with leaves and the stand of
pampas grass sharp enough to slice your fingers.

Home is one bathroom and the whole family crowded in.

Home is wading into the baptismal pool and Pastor Gaar
dunking you after your public confession; it's shivering
in your wet T-shirt; it's the fear that you are still not
saved, not really.

Home is the hot vinyl of the fold-down seats in your dad's old Datsun truck.

Home is Rotary Park: peering into bluebird boxes and visiting the chipped blue seals that are supposedly fountains but have never been turned on as long as you can remember.

Home is the skittish rabbit in your chest when you try to ride your bike and fall; it is your brother wiping the bloody mess with gauze from his fanny pack; it is the four stitches in your knee after the doctor digs out the gravel.

Home is the bracelets you weave at summer camp, knot after knot of embroidery thread or flat neon plastic.

Home is Frito pies and pineapple Blizzards and three ways to walk to the MacMillian Memorial Library.

Home is the bag of acorns you gather for the squirrels and then forget until orange and white maggots burst the plastic.

Home is flash floods on the one bridge to the next town.

Home is your father's beard against your cheek and your mother pulling the center cinnamon roll out of the pan and popping it into her mouth.

Home is freshly permed hair and the itch of pantyhose.

Home is a boy named Jonathan and the long hair he cuts away in fourth grade; it is the teacher who cries when Jonathan plays the piano in chapel because it is so beautiful.

Home is writing in your journal under the magnolia tree and waiting for your girl's body to find its shape.

Home is your choked throat when you walk down the long hallway in your grandparents' house, and it is not knowing why you feel such terror.

Home is hands that never seem clean, though you wash and wash.

* * *

Home is pancakes, and strawberries, and orange juice mixed with Sprite on Sundays.

Home is buying two-for-a-dollar candy and cheap toys at Perry's on the summer days when Dad lets you tag along to his work one county over.

Home is the smell of barbecue, cornbread, and fried pies.

Home is the Sabine River churned brown with
thunderstorms.

Home is the copperhead lifting its head out of that river,
its dark body etched cursive behind it.

Home is everything you must forget: the back bathroom
door sliding shut, the damp carpet under your naked
skin, your grandfather's sleeves rolled up to the elbow,
the weave of his brown pants, the burning in your
crotch, the ache in your jaw after.

Home is private day schools and plaid uniforms and knee
socks.

Home is worship choruses and praise songs on
Wednesday nights in summer; it's the families tumbling
out into the heat with their Bibles and prayer journals;
it's the questions you cannot quite form in the face of all
those smiles.

Home is June bugs and flying cockroaches clattering
against the ceiling fan on the patio outside a trailer home.

Home is your mother singing "Amazing Grace" and
stroking your hair when you are sick or cannot sleep.

Home is WWJD bracelets, vacation Bible school, and the Jesus fish on car bumpers.

Home is the orthodontist's chair and years of school photos spoiled by braces.

Home is the padded bra you wear even under your sports uniforms.

Home is learning to please.

* * *

Home is where your family doctor is also your Sunday school teacher, and the librarian is your dad's client, and the lady at the pharmacy counter knows your name and that you play piano and where you go to school.

Home is a baseball player chewing a wad of bubble gum at the field by your friend's house; it's the nervous bob of his Adam's apple when he swallows and reaches for your hand.

Home is the girls' locker room and volleyball uniforms and everyone on their period at the same time.

Home is dial-up internet, pagers, and call-waiting.

Home is learning to ignore the racing of your heart
when Mom steers the old silver Toyota van into your
grandparents' driveway; it is Grandaddy making orange
juice in the kitchen, his eyes never meeting yours;
it is the thievery of squirrels in the bird feeders; it is
anywhere but inside your body.

Home is borrowed clothes, Little Debbie snacks from the
Sunoco station, and hair ruined by Sun-In spray.

Home is boys in frayed baseball caps lettered with
TCU and UT and SFA and Texas A&M; it is tanned
hands that stuff those caps into back pockets beside the
rolled-up pages of unfinished homework.

Home is tall glasses of iced tea tornadoed with sugar.

Home is the oil field: pumpjacks and rigs and flared
bleed-off gas, and friends' daddies with their bodies
broken.

Home is the boy you adore in middle school but never
date because he is black and you are white and a coward,
the one you chase around the gym, the one you think of
for years after; it's the dream of being brave and reaching
a finger to his lips and saying, "Yes."

Home is Spanish moss draped from cypress trees.

Home is counting calories. It's being fat; it's being thin.
It's wanting to disappear, although at the time you can't
say why, only that it is more urgent than anything else.

Home is lovely and dear and also small and
small-hearted.

Home is so much wasted land.

* * *

Home is being in a class with the same thirty kids from
first grade to senior year; it's your best friend, Cristi,
throwing up into your lunch box after cheerleading
camp.

Home is the horse in the pasture on County Line Road
that lies on its side on the hottest days and looks dead
but isn't.

Home is the all-white crowd at the Fourth of July weenie
dog race.

Home is your brother rolling down the car windows on
the freeway to mess up your hair because you are late
getting ready for school.

Home is Sunday-night fellowship dinners and *Not that shirt, young lady.*

Home is quinceñeras at rented halls and sequined dresses and hair crisp with hairspray and curling irons.

Home is driver's ed, hardship licenses, and so many trucks.

Home is the "Do You Know Jesus?" pamphlets in the dentist's waiting room.

Home is the dark cave of the Movies 9 theater, the images that flicker over your bare arms, and a boy named Ben who slides his hand up the leg of your shorts.

Home is the week before prom and the news that Jonathan shot himself; it's how, the year before, you stopped returning his calls and ate your yogurt in the back hall to avoid him; it's the memory of leaning your head against his shoulder the year before that; and it's the elementary years tucked still further back, both of you awkward and lonely with your long brown ponytails and baby fat and melancholic thoughts.

Home is Jonathan's funeral and regret in every pocket; it's unfolding the letters he wrote in eighth grade and crying over *shure* and every other misspelled word.

Home is prom, which still happens.

Home is the smell of hot asphalt in the summer and oily rainbows in parking-lot puddles.

Home is your pasted-on smile and the somewhere-else feeling underneath it.

*   *   *

Home is the church praise band and off-tempo drumming and chorus lyrics projected on the blank front wall of the sanctuary.

Home is the freedom of your first car and an Ani DiFranco CD you listen to on drives to nowhere.

Home is years of animals. The cats: wise Clem, who lived to be eighteen; Kissyfur, Dickens, and three-legged NFL, fluffy orange TailBob, and one more named Dog. The trembling brown mutt Barnum who ate plastic and his own poop. A rabbit who disappeared from the hutch one night and whose name you cannot remember.

Home is a rusted swing set and a bike taken over by ivy in the big backyard.

Home is the terror that accretes and repeats long after your grandparents' house has been torn down; it is the terrible trick whereby the worst is still happening, always happening, in a walled-off room of your brain; it is the everyday you who does not know about that suffering, the you who smiles wider, fixes her ponytail, and corrects her Algebra 2 test.

Home is produce codes and scan times and getting paid time and a half when you work as a checker at the grocery store on Sundays.

Home is the raccoon drinking from your mother's hummingbird feeder like a fat baby taking a bottle.

Home is shame and fear and longing and the damp cotton of your underwear giving the lie to your modesty.

Home is your brother away at college and your father away at work and your mother away caring for her sick parents.

Home is your grandfather, shriveled and yellow during the last days of hospice, and the rage and relief several miles beneath your sadness.

Home is so many kinds of worry; home is trying not to cause any trouble.

Home is the empty house when Mom should be home,
the page from *All the Pretty Horses* you keep rereading
in the hospital waiting room, the ICU doors opening
with a buzz; it's her bandaged wrists and the air full of
apologies.

Home is the dewberries you pick in the woods instead of
going to youth group on Sunday night; it's your fingers
and mouth stained purple.

Home is the boys you don't like but tell yourself you do
because that makes things easier.

* * *

Home is your heart breaking because the only way to
leave is to leave.

Home is the essays you write to get yourself into
the School Far Away; it's the tears you cry when the
scholarship award comes; it's knowing that your parents
cannot stop you, would not stop you now, although they
might have, once.

Home is running to the wooded lot that always floods
and cannot be built upon, longing and sadness knotted
in your throat.

Home is already missing the high trees and the cathedral light coming through them and the carpet of pine needles and the damp smell of decay.

Home is your hands thrown out wide, as if you could hold every precious and awful thing washed up here and left behind.

Home is learning that you get to love this place and leave it.

Home is learning that you can leave it and come back, if you want.

Home is what's rooted in you that can't grow or be weeded out until you live somewhere else.

Home is the pain of the past and the pain to come; it is the wrecking ball of truth, however long deferred.

Home is all that you think is the world but will turn out to be just this small place.

Home is you standing where nothing can be built and vowing to build something anyway.

Home is you.

Home is always you.

Island Rodeo Queen
YAMILE SAIED MÉNDEZ

Three miles from the next exit to Andromeda, Utah, population fifteen hundred, our old Chevy Silverado slowed down on the last uphill, then rocked forward and backward, jostling Papi and me in the overheated cabin.

"Keep going, keep going," I chanted, as if the truck could understand me.

Papi said his own kind of muttered prayer behind the wheel. He had to make it to the Spanish class where he taught teachers and medical professionals on Saturdays, and I couldn't be late to horsemanship practice, my weakest queening event.

Public speaking? No problem. I could out-argue my lawyer mom, even if she wasn't exactly practicing. She was still studying for the Utah bar exam.

Presentation? In my abuelita Irma's words, in my parade clothes I was stunning. And having been involved with the Puerto Rican Miss Universe contest for years, she knew a thing or two about pageants.

But queening was more than a beauty contest or a debate. A rodeo queen carried the American flag at events like parades. She was the face of the rodeo, the representative of the sport that ruled out here in the West, and I still didn't know my reining pattern perfectly.

The voice of my horse-riding trainer, Melinda Hale, echoed in my mind. "If you're going to be the next Andromeda rodeo queen, you must be perfect, Coralí. Punctuality is a mark of respect."

Whatever reason I gave her for being late today, she'd say it was an excuse.

"Come on," I said.

The truck tried. But a few seconds later, the engine sputtered its apology, and finally an ominous hiss broke the expectant silence of the desert.

At least it happened after we'd finished delivering our goodies.

"¡Ay, Dios mío!" Papi lamented as he maneuvered the dead truck to the shoulder of the road, out of the way of speeding cars and semis. "¡Ahora sí estamo' chava'o'!"

My native Spanish was rusty from lack of use, but I understood his words. We were screwed in so many ways.

The black cash box on my lap wasn't *that* heavy, but the earnings would've paid for my rodeo fees. Now we'd have to use it to fix the truck unless I dipped into my savings or the money for Abuelita Irma's Western Union was late . . . But no, we could never do that. She depended on that money, even if she protested every time we sent it.

"Nena, use it for your reina contest," she always said. "It makes me happy to see you happy." Now each training had extra meaning. Each queening item I bought became more important because of Abuelita.

"And now?" Papi asked.

Before I could reply, he took out his phone and scrolled through his contacts, although most of the people lived a continent and an ocean away. We'd moved from Puerto Rico to Utah ten years ago, when I was seven. Back then, we were some of the only Spanish speakers in the area, and my parents had a hard time making the kind of friends that became family. But there were a few incondicionales, as Mami called them.

In the States, there was only time for work. And all the work and sacrifices, my parents' and all our family's, were for me and my future. I was their chance for new beginnings and happily-ever-afters, and if I became the next rodeo queen, the scholarship that came with it would open doors to opportunities that now were only dreams. It would certainly make all the years trying to put down roots in this area worth it. When I was the rodeo queen, that would mean there was room for my family this far from home.

"Juan Carlos is already all the way up in Salt Lake," Papi finally said.

He'd met Juan Carlos when we first arrived, at the pet-food factory, Papi's main job to this day. Besides being like family, Juan Carlos was one of our customers, the thirty or so Caribbean and Latin American transplants who, like our family, had made a home in this developing valley of dairy farms and cornfields. Our customers had been solid in supporting my dream of becoming Andromeda's new rodeo queen.

A few months ago, during one of our weekly Skype calls, Abuelita Irma had suggested we make pasteles and other Puerto

Rican foods to pay for all my queening expenses. So we did. Our friends shared my Instagram posts with their neighbors and friends. Even non-Latinos eagerly waited for our pasteles. Abuelita's recipes were irresistible. All our customers had so much hope invested in me. And now our truck was dead.

"I'm sorry," I said. Papi patted my shoulder. Encouraged by the gesture, I tentatively took my phone out of my pocket to send an SOS message to Trenton.

Papi huffed, but he didn't complain. We had no other choice; Papi couldn't tell an alternator from a carburetor, and Trent was the one person besides my father who would drop everything to come get me even if I were stuck inside a volcano. And unlike other boys I knew, Trent didn't even expect a kiss in return when he did something nice for me, like invite me to homecoming or prom.

I couldn't say he was my boyfriend; our relationship was in a murky in-between. Everything else in my life was *in between*, so why not him? Maybe next year, after my queening responsibilities were fulfilled, we could date. But first I had to win.

I sent the text and immediately put my phone away before I was tempted to check my social media. Ever since I'd become a finalist, my mentions were a mixture of pride and good wishes, doubts that I had what it took to represent the town, and sometimes even hateful private messages from anonymous accounts. I never told my parents, Trent, or Melinda. I didn't want to give haters the power to make my family and friends unhappy, but the truth was, the seed of doubt had taken root in my heart. With the rodeo only a week away, the dark voices blared louder than the positive ones.

"It's like being inside an oven!" Papi said, pointing at the thermometer in the dashboard. It marked triple digits already in early June. The air outside the truck shimmered with heat.

"At least we have empanadillas and drinks in the cooler. Do you want a malta?"

Papi considered my offer for a second, then said, "Okay. It's too hot to wait inside the truck anyway."

We got out of the truck, and carefully, Papi opened the hood. He swore again and stepped back to avoid the hissing steam. In the meantime, I went around to the back and got a couple of bottles of Malta India, still perfectly cold and sweet. I handed one to Papi and we sipped, the flavor taking me back to hot days like these when we went to Jobos Beach in Cabo Rojo, and we let the sun burn our dark skin while Mami surfed the ocean waves that crashed around us. I'd loved how the water chilled my small feet and covered them with sea foam.

The mountains on the east of I-15 were still snowcapped. It had snowed in the canyons only last week. Now in the valley, I could've baked cookies on the top of the truck.

"Did the boy reply?" Papi asked, drying his sweat with a towel that he kept in his back pocket.

Despite calling him "the boy," Papi loved Trent like everyone else who knew him. Melinda, his mom, my riding teacher, had an impeccable reputation for raising sons and horses. A former Utah State Rodeo Queen, she was the one who got me into rodeoing when she noticed my eight-year-old awkwardness, which made me feel like a newborn colt trying to find its legs. My love for horses had opened the door to a world I hadn't even known existed.

"He'll come," I said, licking the sweetness of the soda off my lips. Gritty reddish desert sand flew into my face when a semi and a minivan drove past. No sooner had the dust settled than I realized the minivan had stopped. A man a little older than Papi got out and walked toward us, his legs bowed in true cowboy fashion.

"You folks need help?" he asked, holding his white hat so the wind wouldn't blow it away.

The van's passenger-side mirror reflected a beautiful brunette woman. When we made eye contact, I smiled at her. She glanced at the malta in my hand and shook her head before going back to looking at her phone. Automatically, I put the malta back in the cooler, heat burning my face. The amber bottle made it look like beer, and I had a reputation to protect.

"We got overheated," Papi said. His accent turned much stronger when he got nervous.

The man took a look at the engine and after a few seconds said, "I have some coolant that can help."

Papi's shoulders relaxed. "Great. Thanks."

The man came back with a bottle of blue liquid, and while he worked on our truck, he asked, "Where are you from?"

Every time we met someone new, it was only a matter of minutes before we got that question. The man's tone was friendly, though, so I guess that's why Papi went with the least confrontational answer. "We live in Andromeda now, but we're from Puerto Rico."

The man's face lit up. "I've been to San Juan on a cruise! Beautiful place!" Then a cloud dampened his enthusiasm. "How are things there now?"

An uncomfortable silence fell on us. Even without looking

at Papi, I knew he was probably considering how much to say.

"You know," Papi answered, "the metropolitan area is booming, but the rest of the island is still suffering." He usually didn't share so much, but he must have seen something in the man that encouraged him to open up.

The man nodded as if he understood, but did he really? Even *I* had a hard time picturing what Abuelita Irma had gone through, not only during the actual storm but also the terrifying days after, when her world resembled a postapocalyptic movie. The storm had blown the roof off her house, and when she'd come outside, all she'd seen was the main highway covered with mud and dead palm trees and bushes, torn buildings and electricity poles, and at night, unimaginable darkness.

We couldn't get in touch with her for ten whole days. Ten days and sleepless nights of fear and agony for her and for us, unable to help her. When a neighbor who miraculously had a signal one day let her borrow his phone and she could finally tell us how things were—that her town had no water or electricity, that some elderly neighbors whose house was far from the main road had died in their beds before anyone could help them—it seemed she was narrating the plot of a horror film. Things still weren't that much better, especially out in the small towns. Electricity went out every time it rained or the wind blew, but Abuelita wouldn't leave her island.

Hurricane season had just started again at the beginning of the month. It hurt too much to think about it; I wished we weren't talking about the situation back home, especially when the man spoke again.

"Well," he drawled, "our country has enough problems of our own. Now that Puerto Rico is back on its feet, they have to help themselves. I mean, we can't be the saviors of the world."

Papi winced as if the man had punched him.

"Puerto Ricans are American citizens too, you know," I blurted, a little louder than would be considered polite. Unlike Papi, I didn't have a trace of an accent, and the man looked taken aback.

"Coralí . . ." my dad said, and made a calm-down gesture. My face heated up, and it had nothing to do with the temperature.

Had I overreacted? I wished I could take my words back. A rodeo queen had to be diplomatic and nice to everyone, after all. But there had definitely been a judgy tone in the man's voice, and I couldn't remain silent.

"I'm sorry if it sounded like I have anything against the island. I don't," the man said, putting his hands up in a conciliatory sign. "Like I said, I love the place. It's beautiful."

As if he could sense how uncomfortable I was, he looked at me for the first time. His eyes widened in recognition. "I know who you are!" he exclaimed. "The surfer who wants to be a rodeo queen!"

Uneasy about correcting him again, I bit my next words. I wasn't a surfer just because I was Puerto Rican. Maybe in my riding jeans and sweat-stained long-sleeved T-shirt I was far from the perfect image of a rodeo queen, but no one could expect me to look regal at all times, right? I just shifted in place. The wind whipped my unruly hair into my face.

"Actually, she was never much of a surfer, but she sure has a way with horses." Papi's voice spilled pride for me.

"Nice to meet you," the man said, and shook my hand. His palm was calloused exactly in the same places mine were from the rub of the leather reins.

"I can never pronounce your name, Corral," the man said apologetically, and I tried not to flinch at how he'd butchered it. "But I've seen you in some events, and let me tell you, for being a Spanish girl, your form on the horse is a thing of beauty." He glanced at his minivan and continued, "My sister Kaylee was the Andromeda queen when she was in high school, and the queens after her have been fantastic too. Theirs are big boots to fill, but the Western way of life has room for all if they adapt to it, don't you think?"

I looked down at my dusty checkered Vans as I considered which part of his statement to address first: the fact that he'd called me Spanish, or that I had to prove I was adapting to the gold standard of the Western way of life. Wasn't the fact that I was a good rider proof that I had adapted to it? At what point would I get to be just "one of the girls," someone who belonged, and not someone constantly on trial? Usually, though, when I tried to correct a misconception, people thought I was being argumentative, and in this moment I didn't have the energy to find the perfect words so as not to hurt his feelings.

Papi coughed like he wanted to get my attention before I busted a gasket, but when I looked up, I saw Trent's blue Durango shimmering in the heat of the freeway, speeding in our direction.

If the happiness inside me could somehow be licensed, prescribed, and sold, every sadness in the world would be eradicated forever.

"He finally shows up," Papi said.

I playfully elbowed him and ran to open Trent's door.

The man who'd stopped to help said goodbye and went back to his minivan, looking at Trent as if he was trying to place him—or maybe place him with *me*. But soon he was gone, the van a speck in the distance.

Trent smiled from ear to ear as he got out of his SUV. We were only three weeks apart in age, his birthday in mid-July and mine at the beginning of August, but he was more than a foot taller than me. He hunched down and I leaned in to kiss his smoothly shaved cheek. Trent's Caribbean-blue eyes flew in my dad's direction, but Papi was grabbing something from the back of the car.

"Hey," Trent said. "The engine overheated?" He rummaged in the trunk for a bottle of coolant. "I think this will patch you up until we can get you to the exit."

"We got it!" Papi bellowed, turning the truck's engine on. After a small cough, the truck came back to life.

Trent sent me a questioning look and I shrugged.

"¡Vámonos!" Papi exclaimed.

"Papi . . ." I said, hoping I wouldn't have to ask aloud. Trent had come all the way here for nothing. I couldn't let him make the drive back by himself. Besides, he was heading to the ranch anyway, and if I rode with him, I'd make it to practice *almost* on time.

Papi smiled. "I know. I know . . ." he said. "Follow closely behind so I know I won't be stranded again."

Without wasting time, I climbed inside Trent's car and waited for Papi's truck to get back on the freeway. He stayed in the right lane, hazard lights blinking. But hardly any cars drove this section of the freeway, just an occasional semi or a car full of people heading to Mesquite for a weekend of fun.

I fidgeted with the radio and connected my phone to the Bluetooth speakers. Soon, Luis Fonsi and Daddy Yankee were singing the song of a few summers ago, and Trent joined the chorus of "Despacito," the only word he knew, as Papi's truck coasted down the hill toward the exit.

"It will be nice to sleep in after the rodeo, right?" he said when the music switched to Bad Bunny. I lowered the volume because this song had a lot more English than the others I listened to, and Trent blushed during the more colorful sections.

"I can't think that far ahead yet," I said. I hadn't slept in in ages. Since the competition became serious.

There was still so much to do this week that my palms started prickling. The competition for the rodeo queen title included a speech, which I knew even in my sleep. A question-and-answer section followed, in which the judges' main objective was to see how familiar the contestants were with the sport of rodeo, though they sometimes asked about current global events, too. The queen represents the town for a whole year, carrying the American flag with pride and honor. I'd long ago learned all there was to know about rodeo, and I spent every spare moment getting caught up on the news.

My riding uniform of jeans and a light-blue shirt for the reining portion of the contest had been pressed days ago and packed along with the blue dress for the Q&A and the riding dress outfit that Melinda had gifted me: white pants matching an embroidered vest. The one that Mami and I had spent hours modernizing with sequins and expensive Swarovski crystals. Mami had designed and embroidered the Puerto Rican and the American flags entwined inside a heart. She spent months finishing it. It had taken Melinda hours to tailor it to fit my curves and short stature and to give me the freedom I needed to parade on a horse.

I could picture myself acing the speech and the questions, but every time I tried to see myself performing my reining pattern flawlessly, the ugly private messages blared in my mind, until I saw myself fumbling with the reins and falling, looking ridiculous in front of the whole town. Pretty clothes could only help my confidence so much when my insecurities were so loud.

A shuddering sigh left my lips, but the pressure in my chest didn't ease up.

"I just know you're going to get it," Trent said softly, recognizing my nerves. "The judges will love you."

I smiled at him, but the tension didn't leave my pinched shoulders. For me, a people pleaser, an only daughter who had to check off every single item on my parents' unspoken list of expected achievements, not being adored by everyone was a thorn in my heart. A sign of failure. But how did I tell Trent this without sounding vain and petty?

Just like most people didn't understand that our island still needed help after the hurricane, I didn't think he understood my fears that my background and my present didn't match up. I'd tried to explain this to him, but he always said not to pay attention to the haters, so I'd stopped bringing up the topic.

I just looked ahead at the road and the mountains, and the endless sky that shone bright blue as if it were a lake above us. I could almost hear the song of the water.

Once we made sure Papi was safely on his way to his class at the library, Trent drove me to the arena. The familiar scent of horse manure tickled my nose, and the sun glared off the metal of the barn's roof, blinding me. I squinted and saw Melinda waiting for me at the barn entrance. Sweat prickled my underarms, but she went back in as soon as she saw me arrive.

"See you later," Trent said.

I waved at him over my shoulder, and after putting my boots on, I headed for the corral, where Sugar Daddy, a painted horse, was waiting for me. He was twenty-one in human years but acted like he was ten. We knew each other's quirks, but he was spontaneous and mischievous, which made him perfect for practicing. For the actual competition, I'd have to ride a horse I'd choose randomly by selecting a number from a lottery bowl. This was supposed to make it fair for all the participants, but I was nervous just thinking about it. Horses could sense fear and insecurity. With anyone else, I could fake my confidence, but the horse would notice my real feelings as soon as I got close. I had to earn its respect.

Sugar Daddy greeted me with a twitch of his ears.

"¿Que pasó, viejo?" I asked, and he whinnied, protesting that I was calling him old man. While I placed and adjusted the saddle, he flicked his long tail, trying to swat my back. I was ready for his treachery, though. I moved out of the way just before his prickly tail could hit its target. He snorted, and I laughed as I guided him to the indoor arena.

Three little girls who couldn't have been older than ten were walking out, probably just finished with riding lessons. One was golden blond like Trent, and the other two were as dark as I was. Sisters, most likely, and probably Latinas. The trio was arguing in hushed voices, but I caught the last words the older Latina girl was telling the younger: " . . . not like you can become a queen, Jazzy. Some girls are cut out for royalty, and others—"

Her jaw fell when she and I made eye contact.

After a couple of seconds of awkwardness, she asked, "Are you Coralí Estrada?"

The other two girls stared from me to their other friend in wonder.

"Hi, Jazzy," I said, and the blond girl softly elbowed the smaller morenita, who seemed not to remember how to speak. "Maybe some girls seem like they aren't cut out to be royalty." I paused, seeing a glimpse of my younger self in her. What would younger me have needed to know? "Girls—even girls like us— aren't like fabric or leather. We aren't *cut out* to be—or not to be—anything. We're like water and light. You can fit into any spaces you want to fit into, okay?"

In my heart, the words felt hollow and fake, like something I'd recite at school or what I'd write in a yearbook for someone I never really got to know. If I didn't win the crown, would I still feel like I fit in here, in this town?

As if reading my mind, Jazzy said, "My cousin that lives in Nephi says you won't win. The girl from Provo has family in the area, and the judges will go for someone local anyway."

I knew what she really meant by local: *not Latina.*

The blond girl nodded.

I swallowed, staring at the small girls. They were just repeating stuff they'd heard at home and in other places; I shouldn't take it personally. Inside, though, a hurricane to rival Huracán María bellowed in fury.

"I *am* local," I said.

The girls raised their eyebrows, skeptical, and walked on, leaving me rooted to the ground, the horse flicking his tail at my legs for me to move him to the shade.

Although I wanted to pretend their words hadn't hurt, I understood why the girls didn't believe I could win this rodeo. I'd never met a rodeo queen who looked like me either. But the prize, a scholarship to Utah State University provided by the Daughters of the Pioneers, was too big to let go just because some people didn't believe I could win it. My parents would do anything to put me through college, but I wanted to do something to make their lives easier, and for us not to go into debt for my education. I had to win.

The girls left, whispering furiously, and Jazzy looked at me over her shoulder. I couldn't even smile at her through the doubts in her eyes, the same doubts that screamed in my mind.

Sugar Daddy nickered and bumped his nose against my back, so I quickened my pace, the gravel crunching under my boots.

"I'm going," I whisper-shouted.

My eyes hadn't adjusted to the dim light of the arena after the brightness outside when Melinda's voice bellowed, "Late again, Coralí." She shook her head. "Even Sugar Daddy knows the first rule of rodeoing is *Crowns are won on the practice rink.* Don't be late for the coronation."

Melinda held the reins for me. I jumped in the saddle, and Sugar Daddy trotted to the hay feeders hanging from the fence, the opposite of what I wanted him to do.

"Control him," Melinda said, her voice sharp and matter-of-fact. "Relax your shoulders and unclench your jaw. You're too tense."

I exhaled in an attempt to relax my upper body while I pressed Sugar Daddy with my legs, trying to lead him on a trot around the arena to warm up. When he stubbornly kept going to the hay, I pulled the reins, the knots in the ropes biting into my calloused hands. Sugar Daddy tossed his mane, but he did as I wanted, and soon he fell into an easy canter. I could feel that he wanted to let go and run, but I kept firm pressure on his bit, and soon we synchronized our breathing and, I imagined, our hearts.

Melinda clapped, and Sugar's ears twitched again. He started heading toward the entrance of the arena, but just because I could, I pulled on the reins again for him to go around the perimeter once more before heading to the entrance to do our first reining practice of the day. Although he'd been the one trotting, my heart was racing, my breath coming out in gusts.

The horse fidgeted on the goal line at the arena entrance. I sighed, trying to ground myself in the moment, seeing myself re-creating the eight maneuvers of my pattern around three markers that sat like an isosceles triangle.

Melinda yelled, "Hiya!"

Sugar Daddy bolted before I was ready, and in the millisecond it took me to recover, I imagined myself falling through the air. It was only a moment, but Sugar Daddy sensed my distraction. He turned before we had completed our first left circle.

"No!" I gasped, and tugged the reins.

He circled to the right sharply, and then he beelined to Melinda, who waited for him with a grim expression.

By the time she clicked on the chronometer, I was out of breath. My abs clenched with the effort to stay balanced on the misbehaving horse.

"He didn't even finish the first maneuver," Melinda said.

She didn't need to add anything else. If I didn't complete the first maneuver, it didn't matter if the rest of the seven in the pattern were perfect. I'd score no points.

If I couldn't control a horse I rode every week, how did I expect to control one I had no connection with?

"I'll try again," I said.

This time I kept pressure on the bit the whole run.

Run down the middle, past the end marker, left rollback. First maneuver complete.

On to the second maneuver. Run down the middle, past the other end marker, right rollback.

I counted to three under my breath. Run down the middle past center marker, stop, back up, and hesitate. Sugar Daddy didn't like hesitating, and he bolted for maneuver four before I was ready.

I clenched my teeth until my jaw hurt.

Four right spins.

I guided my horse to the next maneuver, and before he hesitated, I was dizzy, breathing fast.

He usually liked what came next, so I left the reins a little looser than I should've.

Wide circles to the left—large fast, small slow, large fast, and then a charge.

Before I got my bearings, he took me by surprise and headed toward Melinda before we completed maneuvers seven and eight.

The tension bubbled underneath Sugar's skin, matching my disappointment.

"Again," I said, and before Melinda got the clock reset,

Sugar shot out. When I leaned forward to better move with him, I lost one of the reins. As he flashed around the first marker, Melinda's voice rose, trying to get his attention.

She tried to intercept him before the second marker, but he changed course and headed to the center of the arena. In the meantime, I managed to grab the fallen rein. But it was too late to recover from this blunder. Sugar reared his head, braking his run.

I wasn't ready for the change of speed. Inertia sent me flying over Sugar's head, and I landed on the rubber that covered the arena floor. I rolled, curling my body and protecting my head. My ears thundered with my rushing blood and Melinda's voice as she told off Sugar Daddy, who cantered to the hay hanging from baskets on the fence. It took a moment for me to understand what had happened.

When I was learning how to ride, I'd fallen once, but never since. And never like this. I'd always told myself I could deal with other people's doubts, that I fed on people underestimating me. But the rodeo was less than a week away, and I wasn't dealing at all.

I stood up, my whole soul aching, and brushed the rubber dust from my clothes.

"Are you okay?" Melinda's blue eyes, darker than Trent's and with an intensity his didn't have, bored into me.

Unable to speak, I nodded. If a tongue-lashing was coming for everything I'd done wrong, I had to take it stoically. Squaring my shoulders, I raised my chin.

"You're too distracted, Corali." Her voice was soft, but the words cut me deeper than the sharpest knife. She pressed her hand on my shoulder just like she did when she wanted to soothe a panicked horse. "Let's end this practice now. You have a week to figure out what you really want."

With that, she walked out of the arena, taking the horse with her.

As the week stretched on, Melinda's question never left my mind. What *did* I really want?

The more I thought about it—as I exercised at the gym, helped Mami with the laundry, and practiced with Sugar Daddy—the more I realized that the answer was complicated, full of layers.

The part of me that was an island girl—that would be forever—wanted to swim in the blue ocean, hug my grandmother, and help her rebuild her home. The wannabe rodeo queen, however, thought only about the future. She was all focus and determination. She fit so completely into a Western lifestyle that she sought to claim a crown that had only ever been bestowed on girls whose families had been in this area for generations. She was the answer to countless family prayers and promises whispered before an altar.

I didn't know how to stretch myself to be both at the same time.

The night before the rodeo, Mami sang me a lullaby as calming as the waves of the ocean from my childhood.

I woke before dawn, restless, cocooned in the blanket Mami had placed on me. I could still smell the traces of the empanadillas and the pasteles I'd delivered last week, before I fell from the horse. I thought about the people who'd supported me all summer, listening to my dreams and nodding their heads even when those dreams seemed incomprehensible to them, ridiculous even. An island girl who wanted to become a rodeo queen and represent the whole town? Perhaps I'd been too naive. Perhaps I didn't have what was required to wear the crown.

There was no way I'd go back to sleep, so I rolled over and switched on my phone. A flood of notifications dinged through my silent room.

From Jazzy, who'd followed me on Instagram since the day we'd met: "After the rodeo, will you sign my hat? For me you're already a queen."

The man who'd helped us in the highway had commented on the official rodeo page, saying, "Best of luck, surfer queen! Your island will be proud of all your hard work. As are we." My chest swelled with emotion. Maybe when he'd seen me in my old T-shirt and worn pants, he'd seen all I was ready to sacrifice to represent the Western way of life he loved so much.

Friends from school sent me their good wishes. Even one of the girls competing against me, the one from Provo, said she was proud of sharing this journey with me.

Family from Puerto Rico I hadn't seen in years commented with crown emojis and hearts. Their love and confidence traveled over the distance and warmed my heart.

But it was Abuelita Irma's message that pierced through the fog of fear and self-doubt. She sent me a video from her kitchen. It had still been dark when she made it, and in the background the coquí frogs and night birds sang their songs. "You're the queen of my life," she said. "Whether you win the crown or not, what makes you a warrior is that you keep trying. Seeing you live your dreams makes the distance a little easier to bear, mamita. Your light shines bright, Coralí!" She blew me a kiss and I felt it in my soul.

That day at the barn I'd told Jazzy, *Girls aren't like fabric or leather. We're like water and light. You can fit into any spaces you want to fit into.* When the words left my mouth, they'd tasted like lies. But maybe it was a part of me that I hadn't wanted to recognize speaking up for the first time. What if this part was the one that filled in the gap of who I'd been, where I came from, and the person growing inside my heart if I was brave enough to let her bloom?

Some people thought that, to become a rodeo queen, I had to shed all the parts of me that didn't perfectly match up with the Western way of life. But after all, what was this way of life based on? Its foundations were the same values I'd grown up with in my immigrant family: courage, optimism, hard work, community.

It took courage to leave one's country and start anew in a foreign place. It took courage to wake up every morning to face the unknown. Courage was getting up on the horse after the worst, most embarrassing fall of your life.

Without optimism, how did Abuelita Irma tend to her orchids again? How could a little eight-year-old get on a horse and pretend she could fly?

And hard work? I'd learned that work dignifies—even if, like Papi, you were a professor mixing dog food, reciting poetry in your mind so you wouldn't forget the rhythm of your mother tongue. Hard work was coming home from teaching all day and making pasteles and empanadas so your daughter could afford to take riding lessons, like Mami did.

I dressed in silence, trying to savor every second.

The original outfit that Melinda had given me had been expensive to start with. I couldn't put a price to the dreams and hopes sewn onto the fabric.

After putting it on, I put on my well-worn and -loved brown leather boots that molded to my feet like gloves. The ocean-blue hat Papi had given me for Valentine's sat on my dresser, and when it crowned my head, its weight felt like a blessing.

Mami and Papi waited for me in the kitchen; their faces lit up when they saw me. I wished I could gather that light and save it for later, so it could help fill in the blanks of me that weren't fully formed yet. I was seventeen, and while part of me felt like an adult, how many parts were still waiting to develop?

I wasn't sure, but I was optimistic. I couldn't wait to see.

Later, after I delivered my speech from the heart, embracing my Puertoricanness and my Western life, as the sun beat down on the arena, I sat on a white-spotted bay horse called Patchwork, waiting at the goal line. Patchwork's anticipation to perform our reining pattern exuded from him, or maybe it was my anticipation that he felt and amplified. I smiled at my friends and family, who roared back cheers and encouragement. Papi and Mami sat next to Trent and waved Puerto Rican and American flags. Melinda smiled because she could see I now knew what I wanted.

The sign went off for me to shoot out to the left for the first maneuver, and the horse followed my lead. Each section of the pattern felt like a part of me, the island girl, the Western girl, and the third, the unknown part of me filled with hope and light that contained multitudes.

On the horse, I moved with the grace I'd learned from my salsa-dancing father and the speed of my surfing mother. I commanded the horse with all the authority I'd learned from my trainer, Melinda. I was unstoppable. I felt like one more star in my town, Andromeda, a galaxy tucked in the mountains.

And I let my light shine and spread to fill in the gaps.

Grandpa
RANDY DuBURKE

I HADN'T BEEN TO GEORGIA IN FOUR YEARS. NOT SINCE GRANDPA'S FUNERAL.

MOM DIDN'T LIKE THE IDEA OF ME GOING THERE ALONE, BUT SHE AND DAD HAD TOO MUCH WORK TO DO TO COME ALONG.

DAD SAID, "COME ON, NOW! HE'S A BIG OL' BOY. HE'S FIFTEEN."

HE LOOKED AT ME.

"YOU CAN GO ALONE THIS TIME, RIGHT?"

AFTER WE PASSED THROUGH WASHINGTON, JUNIOR TURNED ONTO A TREE-LINED DIRT ROAD. WE CRUISED PAST A FEW HOUSES AND A FARM UNTIL WE MADE ANOTHER TURN ONTO A SMALLER DIRT ROAD THAT LED TO GRANDMA'S HOUSE.

Wellllll, look at you! You talla than Grandma by a head!

Welcome home.

COME SUNDAY, I WENT WITH JUNIOR AND GRANDMA TO SERVICE AT THE CHAPEL WHERE GRANDPA USED TO PREACH.

I HADN'T SET FOOT IN THE PLACE SINCE GRANDPA'S FUNERAL.

AFTER CHURCH ENDED, GRANDMA TOOK ME AROUND TO HER FRIENDS. I THOUGHT I'D REMEMBER SOME OF THEM, BUT I DIDN'T.

THEY ALL SEEMED TO REMEMBER ME, THOUGH.

THE NEXT FEW DAYS FOLDED IN ON THEMSELVES. I HELPED JUNIOR WITH THE CHICKENS, HELPED GRANDMA WITH THE CHORES. AND A LOT OF TIME I JUST SAT AROUND THINKING.

THE AIR WAS STIFLING. MOSQUITOES WERE EVERYWHERE. NOBODY I USED TO KNOW LIVED HERE ANYMORE. I WISHED I WAS BACK IN BROOKLYN.

THAT'S WHAT I WAS DOING AS I SAT IN THE SHADE ON THE GRASSY BLUFF IN FRONT OF GRANDMA'S HOUSE.

What'cho doin' boy? Why ain't you drawin'?

I told you, Junior, I didn't bring any drawing stuff!

That's a shame. I thought you liked drawin.'

I do. I just... I don't know.

You told me you was gonna make books when you got big.

I NEVER TOLD JUNIOR THAT. I TOLD...

Grandpa?

Hey! Get on down here. Lunch is ready.

Boy, ah'm tellin' you. Ah weren't up on that hill wit'cho!

What's this all about?

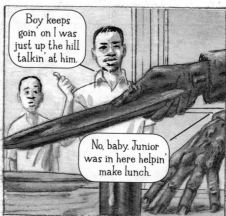

Boy keeps goin on I was just up the hill talkin' at him.

No, baby. Junior was in here helpin' make lunch.

He jus' messed up cause he ain't got no one ta play wit'. Oughtta do some a' your drawin' then you mightn't be so lonely as to make up people to talk to.

Hush now, Junior.

Miss Viola says her girl's boy Lennard is coming tomorrow. You remember him? You and he used to play together when you was little.

YEAH, I REMEMBERED HIM. HE WAS OLDER THAN ME AND HAD BEEN A REAL PRACTICAL JOKER. BUT AT LEAST SOMEBODY WOULD BE AROUND.

THE NEXT DAY I TROTTED OVER TO MISS VIOLA'S. MISS VIOLA WAS AN OLD FRIEND OF MY GRANDPARENTS' AND HAD BEEN ONE OF GRANDPA'S LONGTIME CONGREGANTS.

You sure grown up fine!

Hello Miss Viola. Is ... uh, is Lennard here?

Course he is. Lennard!

Well, don't just stand there. Come out and say hello.

Hey, Lennard.

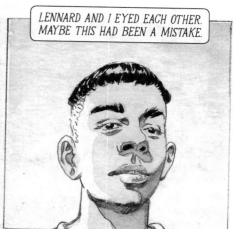

WE WALKED UNTIL WE REACHED AN OLD DRIED-UP WELL. LENNARD PICKED UP A SMALL STONE FROM THE LIP OF THE WELL AND FLIPPED IT INTO THE CENTER. IT TOOK SEVERAL SECONDS FOR IT TO STRIKE BOTTOM.

Remember this?

I told you this went all the way to China? And you believed me!

I was four.

You went home and wrote and drew a whole story around "The Tunnel to China." It had dragons and spaceships and . . . and I don't know what else! It was great!

You showed it to everyone, and people went nuts for it. And your granddad, he really loved it! He talked about it for days.

He did?

Sure he did. You don't remember?

Nuh-uh.

WHEN I GOT BACK TO GRANDMA'S, I GRABBED SOME PAPER AND PENCILS AND HEADED OUTSIDE.

THE LAST NIGHT I WAS AT GRANDMA'S I SHOWED HER AND JUNIOR THE DRAWINGS I HAD MADE.

THEY FLIPPED THROUGH ALL OF THEM: THE CHICKENS, JUNIOR, THE FARM ACROSS THE WAY, GRANDMA'S HOUSE, GRANDMA, AND THE DRAWING WE ALL LIKED THE BEST . . .

. . . GRANDPA.

Best in Show
TIRZAH PRICE

I didn't notice the guy with the camera until I heard the shutter clicking.

It was a ninety-degree day, and space in the wash rack was tight. Herbert was too happy to get some relief from the scorch and humidity to care that his constant shuffling kept slamming me into the rough walls. I braced myself against the corner to keep my balance.

"Dude, you gotta calm down," I told him as he plunged his snout under my hand, the one holding the end of the hose. I placed my thumb over the opening, spraying cold water over his body. Herbert heaved a happy sigh against my leg. His hairy side was warm, and not for the first time I wondered what blip in biology allowed pigs to suffer without enough sweat glands. "Better?" I asked.

When his breathing calmed to happy snuffles, I squirted a generous stream of Dawn dish detergent down his back and got to work lathering him up. Herbert was the best-looking pig I'd

ever raised—straight back, generously shaped shoulders, and
perfect globes for hams. Even if things fell apart in the show
ring on Thursday, we'd stand a decent chance of placing in
market class, I was pretty sure.

I was scrubbing away the stubborn dirt and muck from
Herbert's underside and thinking about ribbons when the
clicking sound finally registered. What really got my attention,
though, was a quick high-pitched giggling. Not wanting to star-
tle Herbert, I slowly straightened and looked over my shoulder.

A guy and a girl around my age stood just beyond the wash
racks, near the pig barn entrance. The guy was pointing a huge
black camera right at me. I looked into the insect eye of the lens
as it clicked again. The girl laughed nervously when she realized they'd been caught.

The photographer brought the camera down and met my
gaze. "I've never seen anyone give a pig a bath before."

"Okay?" I said, my non-response tinged with annoyance. I
tried to tamp it down. Beth, my 4-H leader, was always reminding us that fair week was an opportunity to educate people,
not dismiss them. But it was the Mekawnee County Fair, right
smack in the palm of Michigan. What did he expect?

"We're from Chicago," the girl added, like that explained
everything. I guess it sort of did. Everything but the rudeness.

"Not many pigs in Chicago," the guy added unnecessarily,
and they both laughed.

I tried to attach a smile to my face, but it wouldn't stick. It
didn't help that my shorts and T-shirt were soaked with sweat
and water, and my bare legs were streaked with grime. This
was hardly the photo-op with Herbert I'd been imagining for
months.

"How'd you get him in there?" the blond girl asked. "Does he have a leash?"

"Uh, no." I tried to channel my inner Beth—*Educate, don't dismiss*—and gestured to my pig stick, leaning against the wash rack. "I guided him in. He's trained to follow my lead."

"Oh my God, that's so cute! Did you decorate it yourself?" She picked up my stick, which was nothing more than an old piece of PVC tubing that I'd covered with rainbow-patterned duct tape.

"Yep," I replied tersely. I resisted the urge to snatch it back—the guy was still snapping pictures, and the last thing I needed was photographic evidence of me tussling over a stick to make its rounds on the internet. *Dirty Farm Girl Loses Mind Over PVC Pipe*.

Thankfully, she handed it back as the guy said, "Can you give us a demonstration?"

Herbert stepped on my foot, and I felt all 287 pounds of his check-in weight through my rubber muck boot. "The pig show is Thursday. You can see us in action then."

"We won't be here," the girl explained. "We leave tomorrow."

"So soon?" I asked, my restraint slipping. Luckily, I was kept from unleashing any more snark by someone calling my name.

"Molly! Hey!"

I looked past the Chicagoans to the last person I expected to see: Amoreena Sandoval. A jolt of energy ran down my body—this must have been how Herbert felt when he was doused with cold water.

"Hi!" I squeaked, and promptly dropped the bottle of Dawn. I stooped to pick it up before Herbert tried to eat it. *Pigs*.

Amoreena stepped up to the wash rack, ignoring the two Chicagoans, and I felt more on display than ever. "I thought maybe you'd be around," she said. "What's this guy's name?"

My brain had snagged on *I thought maybe you'd be around*, so it took me a full three seconds to say "Herbert."

"Herbert!" The other girl laughed.

Amoreena edged closer, apparently not caring about the sudsy gray water that swirled around her floral Keds. She was dressed in shorts and a tank top, and her dark curly hair was piled on top of her head in a bun. She didn't look like a fair kid, but at least she was dressed for a fair, unlike the Chicagoans. "Can I?" she asked, nodding at Herbert.

"Go ahead," I said. "He likes to be scratched right behind his ears."

Amoreena reached out a little hesitantly but laughed when Herbert leaned into her touch. "It's like petting a dog."

"Oh my God, this is hysterical!" The Chicago girl's voice shattered the moment, and the shutter clicked again.

Amoreena turned and looked the guy square in the lens. "It's polite to ask first, you know."

He lowered his camera, surprised. "Um, can I?"

She shrugged. "He's Molly's pig."

I was tempted to tell him to delete his pictures of us *and* where to stick his camera—but then Amoreena caught my gaze and winked. She *winked*, and the heat that spread across my cheeks had nothing to do with the sun beating down on us. Instead, I said, "The exhibition barn sells postcards. You can find plenty of livestock photos there."

Not to mention that those photos would be edited and touched up, and the people in them would be dressed in proper show attire, not old grubby work clothes. I noticed Amoreena bite her bottom lip, but the movement didn't quite manage to hold in her smile.

"Oh, well . . . thanks a lot," the guy said, lowering his camera with a confused expression.

"Sure thing," I said, my sarcasm loud to my own ears, and Amoreena added an extra-sweet "Bye! Enjoy the fair!"

They weren't even out of earshot before we burst into laughter.

"Wow," Amoreena said.

"Some people," I agreed.

"I hope you don't mind me butting in like that. I saw them taking your picture from over there"—she waved a hand toward the goat barn—"and I could kinda tell you hadn't seen them."

"Oh. I don't mind. I mean, thanks. For the save." I tried to smile normally, but I couldn't help feeling that I looked pathetically eager. I'd spent most of the last year checking Amoreena's Instagram account daily. I'd become an expert in the tilt of her head in her selfies and at analyzing her use of hashtags. This kind of obsessive attention to detail made me awesome in the show ring but would probably come off kind of creepy if Amoreena ever found out.

Then she smiled. "Besides, I was looking for you."

"Oh!" If I were braver, I'd have added *Why?* But I couldn't bear it if the answer was anything other than *Because I've been crushing on you ever since I sat down at your lunch table last September, Molly*. Instead I said, "Well, you found me!"

I immediately regretted the way my voice tilted to a high pitch. This was why I was better at nontalking activities and competitions.

Amoreena patted Herbert on the head. "And this guy! What do you do after you give him a bath?"

I steadied. I could talk pigs and showmanship all day. "After this, I shave and brush him." When she didn't laugh, I kept going. I explained Herbert's serious lack of sweat glands, how pigs can get easily stressed, and all of the accommodations I made for him, like hanging a box fan over his pen and keeping a spray bottle nearby to spritz him down. She listened with intense fascination, which made me feel like she actually cared about what I had to say beyond getting an interesting anecdote about that one time she went to a county fair.

It did absolutely nothing to lessen my crush on her.

"I still can't get over the no-sweating thing," Amoreena said as I wound down. Herbert was clean now, and I was just running water over him while he panted contentedly. "Like, you'd've thought evolution would've taken care of that."

"Careful the Baptists don't hear you," I quipped.

The Baptist church ran the food truck between the pig barn and the nearest horse stable, and they aggressively peddled Bibles in addition to the best barbeque sandwiches you could find at the fair.

Amoreena laughed. "They don't have much hope of converting me."

And just like that, I was in a spiral of uncertainty and excitement. My Instagram sleuthing had told me that Amoreena was most likely, probably queer—there was a photo from last summer, at her old school, where she stood with a bunch of rainbow-clad friends at what appeared to be a Pride party. Last month, she'd posted a generic "Happy Pride!" message. This was more than I dared to do, and I had no good reason to avoid it. I had come out, quietly, to my parents last year, and they reacted just as I predicted—with tears and hugs and lots of dramatic declarations of love. Most of my friends knew I liked girls, but they rarely brought it up, because I didn't bring it up. Unlike Amoreena, I didn't have queer friends. No one that I could drive two hours with to the nearest city so we could do gay things. All the other openly queer kids in our school did theater, or were in AP classes together, or read serious books about politics. I had more in common with my straight friends.

Then Amoreena showed up. Sat at our lunch table. Didn't laugh when she found out that I lived on a farm or ask if I felt bad for eating my pet cows. Plus, she was beautiful. I had the biggest crush on her, but I had no idea what to do about it, not even when she was standing next to me, asking questions about Herbert.

"I have to get this guy back inside," I told Amoreena abruptly, nodding at Herbert. "Before he gets sunburned."

"Oh, sure!" she said brightly, but she didn't turn to leave.

I drew in a shaky breath. *Come on, Molly. Don't be a weirdo.* "Do you, um, want to meet me inside?"

"Sure!" Amoreena flashed a wide smile, and I returned it before grabbing my rainbow-covered pig stick. I glanced up, and Amoreena was eyeing it. Was she wondering if I was an ally? Or was she picking up what I was putting out there?

Before I could analyze any further, Amoreena disappeared into the barn. I unlatched the wash rack gate and coaxed Herbert through the chute leading inside the barn. It was a good thing he was so well trained, because my mind was elsewhere. Herbert trotted inside, and I nudged him in the direction of his pen with little effort. As I drifted after him, my skin prickled like I was in the middle of the show ring, holding the weight of hundreds of pairs of eyes but only caring about the one gaze that mattered. But instead of the judge, it was all about Amoreena.

"Is this really happening?" I muttered to Herbert as I got him settled in his pen. In true pig fashion, he ignored me completely in favor of snuffling about in his clean sawdust.

Herbert settled under his box fan, and Amoreena glided up next to me. "I know 'cute' is a term usually saved for really small things, but your pig is kind of cute."

I grinned like she had called *me* cute. "He's a good pig. I guess I kind of baby him, but you get attached, you know? I got him when he was only four weeks old. I don't really think about how it might look weird to other people that I give him baths and brush him, or train him to follow me around."

"I mean, some people have cats," Amoreena pointed out.

"I'm not a cat person," I confessed, and hoped that wouldn't be a deal breaker.

"Same. But I think I could be a pig person. When's your show again?"

I couldn't speak at first. What was even happening right now? For nearly a year, we had orbited the same friend group and shared a lunch table. We'd barely spoken one-on-one, and when we had, it was about classes or school events. For the entire month of February, I'd dropped as many hints as possible that I was into girls, and she'd never even looked in my direction. So what had changed? Was it because it was summer and she was bored? I didn't want to look a gift horse in the mouth, but I couldn't wrap my head around this reversal of fortune.

"Thursday," I said finally, and because apparently I wanted to die alone, added, "But you don't have to come."

"I want to," she said. "Only—"

There it was. The *but* I'd been waiting on. I should've known better than to get my hopes up.

"—that's, like, four days away. Wanna, maybe, hang out sometime sooner? Without Herbert? No offense, Herbert."

Herbert was already fast asleep.

"Oh," I said, and then, before I could think better of it, I added, "You mean like a date?"

My cheeks flushed and I glanced around to see if anyone was bearing witness to what was shaping up to be my most embarrassing moment ever. Why'd this have to happen in the pig barn? I'd never be able to set foot in this place again without remembering my humiliation in front of the prettiest girl I'd ever met.

"I mean, yeah?" Amoreena said, nervously drumming her fingers against the gate. "If you want?"

"Really?" I asked, focusing back on her. I did what I'd been too afraid to do and looked her square in the eye. Her brown eyes danced with amusement, but not the kind that was laughing at me.

"Really."

"Yeah!" I agreed too quickly, but it was all I could think of to say. She must have been struck similarly speechless, because we grinned at each other like fools until Tim Wexler yelled, "Incoming!" and his dirty pig streaked past us, squealing its protest all the way to the wash rack.

Maybe it's pathetic to admit that I lived for the second week of July, but it's true. Fair week was my time. The week I'd spent most of the year working and planning for. It was one of the only times when I felt like I wasn't on display for all the things that made me different from other people: being a farm kid; being one of the few sixteen-year-olds who didn't lose interest in 4-H in high school; being the only person in my age bracket to have gotten a perfect score on my Pork Quality Assurance exam. During the Mekawnee County Fair, I wasn't that weird girl who wore overalls unironically. I was president of the Grant Township Pioneers 4-H Club, holder of schedules and keys to the club tack trailer. If people were looking for me, or at me, it was because I had an answer to their question or a solution to their problem.

Which is why I did feel weird about how Amoreena had caught me completely off guard.

We agreed to go out on Tuesday, which had the only gap in my busy fair schedule. Then we exchanged numbers and waved goodbye outside the commerce barn. I spent the rest of my day preparing for fair week to begin in earnest—making sure the last of the barn decorations went up and everyone in my club had weighed in their animals and bathed them. I helped our Clover Buds finish their record books and reminded everyone of the barn duty schedule. It took pretty much all afternoon and into the evening, because every time I tried to go anywhere, even the bathroom, someone was calling, "Hey, Molly, what time's barn duty?" or "Molly! What did Herbert weigh in at?" or "What campsite are you at this year, Molls?"

The excitement hung almost as thick as the humidity, and I made sure to stop and answer every question and say hi to everyone I recognized, but it also felt different somehow, like all the weirdness I felt for not totally belonging at school had infiltrated my fair week confidence. Every time someone called out my name, I jumped a tiny bit. Doubt was slowly rising to engulf me, and I wondered if anyone had seen me with Amoreena and guessed that we were going on a date, as absurd as that was. We were just talking, and there was nothing shocking about that. I tried to tell myself that it was fine, but something like panic still kept crawling up my skin.

"Everything's looking great," Beth said when I found her in the goat barn later that evening. She was reinforcing a pen that contained Cinnamon, a goat belonging to one of the Clover Buds. They should've named him Houdini. I reached out to pet him, and he tried to nibble my fingers. Goats and pigs were kind of similar that way.

"I'm going to double-check the horse barn before dinner," I told her. "The twinkle lights above the stalls keep falling, and if they get within Paco's reach, he'll eat them."

"Take this," Beth said, handing me her staple gun. "I think I'm done. If this goat escapes, he deserves his freedom and I'll deny he was ever here."

One of the reasons I liked Beth so much was because her humor was a little dark and she never apologized for it. She was in her early forties and had been running our club for ten years, even though she didn't have kids of her own. Beth was the only adult I'd come out to aside from my parents. When I told her last fall, she'd just said, "Okay, Molly. You let me know if you need anything." And I knew she'd have my back.

Why couldn't everyone be that cool?

As I took the staple gun, Beth studied me closely.

"What?" I asked.

"You look worn out. Remember, this week is supposed to be fun."

"Yeah, yeah." This was an old topic with us that I didn't want to rehash. I didn't know how to tell her about Amoreena, or if doing so would be weird. I mean, it wasn't like Beth kept me updated about her dating life. Instead I said, "I had some rubberneckers while I was in the wash rack."

"Fair week brings out all types." She pushed her graying brown hair off her forehead. "Don't let them get to you. This is your week."

"Yeah," I agreed, but there was no feeling in it.

"How's Herbert settling in?"

"He's good. He was sleeping when I went to feed."

Beth looked like she didn't quite believe I was telling the whole truth. "When you're done with the lights, come by my site for a hot dog. We'll talk strategy for show day."

Beth and I had done this hundreds of times—talked about everything from pigs and farming to school and college and the future, our dreams and our families, 4-H gossip and funny stories about our club members. But I knew I couldn't ask her what was really on my mind: *How do I go on a date with a girl in this small town without it becoming a major event? How do I not care what people think about me?*

How do I not be afraid?

"Yeah," I said. "I'll be there."

On Tuesday morning, Amoreena texted me to suggest meeting at the fairgrounds, but I shot back, "No! I'll pick you up!"

It wasn't just because I felt the urge to be chivalrous, although that was a big part of it. According to every single romantic comedy I'd ever seen, someone picked someone up on a date. The only thing was that most of those rom-coms had

straight couples, and the one I'd seen with two girls had someone who was still in the closet. My first anxiety attack of the
day was that Amoreena wasn't out to her family and having
a girl pick her up might cause problems, but asking someone
if they were out to their family via text seemed rude. Before I
could stress over it any more, she texted me her address.

Later, I freaked myself out on the drive over by imagining
having to meet her parents as her date—or, worse, having to
pretend we were "just friends" hanging out. But when I pulled
in the driveway, Amoreena bounded out of the house like she'd
been keeping an eye out for me.

When I caught sight of her, I forgot for a moment that I was
behind the wheel of a rusted-out Chevrolet truck older than
me, still smelling faintly of farm despite how much I'd cleaned
and the new air freshener I'd attached to the vent. Amoreena
was wearing a goldenrod sundress, her dark hair down in loose
waves. Before I could do more than just gape, she opened the
passenger door and hopped into the truck. "Hey!"

"Hi," I said, a bit breathless. Not just at the sight of her, but
her presence. It was so big the cab of the old farm truck couldn't
hold her. "You look beautiful."

Her smile was a reflection of how I felt—excited and nervous. "Thanks. You look great, too."

I bit my bottom lip so I wouldn't argue. I was wearing the
only skirt I owned, which was a denim hand-me-down, and one
of my sleeveless button-down show shirts, a red gingham that
Mom had talked me into buying because sexist judges went for
a wholesome Laura Ingalls Wilder vibe. I'd never worn it before
tonight, but I'd knotted it at the waist in an attempt at fashion

and so I wouldn't look like I was headed into the show arena. I wasn't entirely sure it was working.

When Amoreena was settled, I turned the key and the truck started with a roar. "Sorry about this monstrosity," I said above the engine. "I couldn't borrow my mom's car."

"No worries," she said brightly. "I like how high up we are! My mom drives a Prius."

"It's so obnoxious, though. People are always turning to look whenever I accelerate, and when they see a girl behind the wheel . . ." I shook my head to banish thoughts of the lewd gestures that some guys made when they saw a girl in a loud truck.

"Just give them a beauty queen wave." Amoreena demonstrated a robotic wave that made me laugh, even though I knew if I did that it'd only encourage some guys. "So what do you want to do tonight?" she asked.

My hands tightened on the wheel. That was the question that had kept me up all night. The fair seemed like the obvious answer, and I was certain that's where Amoreena expected us to go. It was where everyone would be, but that was exactly why I didn't want to go there.

I sucked in a deep breath and said in a rush, "I thought maybe a movie? If that's okay with you?"

"Sure!" she said, and I relaxed—but only for a second.

It was a short drive to our downtown, which was really only two blocks of old brick buildings, some of them in better shape than others depending on whether they were occupied or not. Businesses came and went a lot, but the theater had been there for as long as I could remember.

When I pulled onto Main, it looked like the set of an

apocalypse movie: the streets and sidewalks were mostly empty, and traffic was nonexistent. Even though there were plenty of spots open, I parked the truck between a minivan and another truck in front of the theater. Parallel parking was something I could do well, and when we were even with the curb, Amoreena said, "That was kind of impressive."

"It's easier in a truck than a car," I told her. "An open bed, an unobstructed view."

"You," she said, "are unexpected."

"Yeah?"

"Yes," she confirmed, and hopped out.

I followed, processing her words. Amoreena made *unexpected* sound like a compliment, but it made me nervous. I had a hard enough time figuring out what I was supposed to do or say on a daily basis without the added complication of being unexpected. Case in point: As we walked toward the small theater, the impulse to reach out and take her hand surged through me. How would she react? Would that be *unexpected* or just weird? I settled for walking really close, our arms just barely brushing.

The theater had only two screens. One was showing a horror movie and one a romantic comedy. When we walked into the blessed AC, I asked, "Which one should we see?"

"I don't do horror," she said.

"Oh, thank God. Me neither."

"Excellent," she said, and I think I could have just held her stare for another hour, except Travis Stockton was behind the counter and he said, "Which showing?" loud enough to make me start.

I didn't look at him as I dug around in my bag for the cash and Amoreena told him what movie we wanted. When I handed him a twenty, he cut a look between me and Amoreena that made me stiffen just slightly. I smiled weakly while he printed our tickets and handed me my change.

"Enjoy the show," he deadpanned.

"Thanks!" Amoreena said brightly. To me she added, "You got the tickets, I'm getting popcorn."

"You don't—"

"Yes, I do! Don't argue!"

She bounced up to the concession stand while I hovered awkwardly behind her, trying not to sneak glances at Travis. Was that just how he talked or was he expressing disapproval? I didn't really know him, but that didn't stop me from desperately wondering what he was thinking about us. Did we look like two friends? More than friends?

"Ready?" Amoreena asked, popcorn bag in hand.

I smiled to cover up my uncertainty. "Yeah!"

Only half a dozen people sat inside the theater, clustered around the center seats. "Front or back?" Amoreena asked.

Normally I liked to sit in the second or third row. But if we did that, we'd have to walk past all those people. They'd see us *together*. Would they assume that we were on a date? Probably not. But what if they figured it out? *Calm down, Molly.* This was a small town, not 1955. But fear won out, and I replied, "Back." Amoreena picked the row second from the back, and I felt traitorous for appreciating that it was close to the exit, in case we needed a quick escape.

Amoreena offered me the popcorn. "My mom always makes me and my brothers wait until the movie actually starts because otherwise we'd destroy the popcorn before the previews were over."

"But the previews are entertainment, too!"

"Thank you!"

"Besides, this is probably the only theater in the Midwest that gives you free refills on two-dollar popcorn," I added. "You have to eat a bunch so you can get a top-off before the movie starts."

She gasped. "Free popcorn refills? Why didn't anyone tell me this?"

"Best-kept secret in Mekawnee County. If everyone knew, our tiny theater would be flooded with big-city folk."

Amoreena laughed. "Who knew there were so many perks to small-town living?"

I kept forgetting that Amoreena used to live in a big suburb outside of Detroit. Before I could ask about her old school, the lights dimmed and the previews began to roll. In the dark of the theater, I tried to relax. No matter how many times I'd envisioned going out with Amoreena, I hadn't pictured anything like this. In the fantasyland of my imagination, our date hadn't happened here. It was in some bigger, blander town where we wouldn't run into anyone we knew.

I told myself to relax and tried to block out everything but this moment. I was really good at doing that when I was in the show arena—I could ignore the audience and the other pigs and participants and just focus on myself, my pig, and the judge. But if anything, I was hyperaware of everyone else in the dark theater. Amoreena didn't seem bothered—at the end of each preview, she turned her head just slightly toward me and whispered either "Yes" or "Pass," and when the new Star Wars movie trailer came on, she actually bounced in her seat. I was struck with another thought: *Do I try and hold her hand now? But then how would we balance the popcorn?* Why was this so stressful?

The previews faded, and the opening credits lit up the screen. A vaguely familiar pop song came on and kept playing even when the screen went suddenly black. At first I thought the blackout was on purpose and a new scene would appear on the screen, but after one second, two, three, then five, I looked at Amoreena. A few moments later she looked at me, and then we both glanced at the still-blank screen.

"Um," I said.

"Maybe it's just technical difficulties?" Amoreena offered me more popcorn. The sound kept running without a picture, and a woman's voice talking about how love could be found in the last place you'd expected drifted over the music.

Someone in front of us got up to tell the theater staff what was going on, and after a minute, the sound cut off too. The lights came back up, and Travis walked in. "Sorry, guys," he said. "The bulb burned out and we're out of backups. You can get a refund at the front counter or you can just pop into theater two."

I looked to Amoreena. "I don't do horror," she reminded me.

"Fair enough."

A cascade of emotions tumbled over me as we got up to collect our refund. On the one hand, what the heck were we going to do now? On the other, it was a weird sort of relief to walk back out into the full light.

"Sorry about the bulb," Travis said when we reached the counter. He looked between me and Amoreena. "Are you two together?"

My mouth went dry. Would he ask a straight couple that?

"Yeah," Amoreena said next to me, and Travis nodded and punched some buttons. It didn't register until he was counting out my refund that he was only trying to figure out if he had to refund me one or two tickets.

After I pocketed my money, Amoreena and I stepped back into the sultry night.

"Should we head—"

"Want to go—"

We both stopped, flustered.

"Go ahead," Amoreena said.

"Okay. Well . . . that was a bust. Want to head down to Vinny's?" I thought maybe I could salvage the evening with the corner booth of the diner and some homemade hot chips doused in vinegar and salt.

"Oh. Sure, sounds good."

There had been a ghost of a hesitation there. "Is that okay?"

"Totally!" she said, and smiled so brightly I wanted to believe her.

We left the popcorn in the truck and walked down the block. Most of the storefronts shut down at five p.m., except for the theater, Murphy's Bar, and Vinny's diner. Since it was a Tuesday night, things were pretty quiet. We were pretty quiet ourselves as we walked past closed insurance offices, a medical-supply store, and the lone dentist office in town and rounded the block.

But Vinny's was dark. "Are you kidding me?" I said, and we stopped to read the handwritten sign taped on the door: "Closing at 7 p.m. during fair week. Sorry for the inconvenience."

"Aw, man," Amoreena said. "I was craving their chips, too."

I stood frozen on the sidewalk, running through our options—a short list in this town. The only other establishment open downtown was Murphy's, so that was out. We could head out toward the highway, where there was a McDonald's, a Subway, and a Chinese buffet, but that was a twenty-minute drive at least, and I didn't want to admit to Amoreena that I wasn't sure my old farm truck could make it without overheating. The only thing more embarrassing than driving that truck on a date would be it breaking down and having to call my dad to bail us out.

"I'm sorry," I blurted.

"It's not your fault. Let's go." She nudged me.

"Where?"

"Um, where literally everyone else is tonight? The fair?"

"Oh."

Her head tilted to the side as she stared back at me. "You don't want to?"

That was a loaded question. At the fair, we could get food. We could walk the midway, find a bonfire at the campground, or just hang out in the pig barn.

Amoreena took measure of my hesitation and said, "You don't want to be seen with me?"

"No!" I blurted, too quickly. "That's not it."

Except that was exactly it. Acknowledging it, even just to myself, made me feel the worst kind of humiliation.

Amoreena shook her head and stared past me down the street. "It's fine," she said shortly. "You can just take me home."

"Wait," I said, but she was already heading to the truck.

"I'm not interested in going back into the closet," she said without turning around.

I jogged a few paces to catch up to her. How could I have imagined this moment a million times only to mess it up so spectacularly? Oddly enough, Beth's words came to me then: *Educate, don't dismiss.*

"Sometimes I wish everyone was gay," I blurted. "So I could actually fit in for once."

That got Amoreena to stop. "Yeah?" She shifted her gaze back at me.

"Yeah. I mean, I don't know if you've noticed, but I'm kind of weird." I wasn't trying to be self-deprecating—it was just a fact. "I feel more comfortable with my pig than I do with most humans."

Amoreena waited, like I hadn't said the right thing yet. At least she was listening.

"Everyone acts like coming out is the hardest thing you'll have to do," I said. "But coming out was easy for me. I don't know what to do *after*. I've had a crush on you since September, but I didn't know what to say. And part of me knew that if I did make a move, it would make it more real."

"How would it be more real?" she asked, and she sounded genuinely curious.

"Um, okay. You know Peter W. and Carlos?"

Amoreena nodded. They were in the grade ahead of us.

"The second they started dating, everyone was like, 'Oh, they're the cutest couple, it's so great, blah blah blah.' But those same people are always snapping their fingers around them and won't stop until they kiss. People nominated them Homecoming Kings because it'd piss off Principal Tingey. And, I don't know, maybe they like that attention. But I'd *hate* it. People mostly don't realize I'm queer. I'm not ashamed, and the people who matter know. I just . . . I don't advertise it."

"I get it," Amoreena said, and she didn't sound mad or sarcastic.

"You do?"

She crossed her arms. "In case *you* haven't noticed, I'm one of four Latinx people in school. And one of them is my brother."

"Oh, yeah," I agreed, embarrassed to realize that I'd just assumed she wouldn't understand my conflicted feelings because she seemed so casually, effortlessly out.

"So yeah, I get what it's like to be a little different," she went on, "always waiting for someone to say . . . *something.*"

That was exactly it. I was always on high alert for someone to say something rude or cruel, but even just plain cluelessness gave me anxiety. Maybe other people were better at handling it, but I didn't want to be in showmanship mode 24/7.

Then Amoreena added, "That's partly why it took me for-ever to get up the courage to ask you out."

"*What?*"

Amoreena stepped closer to me. "I had no idea what I was walking into when we first moved here. All my friends thought I was going to be bullied at best and shot on some back-country road at worst."

I only managed to work up a scowl before Amoreena said, "I know, it's not like that here. But in some ways, it's much more of a mixed bag. I don't know where people stand on the whole gay issue, and that's even harder to figure out than how people feel about the fact that my mom is from Colombia and my dad is from Spain. I can't hide this." She gestured at her hair, but I knew she meant her brown skin, her whole self.

"I'm sorry," I murmured, and she shrugged.

"It's the way it is. Listen, I get being cautious—for the longest time I couldn't figure out if you'd even want me to ask you out."

"I definitely did. I mean, I still do. Want to go out with you."

For the first time, I realized how easy I had it. Probably no one would slap a rainbow "gay friendly" sticker on our small town, but no one had bullied me for being queer either, and I could walk around in public without worrying that people were going to judge me for the color of my skin.

But dating Amoreena would definitely change things. It meant opening myself up to other people's judgments and coming out again and again. It meant that I'd have to start sticking up for myself, and for her.

Amoreena pushed her curls back and said, "Do you care what people think about you showing pigs?"

"No," I said automatically. It was true—I'd never cared about what anyone thought about me and my pigs, except the judge.

"Because you love doing it?"

"Yeah."

"Even though there are people who might make fun of pig shows?"

"To be fair, the shows *are* kind of extra."

Amoreena laughed. "Okay, well that aside, you don't let the assholes get you down, right?"

"Right," I agreed. Amoreena stared so steadily at me, I almost forgot how to breathe. "Are we talking about pig shows or you and me?"

"You and me," she said. She took my hand, and my fingers automatically interlaced with hers. I squashed the impulse to look around and see if anyone was noticing us. "We can't control what other people do or say."

"I don't like being taken by surprise," I admitted softly. "It's why I hang out with pigs more than people."

Rather than look alarmed by this, Amoreena laughed. "You're adorable. And I like you. And sometimes, maybe, people will surprise you by being cool. If you give them the chance."

I didn't know if I had that much faith, but I wanted to be brave—especially if it meant that I had a chance with her. "You surprised me when you asked me out."

"You surprised me by saying yes."

I squeezed her hand gently and gathered my courage. "Want to go to the fair?"

We drove to the fairgrounds, passing the popcorn back and forth between us, and I felt a happy jolt each time our hands brushed. After we parked, I showed Amoreena my favorite food truck. We ordered french fries smothered in cheese and ketchup, giant cups of lemonade, and an elephant ear bigger than Amoreena's face. We looked for a spot at the picnic tables under a large tent, but it was a crowded night, so we took our bounty to the relatively quiet pig barn and sat on the bench in my club's supply stall, using the surface of the feed bin as our table. It wasn't quite private, but it wasn't under a spotlight either.

"This," Amoreena declared around bites of cheese-drenched fries, "is definitely better than a movie."

I covered my face with a napkin, and she playfully yanked it down. "I mean it!"

"Well, it's definitely memorable," I agreed. "Not many girls can say they spent their first date with a pig."

"I think it's fitting that we ended up here, since Herbert brought us together, in a way."

I couldn't argue with that. "To Herbert," I said, raising my lemonade cup in his direction. He was passed out on his sawdust and didn't even budge.

"To Herbert," Amoreena echoed, raising her own cup. "Man, he looks ready to go home."

I let out a nervous noise, halfway between a gasp and a snort.

"What?" Amoreena asked.

"Herbert isn't going home after this. I mean, he is going home. The *ultimate* home."

Amoreena's eyes widened as she caught my meaning. "You mean he's . . ."

"He's making his transition into bacon," I confirmed. "Everyone here is."

Amoreena surveyed the couple hundred slumbering, snuffling pigs in the barn. "That is so *sad.*"

"It kind of is," I acknowledged.

"Poor pigs!"

"But bacon," I reminded her.

And then, despite her sad expression, she giggled. "But bacon," she agreed. She set down her lemonade and pulled out her phone. "Okay, since his days are limited and he may be a Mekawnee County Fair star very soon, I want a selfie with Herbert."

She angled her phone to catch Herbert snoring in his pen behind her, and I felt a stupid smile stretch across my face. It didn't slip once, not even when a bunch of 4-H kids came in through the far barn entrance.

"Aren't you going to selfie with me?" Amoreena tilted her head toward me, and I moved closer to her on the bench. I wasn't quite in the frame, so I scooched even closer, until our sides were touching and her scent—something floral, with a slight spicy tang—overwhelmed me, which is the only explanation for my bravery. I slipped my arm around her as she adjusted the camera to get both of us and Herbert in the shot. When I smiled, I wasn't looking at the little black eye of camera. I was taking in the two of us on the screen, out in the open. I didn't care that my face was too shiny in the heat or that the lighting was weird—we looked happy. I *was* happy.

I turned right before Amoreena took the picture, nerves giving way to determination—just like in the show arena. My lips found the curve of her cheek, and I brushed a kiss on her warm skin just as she took the photo.

Amoreena lowered her phone and turned her head so that only a breath separated us. "You," she whispered, "are definitely unexpected."

As I closed the distance between our lips, I decided that was definitely a good thing.

Praise the Lord and Pass the Little Debbies
A (Mostly) True Story
DAVID MACINNIS GILL

On a Sunday a couple of months after his little sister, Lisa Ann, died, Coby sat on the front porch with his dog, Peanut. It was late fall in Fairview, Georgia, when leaves were the color of pumpkin pie, and the air smelled like fires burning in the distance.

Peanut was small and light brown, with a corkscrew tail and pointed black-tipped ears. He was what Coby's daddy called a Heinz 57, meaning a mutt of so many different breeds, nobody knew what to call him. Coby was a mutt, too, with light-brown hair clipped high and tight, wearing hand-me-down Sunday dress clothes—white shirt, black pants, and a clip-on red bow tie. Peanut was dressed in his birthday suit, being a dog and all.

"Mama's singing, Peanut," Coby said. "That's a good sign, don't you think?"

Inside, Mama was cleaning house while singing along to Elvis. She had a sweet and lilting voice. Coby was always glad to hear it. Sunday mornings that smelled like Pine-Sol and sounded like the King of Rock 'n' Roll were good signs. It meant Mama was in a good mood. Which meant Daddy was in a good mood. Which meant that he hadn't gone down to the pool hall last night and come home with half his paycheck gambled away. Which meant he wasn't spoiling for a fight that Mama'd be glad to give him.

Daddy hadn't gone out to shoot pool since Lisa's funeral. Mama hadn't cleaned nor put on music, neither. That made a good sign even better.

At three minutes till eight, the sound of the Park City Baptist Church bus, a new 1976 Bluebird painted red and white, drifted up the hill. For the first time in weeks, Coby was waiting for it.

"Bus's early this week," he told Peanut. "C'mon, let's get you put up."

Coby clicked his tongue. The pooch followed him around to the doghouse in the backyard. It sat in the far corner, underneath a peach tree. Coby clicked the chain onto Peanut's collar. Gave his ears a good scratching.

"Be a good boy," Coby said, "and I'll bring you scraps when I get back."

Peanut wagged his tail and barked. He liked scraps. He liked chasing the bus even more, which was why he had to be chained up.

Mama came to the screen door and scowled. A half-smoked Kool hung from her bottom lip. "That mutt better shut up. Your daddy's still sleeping."

"He'll quit soon as the bus leaves."

She took a deep drag of the Kool and flicked ash out a crack in the door. "Got money for the offering?"

Coby patted his shirt pocket. "A dollar."

"I only give you one half-dollar. Where'd the other one come from?"

"Piggy bank."

"Half-dollar's enough for Jesus." She took a long drag and swallowed the smoke. "Keep t'other for yourself."

"Yes, ma'am."

The church bus stopped at Coby's driveway.

"Be good this time," she said, and unlatched the screen door. "No getting kicked out of Sunday school again."

"Okay, Mama," he said, and her answer was drowned out by the bus horn.

"Hold your damn horses!" she yelled, and let the screen slam shut.

Coby boarded the bus, Bible in hand. He waved to the driver, Brother Roy. The bus pastor, Brother Eugene, was waiting on the top step with a welcoming smile and two pieces of Dubble Bubble chewing gum.

"Morning, Brother Coby," he said. "The Lord's happy to see you this bright and shining day. I see that the wreath remains on your door. Is your family still grieving?"

Coby's eyebrows knitted. Is that what the wreath meant? He thought it was just a way to tell folks that there'd been a death in the family and to let them be. They never talked about it. Mama talked about everything else but Lisa, and Daddy never talked at all. Did that mean they were still grieving? Was there an allowance of time for missing your little sister? Was grief like a piece of fruit that went bad after a few weeks? Or could you put it in the freezer and let it keep for a couple months more?

Coby shrugged. "Reckon so."

Brother Eugene looked at him all peculiar. "Have a seat up front so we can talk."

The door closed. The bus started up the steep hill. It whipped around Fine Street's dead end and went back down, brakes squealing. Brother Roy was driving. He liked to make the kids scream. The bus shot down the hill, where all the unchained dogs were lying in wait. As it rolled by, they took off after it.

"One day," Brother Roy told Brother Eugene, "one of them mutts's going to bite off more'n he can chew."

"Careful, Brother," Brother Eugene said. "The Lord loves all his creatures, even the mutts."

"You wanted to talk to me?" Coby asked Brother Eugene.

"Did you think about what we talked about last time you went to Sunday service?" He paused and waited for Coby's response, but none was coming. "About taking the Lord Jesus Christ as your personal savior? Did you forget about it that quick?"

Coby shrugged in reply. Truth was, he felt relieved. Brother Eugene asked every kid every week about getting saved. What Coby thought he was referring to was getting kicked out of Sunday school for asking what the fruit of knowledge was in Genesis and not being satisfied with the answer: a fig. They got kicked out of Eden for partaking of a fig? He'd tried to eat a fig once, and it wasn't worth the effort. Too many seeds. There had to be more to knowledge than that.

"How about you cogitate on an acceptable answer for a while," Brother Eugene said, and turned away. "In the back of the bus."

Fine with him. Coby drifted to the back. He spotted a couple of open seats. One was next to Teresa Young. The other was a completely clear bench next to the exit door. Coby hated that seat. It stank of diesel fumes, and every pothole and bump Brother Roy hit made his tailbone rattle.

"Glad you're back." Teresa grinned at him and patted her seat. "Come tell me about the funeral."

Teresa had dark-red hair, pale skin, and bright freckles that looked like burnt orange glitter on her cheeks. She'd been trying to get Coby to sit beside her ever since summer, when they'd kissed during a few games of Slap, Kiss, and Hug. Wasn't that he minded kissing her. It was kind of fun. Till one night her brother caught Peanut knocking their garbage cans over and shanked him in the belly. Peanut had run screaming all the way up the hill. The gash healed fine. Peanut had an impressive half-moon scar to show for it. But Coby lost all desire to touch lips with the sister of a dog-stabber.

"Ain't much to tell," he said, and sat by the exit.

There was lots to tell. How Mama had come home from work at the mill that morning and found Lisa Ann not breathing. How Mama and Daddy had rushed her to the hospital. How Aunt Ginny had come to take the kids to her house while they waited for news. How Mama and Daddy had come to get them, Mama's eyes swollen shut from crying, and Daddy's eyes red, too. But he didn't feel like telling Teresa any of that. He didn't feel like thinking about it, either, so he tried hard not to.

On the forty-two-minute drive on one-lane winding roads to Park City, which was a neighborhood all the way across the Tennessee state line into downtown Chattanooga, the kids sang songs like "Deep and Wide" and "This Little Light of Mine" and had bubble-blowing contests. The winner got an extra piece of gum. Coby could blow a mean bubble. He specialized in a bubble within a bubble. By the time the bus parked on the hill in front of the Sunday school annex, he had six pieces wadded up in his cheek.

"Chewing gum out," Brother Eugene said as they filed past him into the annex. "The Lord don't like Dubble Bubble under his seats."

Coby deposited the gum wad in the trash. This was a fresh start. He was starting today off on the right foot. He followed the line into the twelve- to fourteen-year-olds' classroom. He sat in the back. Teresa sat next to him. That was all right. He wouldn't dare think about her lips with the brothers watching.

Sister Grace started the lesson. She rolled a felt-covered board closer to the Sunday schoolers. She told them a story about lambs and Jesus and placed cutouts like paper dolls on the board. Her voice was soothing and gentle, and Coby might've fallen asleep listening, if he wasn't so fidgety.

His collar was too tight. The clasp from his clip-on tie dug into his Adam's apple. It'd gotten hot sitting in the room. Especially with Teresa sitting so close. He hated dress shirts and dress pants and dress shoes. Maybe he'd ask why they couldn't come to church in play clothes so they could worship comfortably. But he knew better than to ask.

When Sister Grace was done, a youth pastor name Brother Larry came up front. He greeted them all and allowed how lucky he was to be in the company of such fine, obedient children. Then he looked straight at Coby like an electric wire stretched between them.

He knows about Teresa's lips, Coby thought. His collar got tighter.

"Today's lesson," Brother Larry said, "is about Deuteronomy. Please open your Bibles to chapter twenty-two, verse three. Now, who would like to read the verse?"

Hands went up. Larry pointed to a girl who hadn't volunteered. "Read for us, please. . . . Wait, start over. That was too soft. Lift your voice. Don't leave your light under a bushel."

Coby's eyes started drifting. Brother Larry was saying something about following the rules to the letter and how important it was to take the words literally. Then his voice took on a droning sound. Coby let the words drip over him like water off a duck's back.

"Coby!" Brother Larry hollered. "You are being called up!"

Coby jerked straight up in his chair. "Huh?"

"Read Deuteronomy 23:1, Coby."

Teresa pointed to his spot on the page.

"Thanks." Coby focused on the words. "'He that is wounded—'"

"Louder."

Coby lifted the bushel from his light. "'He that is wounded in the stones, or hath his privy member cut off, shall not enter into the congregation of the Lord.'"

"Finally," the brother said, and pointed to another kid. "Next verse, please."

Coby raised his hand. He couldn't help himself. He had to ask. "When this says stones, does it mean testicles?"

The brother's face went white. "If the Bible says stones, it means stones."

"But we don't have stones in our bodies," Coby said. "Unless you mean kidney stones, and those are bad, so seems like they ought to be cut off."

Teresa raised her hand. "What's a privy member?"

Sister Grace clapped a hand over her mouth. Her shoulders started to shake.

The brother's face went red. His ears glowed like a blacksmith's tongs. "Coby, look what you've started!"

"But I was just asking a question," Coby said.

"Out!" Brother Larry pointed toward the exit. "Out right now."

When Coby didn't get up fast enough, the brother grabbed him by the ear and hauled him into the hallway. "I'll be speaking to your bus pastor." He slammed the door closed, then locked it. "Laughing, Sister Grace?" his voice came through the glass. "You ought to be ashamed."

Coby was waiting alone when the bus pulled up.

Brother Roy opened the door. "What're you doing out so early? Behaving like a heathen again?"

After getting kicked out of Sunday school, Coby had wandered outside, then down the street to a corner market. They had Cokes in the cooler and Little Debbie cakes on the shelf. He'd used his offering money to buy a box of oatmeal creme pies and a quart-size Coke. He ate half the soft and moist cakes walking around in the sunshine and drank the Coke sitting in the shade, savoring the way ice-cold bubbles made his throat scrunch up.

"Where's your tie?" Brother Roy said.

Coby pulled it from his pocket.

"It belongs around your neck." Brother Roy sighed like he was put out. "Get in. I'm about at the end of my rope with you."

Coby started to ask him how long a bus pastor's rope was

but decided he'd rocked the boat enough for one day.

He sat by the exit. He looked out the window till the bus was full. Nobody sat beside him. Not even Teresa. He kept looking till Park City melted away and Chattanooga was a memory.

"Heard there was another altercation in Sunday school," Brother Eugene said, and sat beside Coby without asking leave. "Here's a Little Debbie to cheer you up."

Coby took it. A raisin creme pie. Coby hated raisins. At home, he picked them out, but Brother Eugene didn't like wasting food, and he sure as shooting didn't like squished raisins on the bus floor.

"Thanks," Coby said. He set the cake on his lap and returned to staring. "Funny how nobody ever wants to answer my questions."

"Maybe you're asking the wrong questions." Brother Eugene opened the cellophane wrapper of a Little Debbie. "Or asking them in the wrong way. Tone's important, Coby. You've got to know your place. Nobody likes an unruly child."

Nobody likes to be called a child, either, Coby thought. But his daddy's belt had taught him all about what happens when you get unruly.

He wanted to tell the brother to mind his own business. He didn't know Coby. His grandma had always said that most of us have a red heart full of anger and passion, but she thought Coby's was softer, kind of pale and easy to bruise.

"Eat your Debbie cake," Brother Eugene said. "It'll cheer you up."

Coby took a bite. It was stale and crunchy. Nothing like the oatmeal creme pies he'd bought. The raisins were bitter and hard and not the least bit cheery.

The church bus slowed down on the highway and made the turn onto Fine Street, where the pack of barking dogs started chasing it.

The brother cleared his throat. A sharp cough. "I understand that your sister wasn't baptized before she passed?"

Coby shrugged. "She couldn't talk or walk." Doctors said she had the brain of an infant. It wasn't easy to baptize an eight-year-old baby.

"If the spirit is willing," Brother Eugene said, "the weakness of flesh can be overcome. Your folks never took her to church?"

"My folks never took me to church, neither." He'd decided to ride the church bus because it got him out of the house Sunday mornings, and that was when Mama and Daddy had their knock-down-drag-outs over Daddy coming home drunk after a night of shooting pool. "But here I am."

"That's a real shame, then. An unbaptized child cannot enter the house of the Lord."

"Come again?"

"Scripture is very clear," the pastor said. "We must take Jesus Christ as our personal savior and be baptized before—"

"You're telling me my eight-year-old sister, who never took a step nor said a word in all her life, who died wearing a diaper, ain't going to heaven? You're blaming my folks for that? She never had a chance."

"I didn't say that."

"You sure did."

"Not in so many words."

"How many words you need to say a baby's going straight to hell?" Coby stood up. He pushed the brother and stormed up the aisle. "Stop this bus!"

Brother Roy glanced up in the rearview. Coby saw him look-ing, and their eyes met. Brother Roy made the slightest shake of his head, then yanked the wheel hard to the right.

Thump.

The front wheel of the bus rose and fell. There was a squeal, then a howl of agony. The pack of dogs barked louder. Meaner. They tore off toward Coby's house, chasing something.

Peanut.

His dog had slipped the chain again. He was limping across the yard. Screaming and trying to bite his own hip. The pack caught up to Peanut on the front porch and fell upon him. The commotion brought Mama to the screen door, a look of horror on her face.

Coby beat on the bus door to get out. "Open up! Open up or I swear I'll kill you!"

Brother Roy said something, but Coby could only hear Peanut as he grabbed the handle himself and threw the door open. He sprinted for the attacking pack.

He grabbed dog after dog and threw them off the porch. He reached for Peanut. His dog was wild with pain, and he bit Coby the way he'd bitten the other dogs. Coby picked him up. Held him against his white shirt. He could feel blood seep warm against his skin.

"Mama!" he said, and tried to go inside. "Help me!"

Mama held the door closed. "You'll get blood all over the house."

"We got to take him to the vet!" Coby screamed. "Mama! Let me in!"

Behind Coby, the church bus drove away.

"We ain't wasting good money on no vet," Daddy said as he appeared beside Mama, then took her place. "Take the dog around back, son. Ain't nothing nobody can do but dig a hole."

The next day after school, Brother Eugene and Brother Roy knocked on the front door. Daddy wasn't home from work, and Mama was still sleeping from third shift at the yarn mill.

Coby opened the door. He waited for them to talk.

"Coby," Brother Eugene said. "Please accept our sincerest apology for the loss of your pet dog, Pumpkin."

"Peanut. That's his name." Normally Coby didn't correct grownups, but he figured the brothers should feel sorry for the right dog. "He's dead. Brother Roy run over him, then drove off."

"Well, if y'all kept your mutts from running loose on the road," Brother Roy said, "or if you hadn't distracted my driving, maybe he wouldn't have got run over."

Brother Eugene cut Brother Roy a look. "What Brother Roy means is he's sorry. It was a terrible accident. We'd like to make it up to you."

Something squeaked, and Coby noticed that Brother Roy was hiding a box behind his back.

"What's that?" Coby asked, and tried to lean in for a peek.

Brother Eugene took the box from Brother Roy. He lowered it so that Coby could get a look inside. The squeaking was from a hound dog puppy. It lay on its side in the bottom of the box. Its eyes were blue as the sky, and its belly poked way out.

Brother Eugene scooped the puppy up and pressed it against Coby's chest. "His name's Pepper."

The puppy nuzzled Coby's cheek. Its nose was velvet soft, and it still smelled like milk. Coby smiled and put it back in the box.

"A puppy fixes everything," Brother Roy said.

"I'm inclined to agree with you," Brother Eugene said. "Coby, we'll leave so you and your new friend can get better acquainted."

They left, and Coby closed the door. When he turned around, Mama was standing in the living room, giving him the stink eye.

"Ain't no way that dog's staying in the house," she said, and took a drag on her Kool.

"But—"

"Don't give me no lip, son. You know your daddy don't allow dogs in the house." She walked over and looked inside the box. "That's what they give you for killing your dog?"

"Yes, ma'am."

"If I was you," Mama took another drag of her cigarette and gave the puppy a peculiar look, "I wouldn't get too attached."

The next Sunday, Coby woke up to a quiet house. A bad sign. He got dressed for church. A few minutes later, he heard Mama yelling. Then there was a low voice in answer, followed by the thump of Daddy putting his fist through a wall. Same song, different verse. Daddy had tried to straighten up and fly right after Lisa Ann, but old habits died hard.

With them fighting inside, Coby went outside to wait. He was sitting on the front porch with a cardboard shoebox beside him when the church bus came up the hill. He looked down into the box, then cast his eyes away.

The bus stopped at the driveway. Brother Roy honked and waved for Coby to come on.

Coby didn't move. That bus ain't headed where y'all think it is, he thought. He put the shoebox on his lap.

A moment later, Brother Eugene tromped down the bus steps. He strode up the driveway with a funny look on his face. Not funny ha-ha or even funny strange. More curious than anything else.

"Coby," he said, "we're going to be late."

"I wanted to give you something first."

Inside, Mama cussed a blue streak, and there was another loud thump.

"A thanks for Pepper?" Brother Eugene smiled. "Brother, the look of pure joy on your face was thanks enough for me."

Coby handed him the shoebox. "Open it."

Brother Eugene took the lid off. His broad smile turned to shock. He dropped the box on the driveway and covered his mouth to keep from puking. "What the hell is that?" he said through his clasped fingers.

"Roundworms. That dog was half dead when y'all brought it." Coby stared at Brother Eugene until the brother met his eye. "You lied. A puppy don't fix everything." He got up and brushed off his pants. "So you can take your lies and your dog and your Debbie cakes and go straight to hell."

Coby opened the front door. On the threshold, he hesitated at the sound of his mama's and daddy's angry voices. Then, without looking back, he went inside. He closed the door behind him, and the latch softly clicked shut.

The Cabin
NASUĠRAQ RAINEY HOPSON

Don't let the boogies get into your head, Adah.

I repeated the words over and over like a mantra.

Something shifted outside the cabin.

Stay calm, Adah. Breathe.

I grabbed my aapa's old rusted knife, left behind from an earlier trip. It wobbled, much heavier than my own knife, as I tried to find a good grip. After my small dinner of caribou meat and a cup of melted snow, I'd packed my own knife and cooking pot in my backpack and stowed the pack in the sled outside to make my predawn departure smoother. I had more wolverine traps to set on the way home and wanted to have everything ready to go. How could I have guessed some . . . *thing* would come calling in the middle of the night?

I wasn't afraid of wildlife, but whatever had woken me up wasn't any creature I was familiar with; I was sure of that.

Crunch.

Crunch.

The slow crushing of iced-over snow echoed painfully

loudly in the still air, even muffled as it was by the wooden walls of the cabin. I could tell by the rhythm of the footsteps that the thing walked on two legs.

The dim light of my iPhone's flashlight cast weird shadows on the cabin's textured walls. I scanned the dark space, searching for anything else I could wield as a weapon, but . . . nothing.

Crunch. Crunch.

It couldn't be a person. During deep winter in the vast arctic wild, people didn't walk around in the middle of the night. People didn't travel at night at all, really, unless it was an emergency, and in that case they would call out and ask to use the emergency beacon to summon help. No other hunters were down here that I knew of, and I was the only one with a trapping line this far south, forty miles from the nearest human being.

My body shook with the combination of restrained breathing and adrenaline. Whatever was out there was making its way to the back side of the cabin. There was a single small window there, the size of a laptop screen. If the creature passed by it, I might be able to get a look.

I lifted Aapa's knife, readying myself. I gritted my teeth and flexed my fingers, chiding myself for also leaving my rifle outside the cabin door. But it was well below zero, and since there was no fear of bears this late in the season, I'd left the rifle outside to prevent water from condensing on its surface. Such condensation required significant time to dry thoroughly or you risked a misfire.

Crunch. Crunch.

The footsteps sounded lighter than an adult's. More like how a child's steps sounded in the snow. What *was* this thing?

I turned slowly, always keeping the sound of the crunching

snow in front of me. Then the footsteps stopped. Something clanked, and I heard the creature wiggle the handle of the abandoned cast-iron stove that sat weed- and snow-covered on the east side of the cabin.

More sounds—waxed paper crinkling, then a bundle being picked up and set back down. The creature had rejected my stash of leftover frozen caribou meat. No arctic predator would pass up the chance for free food; even if it was full from an earlier meal, it would take the frozen meat and bury it somewhere for later. If it was an herbivore, it would not be examining anything that smelled of humans and blood, and would definitely be part of a herd or group and not alone.

What *was* this thing?

Come on, I thought. *Pass by the window.*

More crunching, and this time I heard the metallic scrapes and clangs of one of my Conibear traps being moved. The creature was strong, then: my shoulders still ached from carrying and setting the traps all day. The trap banged again, sparking a memory from yesterday, something I'd dismissed as insignificant.

I'd set up three bucket traps that afternoon. After placing the second one, which I'd attached to a large willow right where the black spruce trees met the rolling tundra, I'd taken a bit longer to disguise the trap after setting it. Wolverines, in addition to being incredibly fierce and violent, are also very smart. If they sense a trap, they can snag the bait—smears of rancid bear fat—without getting caught, so disguise is crucial.

As I brushed the snow smooth around the trap site, arranging loose sticks to point the animal in the direction I wanted, I saw movement from the corner of my eye.

I turned to see a short dark figure dart behind a tree about a hundred yards away. As I pulled my rifle from my snow machine and raised it, I whistled loudly, like my aapa had taught me; an animal would poke its head out to investigate the odd noise. When nothing moved, I yelled a quick "Hey!"

Still nothing.

Strapping the rifle across my chest, I hopped on my snow machine. The sound of the vehicle should have made any animal run from the tree, but nothing emerged. I drove off to the side, hoping to get a better view of whatever it was and at the same time putting a little bit more distance between us.

To my surprise, the space behind the tree was empty.

Thoroughly creeped out, I set off down the frozen river toward the cabin, throwing uneasy glances behind me, eager to put miles between me and whatever it was. But as soon as I was settled in the cabin, I had dismissed the sighting as I'd been taught to do. If you run into anything odd in the arctic wilderness, the Elders said, leave it alone.

The trap outside banged again. Was it the same creature I'd glimpsed yesterday? Had it followed me here? Was it watching me? Was it . . . hunting?

My pulse surged, heartbeat drumming in my ears, as I prepared for the thing to move again, to pass the window. But no footsteps came. It was taking its time, examining everything along the cabin walls. Could it be looking for a way in?

I shook my head, remembering the advice of the Elders: *Ignore it.*

No matter what you see or what you hear, just ignore it. Whistling? Ignore it. Distant chatter that drifts in and out of hearing? Ignore it. Footprints that are moose-like but definitely not moose? Ignore them. Weird glowing lights humming along the mountain ridge? Definitely ignore that.

Arctic winters are mostly filled with darkness, and we all grew up hearing stories of the scary things that go bump in the almost-twenty-four-hour-long night—*boogies*, as my aapa called them: the little people with ten times the strength of humans that still hated the Inupiaq tribe from a war lost hundreds of years ago. The willow people that hid in tall bushes and stole items or family members from you as you passed through dense brush. Spirits that came down from the sky that looked like northern lights and removed your head for foot games.

Sometimes hunters would come back with tales of incredible encounters with beings that they'd barely evaded, and sometimes hunters just disappeared, never to be heard from again.

These stories were told half for fun and half as a warning, but the warning wasn't really about supernatural beings. The moral of every story was that you should never panic, because panicking could expose you to real dangers, like extreme cold, falling into water, or becoming vulnerable to known predators. Most of the battle of thriving in the arctic was fighting the thoughts and fears in your own head.

So, yeah. I'd heard the stories. But I never thought they might actually be true. You could go a little insane if you thought about some of the odd stuff too much.

I relaxed my grip on Aapa's knife. There had to be a rational explanation. Maybe the thing prowling around outside was just an especially fat weasel. Or a wolf pup that walked funny and wasn't hungry.

Right. Except weasels aren't that heavy and they love

caribou meat, and it wasn't wolf pup season and all of last year's pups would've been nearly grown, their bodies too heavy to make the light footsteps outside.

I glanced at the personal locator beacon sitting next to a flashlight on the small table by the bed platform. The bright-green plastic glowed, outlining the shape of the device. My iPhone didn't get service this far out in the boonies, but I could set off the PLB, alerting the search-and-rescue people that I needed help. But as far out as I was, it would take a few hours for anyone to arrive, and by then, whatever it was could be long gone and I would have to explain to a group of tired and angry volunteers why I called for help in the middle of the night when I didn't even know what the thing outside was. No. Not the PLB. Not yet anyway. This was only the second time my aapa had let me travel by myself, and I couldn't disappoint him.

Not many women trapped fur-bearing animals in the arctic, and an even smaller number of teenage girls trapped, maybe one or two across the whole region every other generation. My male cousins had complained about a girl taking over this part of my aapa's trapline, though they clearly thought that it would only be a temporary phase, like that year I had bright-blue hair. But I loved trapping, and I loved a challenge, and I knew I had what it took to be a trapper full-time.

Ever since I was five years old and my aapa taught me how to snare ptarmigans by predicting how they behaved, I was hooked. I'd spent the past twelve years learning the languages of trapping and animal behavior, and I never shied away from all the backbreaking labor trapping entailed.

Aapa had been happy to teach me. Inseparable since I was

born, we were so alike, even down to the way we stood with one hip cocked and our arms crossed. When I got old enough, I asked for camping gear and vehicles instead of Barbies and dresses.

I could almost hear my aapa now: *Don't let the boogies get into your head, Adah.* He always said the words in a quiet, measured tone, the one he used when I needed to take what he was teaching seriously.

His warning in my head, I gripped his too-big knife tightly in my right hand and made my way to the back of the cabin. If the creature wouldn't come to the window, I'd have to look out at it. I'd studied animal behavior my whole life. If I knew what this thing was, it would no longer be a nameless *boogie*. I could predict what it would do and make a plan. I grabbed the flashlight off the table on the way; my iPhone battery wouldn't last much longer, plus the flashlight would illuminate much more of the area.

I crouched in front of the back window, slowing my breath to calm down like my aapa had taught me to do before I took a long-distance shot with a rifle.

The footsteps started again, shuffling around the northwest corner. Any second the thing would be in plain view from the window. As soon as the snow crunched beneath the glass, I flicked on the flashlight and held it to the window. The bright LED flooded the snow outside with light.

I blinked. There was nothing there. No creature—and no tracks. Nothing but clean, undisturbed snow.

Before I could process what that meant, shuffling sounds came from the opposite side of the cabin, near the front door. Something shifted its weight in the snow from foot to foot.

How had it moved so quickly—and without leaving any tracks? Everything leaves tracks. Everything. I could hear the weight of this thing breaking through the surface of the snow.

Cursing under my breath, I made my way to the center of the cabin again, holding the knife in front of me. If the creature hadn't already known I was in here, awake and aware of its presence, it definitely knew now.

Quietly, I crept to the front door, which I'd suddenly remembered was only secured with the rope loop. The bear latch, a long piece of thick wood that slid into reinforced wood blocks on either side of the door, was propped against the wall. With one swift movement, I lowered the latch into place, wood scraping against wood. No sooner had I secured the latch than the door jerked inward with a thud.

The thing was trying to get in.

Could the creature see the foam-wrapped rifle leaning against the wall outside? Did it know what it was?

With stiff, cold hands, I checked the bear latch to make sure it was secure, then backed away from the door, panic making me stumble. The door rattled again, straining against the thick wood bar. I gritted my teeth to avoid making a sound and tried to keep my focus on what was going on instead of giving in completely to panic.

As I held up the knife in front of me, my other hand brushed against my pocket and the outline of my phone.

With numb fingers, I unlocked it and swiped till I got the video recorder going. The *ping* of the app indicating I was recording echoed in the small room. The groaning of the door stopped, leaving only the sound of my breathing in the silence.

I crept forward, the whispers of my thick wool socks against the plywood floor sounding impossibly loud and heavy.

I pressed my ear against the cabin door, and almost as if the creature knew what I was doing, it began moving away, crunching the snow as it retreated into the distance.

The silence stretched on—not even a breeze could be heard.

If I was going to retrieve the rifle, it was now or never. I propped the phone near the door, still recording, and while my right hand gripped the knife, my left lifted the bear latch and pushed the door open just enough to slip through. The cold clawed at my bare fingers as subzero air flooded the cabin, but I forced them around the rifle's foam cover. As soon as the weapon was inside, I slammed the door shut and shoved the bear latch back into place.

The noise triggered another sound—snow crunching. Footsteps running back to the door. It rattled again, harder this time.

Ignoring the stiffness in my left hand, I unzipped the rifle cover and loaded a round, the freezing metal burning my frigid fingers. The white of frozen skin cells peppered the rifle's surface.

My body remembered the weight and shape of the rifle, and in one smooth motion, I knelt and lifted it against my shoulder.

Outside, the creature shifted its weight from one foot to the other, as if trying to decide what to do.

I cocked the rifle, the metallic sounds ringing sharp and deadly in the air, and trained it on the door. After what felt like forever, the footsteps moved away, growing quieter and quieter as they passed into the distance.

I waited a breath longer, then lowered the rifle. And noticed my phone was still recording. I picked it up and pressed the button for it to stop. Its clock read 5:26 a.m.—only an hour left before I needed to leave. That was fine. Even though my face and hands stung from the icy rifle and my muscles trembled from exhaustion, there was no way I'd be going back to sleep.

I fed the stove a few small logs, adjusting the damper and vent for a slow burn. I grabbed my rifle and flicked on the safety, then wrapped my sweater carefully around it, hoping the fabric would absorb the beading moisture, and set it aside within arm's reach.

Aapa's knife I kept on my other side, along with the flashlight. I wrapped the sleeping bag around myself, wincing as the cold, silky lining brushed my frostbitten skin. I fished my phone from my pocket and played the video I'd recorded. There was no mistaking the heavy footsteps of the creature running up to the cabin and then backing away. And the rattling of the door was so loud I had to turn down the volume.

A shiver snaked through me, and suddenly I wanted to get home immediately, maybe even leave some of my emergency winter gear behind to lighten my load and shorten the trip. It would be risky riding the snow machine in my exhausted state, unable to see the intricate details of the terrain in the total dark, but fear clawed at my mind, almost convincing me.

Then Aapa's voice found me again: *Don't let the boogies get into your head, Adah.*

In the cabin I was safe, warm, and secure, and I needed the dim half-daylight to see my way home in one piece. The smartest move was to stay here a little longer.

I shoved all the boogies, all the fear and what-ifs, from my mind, closed my eyes, and, in spite of myself, fell asleep.

* * *

An hour later, I opened the door to find the world dim with a barely visible winter sun hovering behind the mountains. I hadn't heard any strange noises in a while; whatever the thing was, I was confident that it had moved on. Now that the threat was gone, I was eager to find evidence of the creature and maybe get some pictures of its footprints to show Aapa. He would know what it was even if I was unable to identify it.

Emerging into the chilly predawn air, I circled the cabin, carefully examining the ground.

Footprints should have shown easily; I had clearly heard the cracking of the snow last night. My phone had even captured the sounds.

But there were only my own footprints. Not even a depression or disturbed snow pile. Everything was clean. Even the wrapped caribou meat didn't show signs of having been moved.

My unease returned, and I packed my gear quickly. Aapa might scold me for packing sloppily, but he'd understand. I scarfed down a protein bar and drank cold coffee from my thermos, threw on my heavy mouton-lined parka and winter gear, and hopped on my snow machine.

The three-hour ride home was uneventful and quiet—too quiet, without even the usual movements of clumsy ptarmigan or winter-hungry rabbits.

It wasn't until I rounded the end of the frozen river and glimpsed my village that the tension finally left my body. With only a hundred houses or so nestled in the bottom of a wide valley surrounded by huge, ancient mountains, Anaktuvuk Pass barely qualified as a village. But it was my home, and I'd never been so happy to see it.

Aapa stood waiting outside our house, his tall, wide form like a mountain. He was dressed in his lightweight winter gear, a shovel in his gloved hands. Neat piles of snow were off to the side, and a level path now led to the front of the house from the road. His dark-skinned face broke into a wide smile as I pulled up, but then worry lines bloomed as he realized I had returned early.

I rolled myself off the snow machine and involuntarily squeaked as he grabbed me and lifted me off the ground in a big bear hug.

"Adah! Panik, you're early!" His voice was muffled by my fur ruff.

I laughed as I extracted myself from his arms and removed my goggles and face mask. "Man, Aapa, something weird happened this morning," I said as I pulled off my heavy parka, not wanting to overheat now that I was moving around. "I think I ran into a *boogie*! A bona fide *boogie*!"

"Ohh? Paniga, I bet you have a story!" He made an overly shocked face with wide eyes. "But you came back all right. If a little early."

My face warmed. "I didn't get as many traps out as I'd planned, but I don't know what was out there. Didn't want to press my luck. I recorded the sound on my phone a little. Whatever it was didn't leave footprints."

"Ohh? Eakanee, well, come inside and tell me and your aaka all about it. We will unpack your gear after you warm up and eat."

Walking into the house, I was greeted with the warm scents of cooking yeast and sweet dough. The short round figure of my aaka stood at the stove with her favorite spatula in hand. Sourdough pancakes bubbled pleasantly on the hot pan after she flipped them over expertly, the sound and smell making my stomach growl.

Aaka ran over, her hug enveloping me in a cloud of hot oil and hotcake batter. "Paniga! So early. Just in time for sourdough, though. Hot from the pan." Her frizzy hair tickled my face before she ran back to the stove to tend her cooking.

"Sit! Eat!" she called over her shoulder, and gestured to the steaming plate of hotcakes on the table. I shimmied free from the rest of my outside gear and left it in a pile at the door, then sat down with Aapa and pulled the hotcakes toward me.

Three maple syrup–drenched pancakes and one glass of water later, I told them of the events of this morning.

When I had finished, I played them the recording on my phone. The heavy footsteps of the mysterious creature filled our small kitchen.

"Sounds like two legs for sure," Aapa said as he scratched the thin stubble on his chin. "But no tracks at all?"

"Not even one, Aapa. Clean snow besides my own footprints. There weren't even secondary markings, like on things it touched."

He leaned back in his chair and grunted. He didn't doubt my ability to read snow tracks; he'd taught me himself. His dark-brown eyes looked over my face for a minute. The worry lines faded a little.

"You did good, Adah. You didn't panic. You did what you were supposed to. You came home safe. Proud of you. Aarigaa. Whoever taught you to be out there really knows what he is doing." He said the last part with a smile and a wink.

I snorted and rolled my eyes. But his words resonated in my head. After all those stories, I finally understood what Aapa and the Elders had been talking about. I'd confronted a mysterious creature last night—a boogie—but that wasn't the only kind of boogie there was. Fear and panic, self-doubt and rash decisions . . . I'd known those were to be avoided, but after last night, it was suddenly clear: Those states of mind were just as much boogies as the creature kind.

Aapa's expression turned serious again. "Maybe you can take over my trapline to the west too next year?"

I sat a bit taller in my chair. I'd confronted both kinds of boogies last night, and I knew I was more than capable of doing it again.

I raised my eyebrows in a silent yes, a wide smile on my face.

There would be boogies, sure. But fear wouldn't be one of them.

A NOTE FROM NASUGRAQ RAINEY HOPSON:
This story and illustration were based on an actual experience we had while visiting our hunting cabin in the spring. My husband is a fur trapper, and he regularly visits the small family cabin for his overnight trips. We have encountered odd things before, which is normal when you spend time in the vast untouched boonies of the Alaskan north.

Black Nail Polish
SHAE CARYS

I'm rushing down the nearly empty hall, trying to get a paper from my locker for fifth period. Then it happens. My ankle collapses like a cheap paper cup and—*slam!*—I spill feet over head into a locker.

Tripping over my own feet is sadly on brand for me. I lie still for a few moments, blinking tears and fuzziness out of my eyes before dragging myself up like a limp marionette and making my way to the office. I hope no one's seen this. The last thing I need are more "klutzy Mads" memes.

I must look like a horror movie extra, because when the admin assistant, Mrs. Anderson, sees me, she turns as white as a printer page and shouts for the school nurse. My bloody forehead and face get cleaned up with alcohol wipes as I fidget under Liz's less-than-gentle ministrations. (At this point, I know her so well, she lets me call her by her first name.)

I frown. "I hope this doesn't screw up cheerleading tryouts tonight."

Liz gives me a gentle pat on the hand. Not promising.

Liz calls my mom and my heart sinks.

I need stitches.

The doctor's office is half an hour away. There's no way I'm going to make tryouts on time.

"It's time to consider a diagnosis of hypermobile Ehlers-Danlos syndrome."

Wait. What? What diagnosis? Stitches—wasn't *that* the diagnosis?

As if to prove a point, Dr. Fields lifts my arm and lets it drop. My elbow points in the air in a way that looks completely normal to me. My mom's face, though, tells me it's not normal. She looks horrified.

Dr. Fields continues: "You dislocated your shoulder twice this summer, and with your ankle going out, plus the widespread pain and fatigue over the last year, I'm ninety percent certain that's what's happening here. I wouldn't even suggest this if I wasn't almost positive, Madison."

Dr. Fields pries my fingers back slowly. As she does so, my mom's eyebrows go up. Okay, not normal. Dr. Fields has me bend down and touch the floor, which I can do with ease. She asks me to stand straight and bend my knees back. Easy. For me, this is showing off. Lauren loves it. It's how she came up with the cheer plan in the first place. With her bubbly personality and my bendiness, we figure we're shoo-ins.

As if she'd been summoned, my phone buzzes and a text from Lauren flashes on my screen.

where r u? ur gonna be late

"Mom." I fidget, jogging my knee up and down, looking

from her to Dr. Fields to the door. "I've got to get to tryouts."

Dr. Fields answers before Mom can. "Tryouts?"

"Varsity cheerleading." Mom smiles. "She's been excited about it for so long."

Dr. Fields's brows draw down as she shakes her head and takes a seat across from us. "I would recommend against it."

The sudden sympathy in her eyes puts me on edge. Whatever I have is just a joint thing, right? Not terminal cancer. So why's she looking at me that way?

"Ehlers-Danlos is progressive," she continues. "The more you stretch your joints past their normal limitations, the earlier you can develop premature arthritis and other significant issues. Issues like more frequent dislocations and partial dislocations, which we call subluxations." She rubs her palms on her thighs, the sympathy hardening a little as her voice turns more serious. "Most people don't develop arthritis until late in life. You could be looking at it in your twenties if you don't treat your body right. You don't want to need joints replaced in your thirties. We want to put that sort of thing off for as long as possible."

Put it off? Is that like . . . not an if but a *when*? I don't want new joints. I'd like to remain more human than robot. My face must show my alarm, because Mom squeezes my hand, her palm warm, sweaty.

"Is there any medicine to treat it, to keep that sort of thing from happening?" Mom's voice is strong but soft. Determined.

Dr. Fields shakes her head. "No medicine, no, not yet."

That's when it sinks in. Cheerleading isn't going to happen. Not tonight. Not ever.

"Most cases are genetic," Dr. Fields continues, "though

the hypermobile kind has yet to be pinpointed in that fashion, which is why I'm giving you a preliminary diagnosis only. Knowing for sure, though, doesn't really change anything. Madison has hypermobile joints, which can create all sorts of problems." She stands, indicating that the conversation is coming to an end. I have a thousand questions, but they're trapped deep in my throat, like a sickness I can't vomit out.

What's going to happen from here? What damage have I already done? Am I a freak of nature? Am I going to die early? Is the pain going to get worse? And how much worse?

Dr. Fields writes a quick prescription. "I recommend physical therapy and NSAIDs—Tylenol, Advil—for pain. Be certain to follow the dosage instructions, especially since Madison is still a teen. Sometimes braces and canes can help with mobility."

"Wait." I find my voice, finally. "I'm gonna need a cane?" This can't be happening. "I'm sixteen."

Dr. Fields's pity is hard to take. "We don't know anything for sure, and, honestly, this isn't my area of expertise. My niece has Ehlers-Danlos, which is pretty much the only reason I know about it. They didn't cover it much in med school. I'll call in a referral for you to a specialist. To my knowledge, the nearest is two hours away. They'll be able to make the final diagnosis." Her brown eyes meet mine again, then look to Mom. "I'd recommend that both of you read more about it. There are some really great communities online." She gives us a wan smile. "The stitches will dissolve, so there's no need to come and get them taken out. Just follow the care instructions, okay?"

I raise a shaky hand to my head. I'd forgotten all about the stitches, but my temple is starting to throb in earnest.

Another message from Lauren pops up. *Where r u???*
Blinking a few times, I reply. *Sorry. Won't make it.*

Twenty minutes later, Mom and I are checked out. We head the half hour from Dr. Fields's office back home to indescribably bland Marie, Indiana.

My phone buzzes. *Is everything OK? Wish u were here.*

Like a foam ball in a nervous hand, my stomach clenches. She's doing it without me. All those plans, and she's completely cool going solo. I stuff my phone into my book bag, then glare at the country roads passing by.

Low corn. Soybeans. Corn. Soybeans. Corn. Soybeans. Dirt. House.

"Are you okay, Mads? With not trying out?" Mom pitches her voice above the radio, and I look over, shrugging a shoulder. "No."

Mom drops it, reaching over to give my knee a gentle squeeze. She's never been the type to press, to push, and right now I'm grateful for that at least.

I look back out the window, watching corn whip by again before an open field stares back at me, drowned with brown pockets of water and black-brown mud. Sometimes the low-lying fields get too wet to plant. Sometimes even good land can't be used because there's something wrong with how it's made.

I know the feeling.

When we get to the only stoplight in Marie, we've already passed four of the sixteen churches that serve the twelve hundred people of this half-a-horse town. I count them. I always do. *First Church of Christ. Friends Church. United Baptist. First Church of Christ.*

Yes. There are two First Churches of Christ. It's widely speculated as to which one was really the first. I say let them fight it out.

Mom pulls up to the curb and parks, grabbing her work bag as I grab my backpack. I head straight to my room without another word and collapse into bed like a Jenga tower. It feels good not to be upright anymore.

I check my phone, but Lauren hasn't messaged again. I toss the phone onto my nightstand, then flip it over for good measure.

When her next text finally comes, my phone startles me. I must have dozed off. Fumbling, I lift my phone and drop it directly onto my face. "Dammit!" I rub my stinging nose and haul the phone back up.

Lauren: *Hey, so—what happened? Why weren't u at tryouts?*

Me: *Tripped into locker. Had to get stitches.*

L: *Oh damn!* ☹ *How many?*

Me: *7. Doc says I can't do cheer*

L: *Cuz of stitches???*

Me: *No some disorder I have*

L: *is it bad???*

Me: *dunno*

L: *k. I'll see u in class?*

Me: *sure maybe we can hang after school*

L: *I've got practice and library after for SAT prep, maybe later this week?*

Me: *you made it?*

L: *yeah I did*
Me: . . .
Me: . . .
Me: *cool*

When I drop the phone this time, at least it's not on my face, even though I'm pretty sure it's numb like the rest of me. It feels clichéd to be hurt about my BFF being a cheerleader and me on the sidelines. It's not like it matters—there aren't enough people in my high school for popularity to even really be a thing. We all know each other too well. Like, I know that Sammy used to have buckteeth, even though she's gorgeous now. I know that John used to be the shortest boy in class before he shot up to be six foot five sophomore year. Just like they know I've tripped over my own feet and hurt myself every week. I've been Madison the bendy wunderkind, Madison the klutz, since pre-K.

I grab my laptop and look it up, this thing Dr. Fields says I have. I spell it wrong the first time but find the website I need. The first thing that pops up are the symptoms. As I scan the list, some make sense. *Loose joints, dislocations, subluxations, early onset of osteoarthritis.* Last summer I missed a drop-off in the path while hiking with Lauren and dislocated my shoulder. I fell off my bed and did the same thing. My ankles aren't good. My back hurts, like my grandpa always complains about, and my knees let me know when it's about to rain, just like his.

As I keep reading, it gets weirder. *Fragile, soft skin, severe scarring.* I touch my head. Is my forehead going to scar? *Molluscoid pseudotumors, organ rupture, scoliosis, gum disease . . .*

I snap the lid of my laptop down and shove the computer aside. It's way worse than Dr. Fields suggested. Maybe I'm just flexible. Maybe this is all for nothing. Maybe I'll be able to try out next year.

Still. I can't shake the feeling that this explains so much. Tripping over my own feet at least twice a week. The times I popped my knee out while screwing around with Lauren in the front yard, learning somersaults and flips. The way I bruise so easily—"like a peach," my mom always says.

I pull my pinkie backward like Dr. Fields did, over and over again. I watch the knuckle pop in and out of joint at my palm in morbid fascination, sighing. When I stick my thumb up, the tip bends dramatically back. "Party tricks," Lauren calls them.

This stupid stuff I can do—the reason Lauren and I decided that cheerleading would be perfect for us in spite of my clumsiness—is my undoing.

Shit.

Stuffing my pillow over my face, I let out a long frustrated scream.

When morning comes, my encounter with the mirror is the stuff of legend. The bruise takes up nearly half my face, vivid and blue. It spreads out around the stitches like someone broke open an ink pen and spilled it over my skin, a Rorschach test on my forehead and temple and cheek. *Tell me, what do you see? Failure? Suckitude?* No amount of makeup is going to cover that.

I am not going to school today. Mom agrees to let me stay home for three days, the max I'm allowed without being truant. After that it's the weekend. At least the Rorschach should be mostly gone by Monday.

* * *

I'm half asleep when it comes on, my favorite movie. The week we had the flu, Lauren and I obsessively watched it: *Dead Hexy,* a film about best friends who find out they're witches from rival families. The dialogue's fun, the story's hokey, but the friendship is to die for. Literally. That's the tagline.

Watching it, remembering, makes me ache. I haven't spoken to Lauren in the three days I've been home from school, aside from a brief exchange about the status of my face, and she hasn't messaged. I'm sure she's just been busy.

I pick up my phone and flip through it to the photos from a few Halloweens ago. One brunette (me), one blonde (her), decked out in witchy gear, black lipstick, and black nail polish. We were a spectacle, but that happens when there are only twelve hundred people in a town. Everyone notices everything. Even on Halloween.

We had so much fun.

I check my notifications and see an older one from the school message board the day I hurt myself. It's a GIF of someone falling down, flailing, rewinding, and flailing again.

#MadstheKlutz

It has so many views.

Someone must have seen me face-plant into the locker after all. Just my luck. I debate popping onto my account and reaming them out, letting them know I'm sick, but I don't exactly relish the idea of being a social pariah because I've got some bizarro disorder that no one's ever heard of or understands. They'd probably treat me like a leper or worse—with kid gloves.

When I close the window, I see the picture of me and Lauren again, all wide smiles and black lips.

I'm sick of being *#MadstheKlutz,* even if there's a reason.

I'm sick of being okay with everything, of being this too-flexible thumbs-up.

I'd rather be a middle finger.

I spend the weekend furiously diving through all of my clothing and finding my makeup from Halloween. Anything black gets plucked out, put back in my closet. Dark colors, too. Everything else is tossed in a bin for the Marie Mission thrift store.

There's something exciting about doing this, changing everything up. Reinventing myself. Taking control back. As if I can say *Screw you, collagen; I make the rules here.* I use my Christmas gift cards at the mall an hour away, and Mom's glad to get out of town. I think she yearns as much as I do for somewhere that has chain fast food and a store that hasn't been "family owned and operated since 1955." Seeing buildings that are brand-new is nice—it makes me feel like I'm a part of the world and not just forgotten by it.

Mom lets me shop on my own, never having been one to hover, even now.

When I walk into school on Monday, I'm not "the Klutz." I'm a bona fide badass. I never knew there could be shades of black, but I've got four different ones on. The pitch of my boots, the off-black of my tights, the solid dark of my skirt, and the obsidian of my sweater. A black choker with studs rings my neck (the one part of my body I'm A-okay with, since it's thin and graceful). My lips are slashes of midnight on my face, and my eyes are ringed in so much kohl that they watered when I made them up.

It's totally worth it.

Jeff from bio lab heads straight for me, notebook out like he's about to ask me a question. But then he sees me. Really sees me. He cuts a ninety-degree angle and beelines away. Other kids stare and whisper. I've given them a good reason.

It's heady and satisfying, this feeling. Intoxicating, even, and it feels like I imagine magic might feel. Best of all, I can control it. If I can't reinvent myself into Madison the Varsity Cheerleader, I can sure as hell be Madison the Witch.

When the first bell rings, I'm walking down a nearly empty hallway. Someone walks past me too close, almost as if he intends to run into me, and I whip around and *hiss*, like a vampire. It's nothing I would have ever done before, but . . . now I *can*.

When he recoils, I grin.

Oh, *yeah*.

When I see Lauren after first period, she's standing in the hallway in her new cheer uniform, red and gold. For the first full week, the new cheerleaders wear them every day, a mark of pride. The uniform looks perfect on her, and the surge of jealousy that hits me nearly makes me sick. She's laughing and joking with the other new squad members. With their hair up in high ponytails and red scrunchies, they look like long-limbed colorful birds. I look like a raven.

This ungainly fowl . . .

Thanks, sophomore English, and your exhaustive unit on Poe.

When Lauren looks across the hall, her eyebrows rise and her lips fall open in surprise. Our eyes stay locked for a moment before I turn away, the awkwardness searing me. Though probably it shouldn't. You hear about it all the time. People grow apart.

Between classes, Mom texts. She's pulling an unexpected double shift at work. She does this sometimes when the hours are available. Small-town living is cheap, but doctors and specialists aren't, especially since most won't even be in a fifty-mile radius. She's a dental hygienist, so teeth are covered, but the rest of our healthcare is a mix of her crappy insurance and out-of-pocket expenses. Plus gas, of course.

Mom: *Catch a ride w/Lauren?*

Me: *Sure*

Lauren and I haven't really talked for a week, so when I walk up to her after the final bell rings, it almost feels like speaking to a stranger. She closes her locker, and there I am, leaning against her neighbor's.

"Hey."

"Hi." She's eyeing me, uncertain. I can read that on her face plain as day.

"Give me a ride home? Mom's working late."

She glances down at her uniform, fidgeting with her skirt. "I can't, I'm sorry. I have practice." When I say nothing, she gives a small wave and heads down the hall.

Abrupt. It's just abrupt and unlike her. I don't text Mom back. My eyes burning, I wish I'd never asked. I can walk home. It's only a quarter of a mile.

I mark my progress by the familiarity of the weedy lawns, old houses, and vacant lots I pass. The Johnsons. The Smiths. The

Waites. The Hummels. Ms. Mahern's back porch, which smells so strongly of cat pee that even from the sidewalk, fifty feet away, the stench makes my eyes water.

Some homes have newish cars that look out of place with the peeling paint and discolored siding of the dwellings. There are new barbecues and play sets, even in the yards of houses that look like they're ready to fall over. We've all read articles and seen comments online that claim poor people are poor because they're terrible at saving and planning. I don't believe that. No one *wants* to live in poverty, and saving is way easier when you have enough to pay your bills and then some. And let's be real: Forgoing that new barbecue isn't going to get any of these families out of poverty. Are we really saying that poor people shouldn't be able to have things in their lives that bring them joy, just because there's *always* going to be something they "should" be spending their money on instead? That attitude *sucks*.

At first glance, Marie's quite pretty. Quaint, even. There're lush old trees lining the sidewalks, wide patches of verdant (if weedy) lawns, a beautiful blue open sky. It's when you look carefully that you see the town is dying. Most small businesses close almost as soon as they open. Maybe one out of fifty makes it. The pizza place alone has been owned by at least three different families in my lifetime.

I feel like Marie right now. I look okay at a glance, but inside . . . I'm just not.

The lack of clouds makes it hot, and I'm sweating almost instantly. My body doesn't like the heat, fatigue settling heavily on my shoulders. I make it two blocks before my platform

240

boots come off. My fishnets snag on the cracked concrete, the town having neglected the sidewalks in favor of putting in a new baseball diamond last year. After I roll my ankle twice, my left knee and right hip crackle every time I take a step. Soon my back, right knee, and left hip join in the protest, my whole body flaming with agony.

How scary do I look now, how in control, staggering home with sweaty dark hair falling all around my face?

When I stumble into the house, I wipe my face with a towel. Black streaks of kohl cover it. Such a joke.

I can dress up however I want, but underneath I'm still broken.

Mom comes home late with some greasy takeout from Our Pizza House II. I've never been sure why it's named that. There was no Our Pizza House I, so why the sequel? I come down, grab a plate, and retreat to my room to bury my misery in a blanket and a graphic novel from the library.

One text comes from Lauren.

Gonna sit with the squad tomorrow @ lunch so we can hammer out practice sched.

I guess I get to spend lunch alone again. That sucks. Who else am I going to make fun of the school's lame-o attempt at feeding us "healthy" food with? Nachos are not in the veggie food group, no matter how much lettuce you put on them.

Mom pops her head in on the way to bed. It's part of her routine.

"How're you feeling, kiddo?"

I shrug.

"How's Lauren?" She sits down on the bed next to me, atop my blanket.

I don't tell her I walked home. She'll just feel bad.

"She's fine."

"Yeah?" She sighs and brushes her fingers through my bangs. "How's your head?"

"Fine." I say the word again and she frowns. "I'm just tired," I add. That's normal. Fatigue and all.

"Just tired. Okay." She stretches her long pajama-clad legs. "You should have Lauren over soon. I miss her."

I do, too. "She's busy. Cheerleading."

She's silent a long moment. "I'm sorry, Mads."

"Why?" She didn't do this to me. She didn't make Lauren busy or make her pull away like she has.

"It kills me every single bad day you have. I wish I could fix it." Her voice wavers, and she reaches up to clear her eyes with the edge of her scrub sleeve. She said something similar when Dad left, five years ago.

She kisses my forehead, taking care to avoid the bruise.

"I know," I murmur.

"However you want to deal with this . . ." She rubs the side of my face, her thumb coming back a little black, and she holds it up to show me. Thumbs-up. "As long as it doesn't hurt you or anyone else . . . give 'em hell."

At lunch, I see Lauren at the cheerleader table. She's sitting at the end, quiet and staring down at her food. I know that look. She's uncomfortable, maybe even sad.

Standing, I head from my empty table toward the gaggle of

red and gold in the center of the cafeteria. Most of the girls look at me with curiosity, a few with suspicion.

"Hey, L," I say. "Can we chat? Outside, maybe?"

Lauren looks up, startled. She hesitates a moment and then frowns.

"C'mon, Lauren. I just want to talk. I'm not taking you outside to murder you." I cast a glance at the rest of the girls at the table. "Hey, ladies. Great colors. Did you know they match the school's?" I grin as Stacy and Jennifer roll their eyes and Annie mutters "Duh" under her breath.

"I'll be right back," Lauren chirps to the squad, who nod and go back to chatting.

We walk onto the little grassy hill outside the school, still close enough that we can hear the warning bell when it rings. How many times have we hung out here, after lunch and before that bell, talking about TV and stupid stuff, like what our powers would be if we were superheroes or which movie we'd watch first if the world was coming to an end?

When we're far enough, she smiles. "I love the new look."

"You do?" My back hurts, so I sit.

"Yeah, it's tight." Lauren sits next to me and hugs her knees.

"Thanks." I look away, out at the tennis courts and the driveway where the seniors paint their names at the end of the year, only to be painted over by the next year's graduating class. Soon enough, that'll be us. Too soon. Only two years before we're leaving this place for college, and we might not even go to the same one. The number one goal of a small-town kid, at least here, is to get out while you still can. *Stuck* is a bad word in Marie.

"You haven't really talked to me since I found out that I was sick," I say. "Why?"

"You haven't talked to me either, Mads," she points out, her voice rising a little. "And you never even congratulated me on making the squad. That was a big deal." Her frown wobbles, like she can't decide which kind of upset she is—angry or sad. "I just assumed you wanted some space. That maybe all this"— she gestures to her uniform—"was too hard on you, given . . . you know."

I stare at her for a long moment, and I can't decide if I'm the kind of upset that's angry or sad either. I go with instinct. Angry.

"I'm sorry if I wasn't feeling particularly hyped for you on *the day I found out I have a serious health issue.*" My voice is harsh, heavy. I take a shaky breath. "We were going to try out for cheerleading *together.*"

I expect Lauren to apologize. Heck, maybe some selfish part of me even hopes she'll renounce the squad and turn in her red-and-gold uniform. But her eyes harden.

"So, what, you just wanted me not to do it because you couldn't?" Her hair sways as she turns her head, our mascot's sparkly devil horns on her hairband catching the light.

"That's not what I—"

"Look, I get that everything's changed and that sucks, but Mads, I've got my own stuff to worry about. I need to do well on the SATs. You know my grades aren't as good as yours are, and I have to try so much harder. I always have. And adding cheer to my applications will help." Her voice cracks a little. "You can't expect me to be sick with you."

"Lauren, no . . . God, I don't want you to be sick with me." I lock eyes with her. "Just be my *friend*. My best friend."

She sighs. "It's hard to be your best friend when you just cut me out completely. I mean, look at you!" It's my outfit she gestures to now. "You could've warned me about all of this. It's really cool, but you kind of look like you've stopped caring what other people think. That's what's different about us. I *do* care. It's just who I am."

The bell rings before I can say anything else. Lauren stands and leaves me outside to reel at what she's said. I've been so busy faulting her for not being there for me with this joint thing, for not being a good friend. But maybe . . .

Have *I* been a bad friend?

My gaze strays back to the tennis courts, and I worry my lower lip with my teeth as I realize the truth of what she said. With all that happened that day, I never even thought to congratulate her. I take out my phone, scroll through our messages. They don't lie. The sun is bright, almost blindingly so, and it's still so hot outside. I feel hotter, somehow, than when I was walking home yesterday.

I didn't text her back at first, when she told me she'd made the squad and asked where I was. Yeah, I'm dealing with a ton of stuff right now, but that doesn't mean I don't need to think about other people, too.

That night, on a whim, I text Lauren a pic of us at Halloween together, one I kept on my phone favorited, and she messages back almost immediately. A heart-eyes emoji and a single sentence.

How come u never posted this???

I thought I had. It was us. We laughed and danced so hard that night. We were two of a kind, like the girls from *Dead Hexy*, and no one was going to separate us. People avoided us, too, acted like we were terrifying even though it was Halloween. Small-town witches.

I know a little bit about crafting personas now and how they can give you power and confidence you otherwise wouldn't have. My new persona lets me stand out. Lauren's lets her blend in. We're both doing the things we need to do, being who we need to be. I just hope those people can still be friends.

The next day, I have to pass the cheer table to get a water from the vending machine. I'm wearing my armor, black from head to toe, lips a lush wine, and I refreshed my nails this morning. As I approach, the same hush falls as yesterday. Every eye is on me. I don't think I'll ever get sick of the little rush I feel when it happens, now that it's in my power to control the attention.

When I catch Lauren's eye, I almost say hi, but I don't want to put her on the spot. She doesn't deserve that.

A few of the girls surprise me by saying hey, and I nod as I keep walking. I'm almost past the table when my ankle gives out and I stumble, just barely catching myself on the back of a chair.

Laughter rings out. Of course it would happen here, in front of the squad.

"Klutz much?" someone says.

Anger clouds my vision, tears burning hot, but I right myself and keep going. I won't make a scene here, for Lauren's sake.

"Shut it, Jen." Lauren's voice.

I turn to see Jen straightening up, her lip curling.

"Excuse me?" Jen says to Lauren. "Just because you think you're some goth now, too . . ." She rolls her eyes.

The head cheerleader, Lina, casts Jen a look, and Jen sinks back into her seat. "Whatever."

Goth? I look at Lauren in her uniform, confused. What the heck was Jen even talking about? Still, I nod at Lauren in thanks. She had my back.

I'm heading to my empty table when I hear her voice, closer this time.

"Mads!"

I turn around and see Lauren crossing the lunch room to me. Everyone's still staring, though it's different now. I can't control this stare. Nervousness fills me like a blast of hot air.

Lauren smiles and holds up her hand, the back of it to me.

Her nails are painted black.

"Got room for one more at this table?" she asks.

"Always."

Maybe my new persona—someone who's too cool, too tough to care—can't be friends with the girl Lauren needs to be now. But if she can change a little, if her persona can make room for me, then, hell, so can I. There are plenty of things I can't change, like being sick, but there are lots of little things I can. Maybe I can be the girl who answers texts, supports my friend, and listens to her problems even when I'm dealing with my own.

Maybe I don't have to be a middle finger. But I'm keeping the black.

Secret Menu

Veeda Bybee

ring ring

SAWADEE-KA!

The usual? Pad Thai and—

THAT FISH LOOKS GOOD! I'LL HAVE WHAT THEY'RE HAVING!

Grandma, those dishes look spicy. I don't know if I can handle the heat.

We don't usually make these dishes for customers. They're on the *secret* menu!

Can I order from the secret menu? I need some excitement in this small town!

I'll ask my dad!

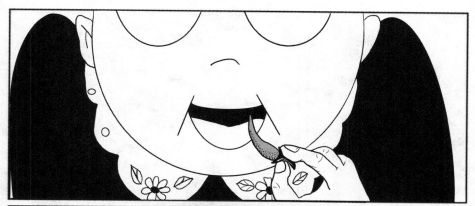

YUM!
YUM!
YUM!
YUM!
YUM!

Pull Up a Seat Around the Stove
JOSEPH BRUCHAC

I grew up at the edge of town. Quite literally. The town line for the city of Saratoga Springs was exactly one-half mile south of my grandparents' house, country store, and gas station, on the corner of Route 9N and Middle Grove Road. The center of town was only two miles to the south. But insofar as my experiences and view of life were concerned, that distance might as well have been from here to the moon.

Part of it was because I was being raised by a different sort of family. I lived with my mother's parents, even though my mom, dad, and younger sister, Mary Ann, lived only a mile up the road. That family division was, I was told then, intended to help make ends meet. No one had much money back in the mid-1940s, and sharing the child-rearing time and expenses between two families made some sort of sense.

Who my grandparents were was different as well. My grandfather Jesse was Abenaki Indian, though it was not something he'd ever talk about, no matter how many times I asked. (One thing I did know was that he'd left school in the fourth grade—by jumping out a window and never coming back—because the other kids kept calling him a dirty Indian.) He did everything he could to distance himself from that heritage, even though it was visible in his features and the color of his skin. He was so dark-skinned that, while he claimed French descent, I heard people say he was "as black as an Abenaki." Others would actually use the N-word to describe Grampa. Though no one ever did that where he might hear them. (Jesse Bowman was usually a quiet person and generous to a fault, but he was also notoriously tough and known to be good with his fists.)

Grampa understood the land and the waters. He taught me about the woods, about fishing and hunting, and the sort of balance that comes from living in a way that respects everyone and everything around you.

Not that he ever said that. He modeled it, but as far as actually saying that something he taught me was Indian, that never happened. It was only later in life that I was able to pick out certain things he said or did as tying directly into Native American practices. For example, no matter what I did at home, I was never spanked the way most of the other kids in town were by their parents. Corporal punishment was an accepted part of school life, too. One of my very distinct memories of School Number Two was the paddle that was kept prominently displayed in the principal's office and used regularly.

"Sonny," my grandfather said, using my childhood nickname, "my father never hit me. If I done wrong, he'd just talk to me or tell me a story."

But when I asked Grampa what sort of stories he heard, he'd just say they were "old" and he didn't remember them.

I have to admit that as a child I felt neither pride nor pain about that Native part of my ancestry. I didn't know enough for either yet, and I'd see only later in life how that Indian blood might make a difference. Nevertheless, my awareness of my grandfather's repressed ancestry affected me deeply. I loved my grandfather and wanted to know more about him. Not hearing those stories made me even more eager to learn them—and to find out more about that Abenaki heritage no one would ever talk about. That may be hard for someone who's not a person of Abenaki ancestry in northern New York or Vermont to understand. My grandfather's unwillingness to talk about or even acknowledge his heritage was characteristic of countless Abenaki families, even into the second half of the twentieth century. "Hiding in plain sight" was a survival technique for Native people in our area who saw "visible" Indians forced from their homelands in the eighteenth and nineteenth centuries and targeted for sterilization in Vermont in the 1930s. If anyone asked someone Native and living outside a reservation community in New England if they were Indian, the most common answer you'd get was what my grandfather would say: "I'm French," referring to being French Canadian.

Even friendly non-Indian neighbors might help keep up that charade. When my grandfather passed on, more than one person who came to his funeral took me aside and said, "Your grandfather was Abenaki." And when I replied, "I knew that," they were surprised.

Curiosity about Grampa's Native background inspired the search for my own Indian identity that would lead me to start visiting other Native American elders—Abenakis and Iroquois—in my late teens and begin collecting and writing down the stories denied me as a child. Some of those, such as the story of the thirteen moons on Turtle's back or how Fox tricked Bear, were ones I'd heard as a child from such "professional Indians" as Maurice Dennis at a tourist attraction called the Enchanted Forest and Swift Eagle at another such make-believe place named Frontier Town, and then again from them with new ears as an adult. It's part of what turned me into a writer.

MY GRANDFATHER'S HOE

The handle was one
that he made himself,
a strong maple sapling
cut and shaped
to replace the weaker
store-bought one
that broke after only
four springs of use.

The head had been shaped
by a local smith,
iron pounded and bent
into a tool
that, sharpened, was
the woe of any weed.

When I first tried
to use that hoe,
it was too heavy

for my five-year-old hands,
though Grampa praised
the effort I made
before lifting it from
my blistering palms, saying,
"I'll just finish
off these here rows."

Where did it go,
that beloved hoe
Grampa relied upon
for more springs
than I could even
imagine back then?

A year ago,
while digging up soil
where I still plant
corn, beans, and squash,
the three sweet sisters
that sustain us,
I found a piece
of rusted iron.

It still held some
of the well-used shape
of what it had once been.

I did not try
to salvage it

or hang it up
upon the wall
as some sort of souvenir.

Instead, with the spade,
I buried it deeper,
knowing its presence,
remembered or forgotten,
held in the earth
my grandfather loved,
was more than enough
of a blessing.

Although he was well versed in the workings of the natural world, my grandfather could barely read or write much more than his name. That made it a puzzle to many that he was accepted by the woman he married. My grandmother Marion was a highly educated woman. Not only had she graduated from Lucy Scribner's Young Women's Industrial Club, which would become Skidmore College, she had gone on to graduate from Albany Law School and pass the bar. Grampa Jesse had been the hired hand working for her parents. But she saw something finer and stronger in him than in the other more book-educated men around her. Their romance was a sort of scandal. My great-grandparents had tried to nip it in the bud; they sent my grandmother to Virginia to stay with her next-older brother, Orvis Dunham, who was managing a hotel in Warm Springs. My grandfather, though, followed her there and got a job working in the hotel to be close to her. When he was nearly killed in an accident involving a dumbwaiter, dragged up two floors through the shaft, it was my grandmother who nursed him to health and brought him back north. Seeing how set her mind was, my great-grandparents gave in, and she and Grampa were married not long after.

For whatever reason, whether it was due to her marrying "below her class" (as I once overheard someone put it) or the lack of opportunities for women lawyers, my grandmother never practiced law, unlike her older brother, Wyllis, who became the town lawyer for nearby Corinth. But she was a notary public who drew up deeds and other legal papers for people and had been town clerk for Greenfield. Marion Dunham Bowman was the only Democrat on the school board. She was also a voracious reader. I grew up in a house that had books in every room, and as a result I was already devouring all of Dickens, Sir Walter Scott, Stevenson, and countless collections of poetry by the age of seven. That was, I am sure, the second thing that turned me into a writer. Having access to all those books. Reading them gave me ideas of my own that I started to write down in the backs of my school notebooks as early as second grade. Those first stories of mine, which my grandmother praised to the skies, were mostly about animals— ones I'd encountered in the tales I read, like those in Rudyard Kipling's wonderful *Jungle Book*, or animals I knew in real life, like our dogs and cats, our pigs and chickens, and the animals I saw in the woods around our house.

Another thing that made my family different was that we were sort of farmers. I say "sort of" because we were not earning our living from farming, like Harold Hall two miles up the road, who ran a dairy with fifty milk cows, or Grama's youngest brother, Harry, around the corner on Lester Park Road, who raised rabbits and brought his vegetables to our store for my grandparents to sell. In addition to the one-room general store and gas station out front—a building separated from the house—we had only three acres in back, taken up by a small woodlot, a former barn, a henhouse, a pigpen, a field of hay, and a quarter-acre vegetable garden. Slopping the always-hungry hogs, spreading out sprays of feed for the chickens, weeding, and hoeing were part of my daily life.

SLOPPING THE HOGS. 1951

My grandfather handed me the bucket,
day just breaking down Splinterville Hill.
Then, eyes still filled with sleep,
leaned to one side against the weight,
I trudged out to the Little House pen,
where the smell of pigs was strong and sweet
as the scent of ferment in the galvanized pail.

"Sooo-eeee, pigpigpig," I called,
voice thin in the throat of dawn.
My stick cracked ice in their trough
as hogs stirred up from straw,
mud tinkling like bells under trotters,
frost in the weeds a froth of diamond.

One leg over the fence as they rooted,
bristled backs rough against my wrist,
I leaned out to stroke
a nose aglisten like a doll's china face,

thinking of pig lore I'd been taught,
how a boar would eat anything—even a snake.

I'd heard of the boy up North Creek Road
who fell into the pen and was eaten by swine
his farmer father still slaughtered for bacon,
yet I swayed back and forth, innocent in my balance.

Slops for the hogs—say it with me now, friends,
as I call, call myself back with simple words,
which ease back that fence-sitting dawn,
defying even the dreams of falling.

It was also my job to lug water. We did have running water
from our well—but sometimes I was the one who did the running when the water pump in the cellar needed some tinkering,
as my Grampa put it. While he was down there banging away
at the cussed thing, I'd be going back and forth with a bucket,
drawing water from the hand pump. That pump was outside
under the blue spruce tree—next to the chopping block where
Grampa both split wood for the stove and brought about the
inevitable demise of any chicken who'd stopped laying eggs and
in so doing designated itself for Sunday dinner.

That's not to say we were without modern conveniences.
We had electric lights in most of the house's nine rooms. We
had a vacuum cleaner that sort of worked, even though we
often had to sweep up after using it—especially when it decided
to spit out more dirt than it sucked in, creating a miniature
Saharan dust storm. And from 1949, when I was six years old,
Grama no longer used a bucket and a washboard for doing our

laundry. We had us a wringer washer that ran off the one elec-
trical outlet in the kitchen. I'd help roll it out of the corner, its
white porcelain sides cool as Alaska as I leaned my shoulder
into it. Then I'd help fill it with buckets of warm water from the
sink. Though now and then—when the heater in the cellar was
having an off day—we'd have to settle for water heated in the
big black pot we kept on the woodstove.

Once the washer was plugged in and it got down to business,
I'd sit on the floor, listening to the churning and ever-changing
symphony of suds and water and clothes sloshing around in
its depths. Now and then it would shudder or even give a little
jump, one of its four wheels lifting off the floor to thud down
again a second later. At times its rough music was like the
sounds of the ocean waves I'd never experienced in person but
heard as we sat around the big brown Philco in the evenings, listening to radio dramas. Thanks to that washer's sound effects,
I could envision myself on a ship far at sea or on some tropical
beach. After my imaginary voyage ended when the wash cycle
was done, it was time to drain the soapy water into the sink,
using the handy hose attached to the machine's nether parts.
I'd pour in buckets of cool water for the rinse and, when that
was done, help my grandmother feed the clean clothes through
the top wringer, its twin rollers turning with such force that the
clothes snaked between them came out nearly dry.

THE WRINGER WASHER, 1949

When the time came
to roll out the old washer,

that job I was first given
when I was seven,
my grandmother would raise
a cautioning hand.

"Watch your fingers, Sonny,"
she would say.
"Get them caught and
they'll end up flat as a pancake."

I always liked the thrill those words created.
That threat of danger appealed to me.

Still, I always, more or less,
heeded her serious admonition,
never doing more when her back was turned
than holding on to the end of a sheet
as it was drawn in closer and closer
to those hungry, whirring wringers,
before letting go at the very last second.

When the cord was finally unplugged,
all my digits intact, I'd help roll the machine
back into the corner, where it lurked
beside the friendly Kalamazoo cookstove.

Then, when my grandmother was safely gone
I'd place both of my hands
on the rubbery rollers and whisper,
"You can't get me!"

Filling the big old wood box for the Kalamazoo cookstove was another of my chores—twice daily in winter. In more ways than one, that old porcelain stove was the heart of the house. It kept us warm better than the clanking radiators. Every bite of the unforgettable meals my grandmother made—sometimes for as many as ten people when there were guests, other family members, or boarders at the table—was cooked on its top or inside its oven. The oven's temperature was set, as Grampa put it, by guess and by gosh. (At that time, we were still almost a decade away from such things as a gas stove whose heat could be varied with a control knob.)

The stove was also the place—right behind it, to be exact—where Samantha, our gray cat, had her yearly litter of kittens. Its cozy, hidden security made it as safe and special a place for her as it was for me. I was always the one designated, after we'd given them enough time to reach the handling size, to crawl in and bring their warm, squirming little bodies out so we could take a look before carefully putting them back with their patient mother.

Though nowadays it's ethical practice to have cats spayed or neutered, in those farming years in Greenfield, there was seldom such a thing as an unwanted kitten. And since everyone knew Sam to be a very special cat, there were plenty of takers for her offspring once they were large enough to be adopted. A cat in the house eliminated the need for mousetraps, and a bevy of barn cats was better insurance than poison against rats getting into your grain. All Grampa had to do was sit out in front of the store with Sam and her little ones in a big cardboard box by his side. Most times, by the end of the first day, those kittens would have been adopted by grateful customers come to get gas or pick up groceries.

I haven't mentioned childhood friends, and that's because I didn't really have many. Even when I first joined a Cub Scout group in Saratoga I was not part of the crowd. I was—a term I heard often—a hick. Back then Greenfield was mostly a mix of forest and farms, while Saratoga prided itself on being a city with big hotels (though most were in decline during my childhood) and a world-famous racetrack and mineral spa. Just being from Greenfield and not Saratoga meant I was a country bumpkin, even though my vocabulary was bigger than any of the Saratoga kids' and I always had the highest grade average in my class. So it may have been that they were a little intimidated by my intelligence. My teachers, though, loved me—"my precious second grader Joey," as Mrs. Monthony always referred to me, even when I visited her forty years later.

My teachers celebrated and praised my writing, which I think made others of my age jealous. I was not yet socialized enough to realize you didn't always have to act like the brightest coin in the change drawer. I hadn't gotten my growth—even by my third year in high school—but it didn't keep me from being mouthy. Fourteen-year-old me once observed that the "intellectual attainment" of a classmate who outweighed me by a hundred pounds was "sadly out of proportion" to his "Neanderthal physiognomy." That got me a bruising.

What I realize now is that, in some ways, being an outsider was a blessing. (It's amazing how many writers I now know who had that feeling of being a misfit or different when they were children.) I had more time for introspection than the popular kids. I might not have had friends, but I had books and the time and desire to write. And as I buried myself in reading or writing poems and stories, I was learning to process things in ways that would help me become the writer I am now. As a child, I never met any real living writers. All the writers I knew of either lived far away or had died as long ago as Shakespeare. The writers I loved—such as Kipling—showed me how to see things as stories, so much so that now, when I think about the events of my life when I was a rural kid, they shape themselves into narratives and not just unconnected incidents.

When the weather was good enough, my grandparents and I would sit outside in the wooden chairs my grandfather made. This was, you understand, a time before television. It was not until I was in fourth grade that our first television entered our lives and a set with a six-inch-wide screen was set up in our living room. However, it didn't rule our routine. Admittedly, we could get three whole channels on a good day, but even during my teenage years, our summer evenings were seldom spent inside in front of a screen.

Instead, the never-boring shows we watched were the flow of traffic on the road, the birds in the nearby trees, and the ever-changing colors of my grandmother's gardens out front. The shrubs and flowers she planted—curated, more like—were colorful as a quilt, never the same from week to week. I've come to think of them in later years as the poems she never wrote, a gift to be shared with anyone who saw them. From the beds of crocuses, tulips, and daffodils in early spring to the lilacs of summer and the chrysanthemums of fall, there was always a feast for your eyes being offered up. And those flower feasts were just as appreciated by the birds and insects. My favorites

were the hummingbirds that would circle my head as I stood by
the tall stalks of hollyhocks and the hummingbird moths that
came at dusk to bury their proboscises in the deepest blooms.

MARION DUNHAM BOWMAN
STANDING IN HER GARDEN, 1951

My grandfather's garden was in back,
where squash and beans and corn intertwined.
Hers was in front and said to be
one of the finest in all the county.
It was just to the right of the general store
they ran together thirty years,
and as he handed out the gold,
the purple and green of popsicles,
she offered up the red of tulip,
sunglow of daffodil, flare of rose.
Perennial, annual, bush, and flower
waxed and waned through growing seasons
each year until the first hard frost.

I knew no words to answer then
when one of the Atwell boys said to them:
"What the hell good is all them flowers?"
But last spring a shrub I never planted
came up again from dormant roots
to open a yellow arc of blossoms
at the edge of the lawn that was her garden—
    one image from the poems she never wrote.

I had a real stake in those gardens. By the time I was thirteen, I was doing almost all of the digging and planting—under Grama's close supervision, since everything had to be done "the right way." There was true artistry and care in the design of that garden. In summer and early fall, I'd climb into the old blue Plymouth with Grama so we could scout out new flowers. We'd drive the back roads till she saw something that caught her eye—perhaps a different color of double hollyhock or dahlia or balloon flower. We'd stop and she'd either knock on the door or go up to the woman outside working in that garden. They'd chat some, sociable-like, before Grama would come back with seeds or a cutting or a small plant she and the other woman dug up. The friendships she struck up that way would last for years. And that sharing of flowers was the same, of course, for any plant lover who stopped at our corner.

There was another reason we sat out front as we did; it was more convenient for the conveniences. The only bathroom in the house—and it was a full bath, with a tub, sink, and toilet—was on the second floor. However, built into the outside wall of the general store—the *station*, as we called it—were a men's room and a women's room. Each had a little sink, an actual flushing toilet like the one upstairs in our house, and even a radiator that generally worked. A darn sight better, as Grampa said, than the crescent-moon-windowed outhouses that had served the same purpose not that long before my time. My grandparents' bedroom (next to mine) was downstairs. Since my grandmother took in tourists in the summer—most of whom were in town for the racing season at the famous Saratoga tracks—the four upstairs rooms and their shared bathroom were off-limits for us a good part of the year. In the summer we took sponge baths in the kitchen sink and used the toilets in the station. But even though their summer accommodations were better than ours, I never felt as if those paying visitors looked down on us. Those tourists, most of whom came back every year, were like part of our family and treated my grandparents with great respect. With the bathroom unavailable during the tourist season and going outdoors in the night undesirable, the only option for us during those times was the one kept shoved under my grand-parents' bed: a deep-bowled chamber pot.

From my seventh year on all the way into my junior year in high school, I was the one delegated to trudge out to the pub-lic restroom on the other side of the station each day to empty that sloshing, odiferous chamber pot into the men's room com-mode. After that daily task, I would renew my acquaintance with a good bit of soap and a lot of hot water. It was not until my grandmother passed on that I found out that the herculean labor of taking out the pot had been my mother's when she was my age. I realized that two days after my grandmother's funeral, when I watched my mother carry the old ceramic chamber pot out behind the house, where she smashed it into pieces with the biggest rock she could lift.

My grandmother's sudden death from bone cancer left a huge gap in my sixteen-year-old life and that of my grandfather. My parents tried their best to be supportive—though they were awkward about it, as our relationship was strained in my youth. There was talk of my moving in with them, but I'd have none of it. Grampa needed help at the store—where my grandmother had done everything from helping pump gas to ordering things and keeping the books. Plus we'd always relied on Grama for all the cooking. Aside from the one thing my grandfather knew how to make—baked beans—I had to take over the kitchen duties. Which, thanks to TV dinners I could heat up in our new gas oven, I managed pretty well.

At the same time, I started to grow and fill out. I'd always been muscular—that favorite pastime of tree-climbing had helped develop my arms and chest—but I'd been short. By the fall of 1959 I'd sprouted up to six-two and weighed 195 pounds. My classmates were amazed, and when I went out for football senior year and became the right tackle on a championship team, they were even more surprised.

My coaches weren't, though. "You farm boys," Coach Tibbetts said, "with all those muscles you build up from working outside, you usually make good linemen." Then I joined the wrestling team and, as the first-string heavyweight, won the conference championship and took third in sectionals. All of a sudden, I had lots of friends, including bullies who'd picked on me in the past.

My grandfather came to every ball game and wrestling match, and when groups of us went out for pizza afterward, he was always with me, at seventy-four almost as much a kid as the teenagers around him. I had not yet learned enough social graces to actually date a girl—that and my shyness held me back. But I did have friends among the girls in my classes who appreciated my sense of humor, as well as the respect and politeness that my grandmother had drilled into me as the only way to relate to women.

And I was doing even more reading—everything from poetry to sci-fi and history and popular fiction. My writing was sophisticated enough now for me to win a countywide "Speak for Democracy" contest for an essay I wrote, and I was still writing poetry in English classes. I'd decided I was going to become a naturalist and write about the natural world like my favorite writers, Edwin Way Teale and John Muir. I won a New York State Regents Scholarship, and then, without any help from school counselors or my parents, I applied to Cornell University and was accepted into the School of Agriculture.

It was at Cornell that my future vocation as a writer became clear for me. After taking two creative-writing classes, I switched my major to English, became an editor of the school literary magazine, and saw my poems published for the first time—poems that often drew on my memories of my rural childhood.

FEED SACKS

We bought the ones with patterns on them,
pastel flowers dusted by the pollen of dry mash.
Grandma sewed them into blue shirts, pink dresses,
purple aprons worn in the kitchen, tucked up
to cradle cracked corn for the Rhode Island Reds
and bring back the troves of speckled eggs
I dug from the warmth of henhouse straw.

Those garments meant more
than that we farm people
were too poor to waste.
We always set an extra place
each night for dinner,
knowing that sharing
with any stranger

who might happen by
would be a blessing.

Today, in an age of new poverty,
when even earth and air seem to be
made to use and throw away,
I remember a feed sack shirt,
humble and useful, circling
my body with the warmth of a time
when we were who we were, and what we wore
was still linked to a simple pride,
close enough to the land
to neither know nor care about fashion.

There's much more to my story, of course. My 1997 auto-
biography, *Bowman's Store*, captured on its pages many of the
experiences of my early life. But what's even more clear to me
now, looking back on those years of my rural childhood, is
how much the person I became was shaped by that place. As I
write these words, looking out the window at the woods I knew
as a child, I know that wherever I've gone, wherever I travel,
Bowman's Store has been and always will be in my heart.

Home Waits
ESTELLE LAURE

Fourteen-year-old Sunbow Rain Bronson was trying to pray the
ghosts away . . . again.

Praying wasn't something she had done much in her lifetime. She was more the beat-a-drum-in-the-woods type, but
lately she felt she had been backed into a proverbial corner,
because frankly, as far as anyone could tell, Sunny was losing
it. And so there she was, flat on her belly, palms together, eyes
closed, whispering pleas into the near dark.

"Are you freaking serious?" Molly dropped her head so it
appeared, disembodied and upside down, over Sunny's bottom
bunk. *"Candles?"* Molly snuffled. "Unbe*liev*able. Do you know
what Miss Sam will do to us if she finds you with those? She
will flay your skin from your body and hang it from a flagpole."

Miss Sam was the dorm mother. Small. Fierce. Somewhere
in her thirties, probably.

Molly's eyes darted to Sunny's makeshift altar, and Sunny
hovered over it protectively, though there was no way to block
the flicker.

Sunny worried about the amount of blood that must be in Molly's head by now, upside down as she was. Sunny wanted to tell Molly to get herself upright, but Molly simply stared at her.

It had been snowing for days and had finally stopped last night, leaving the world coated in white fur. It seemed to have made everyone at the school feel somewhat magical, in the mood for frolics and snow angels, while Sunny imagined herself slowly going insane in a room with no borders and no lines, only never-ending white seamlessly melting into never-ending gray at the horizon line.

"Anyway, that's not the point. We have a Spanish final in like"—Molly disappeared, then reappeared a few moments later, brown hair cascading around her head—"four hours. I *need* to sleep."

Sunny couldn't explain herself, though that seemed to be what Molly was waiting for. Intellectually, she understood perfectly well that she was safe. She was in a cushy boarding school at the edge of Boston, surrounded by people whose only job was to see that she was kept comfortable enough. People who worked at the school were objectively cool, and weird in their own New Englandy way. When the students were permitted to leave the campus, which was not often, Sunny admired the architecture, the electric resilience coursing through the streets, the way people seemed to laugh harder and louder than in other places.

"You know," Molly said, her tone a little gentler than before. "It's a little . . . *off* or something. The way you taped their faces on the candles like that. It's a little *worrying*, isn't it?"

Sunny's ghosts—Georgia O'Keeffe, Millicent Rogers, and

Mabel Dodge Luhan, whose pictures she had printed and taped onto some cheap dollar store candles—were some of the great ladies of her hometown of Taos, New Mexico, pioneers of one sort or another. They had appeared in October and had been with her since. She knew candles were contraband. She also knew that the logic of what she was attempting to do by purchasing, decorating, and burning those candles was likely flawed, but she had to try something because the ghosts were slowly taking over.

Sunny's praying had not had the desired effect, of course. Instead of backing down, the ghosts began to visit her more frequently, appearing in the cafeteria at lunch, showing up during class, crowding the teachers, pointing fingers at them, scoffing, observing. They did not seem to have a purpose at all, but rather seemed to be there solely to make life more complicated for Sunny, and to make her question everything she knew to be true about reality. They seemed to be there so Sunny would come unhinged. But Sunny didn't know what else to do, so she returned to her praying, hoping some sort of combination of introspection and humility would lead to understanding and perhaps even relief.

Georgia would sometimes paint, her dark eyes burrowing into her subject, hair falling across her cheeks. Millicent swanned around any given person, boa draped over her neck, commenting on the person's terrible fashion sense, while Sunny resisted the temptation to tell her she had probably overplucked her eyebrows a little. And then there was Mabel, who liked to wear colorful blankets over her shoulders and always had a pad of paper and a pen in hand.

When Molly sighed heavily, Sunny said, "I'm sorry I've kept you up. I didn't think I'd be bothering you. I thought you'd be asleep. I'm not going to burn the place down, I promise."

"Fine," Molly said. "I'm going to barf if I stay upside down anymore. You want to stage expulsion-worthy rituals, that's your choice, but if you start having visions of razors and ropes, you better get some help."

"Molly," Sunny countered seriously. "I am not suicidal." That was true. But she didn't tell her the next part. That sometimes, although she wouldn't hurt herself, she felt like she couldn't do another day in this place without suffocating. Without being smothered. She couldn't do *this*.

"Okay." Molly yawned loudly. Her head disappeared, and a few minutes later she was snoring.

Sunny felt she hadn't slept in weeks, and every movement of her own eyes in their sockets ached. She vibrated lightly.

Awake asleep.

Asleep awake.

I've been absolutely terrified every moment of my life, Georgia said, crouched in the corner, gazing outward, *and I've never let it keep me from doing a single thing that I wanted to do.*

They do as they please, they say what they think, and nobody cares, for everyone is busy doing likewise, Mabel offered.

Sunny gripped her head with both hands and began to cry into the pillow her mother had embroidered with her initials three months ago, before she had left her home to come here to this strange place, alone.

Sunny's grandfather had seemed small to her the day he received her acceptance to St. Anthony's. Because he had commandeered the entire application process, the letter had gone to him, and as a result, she had never once felt that it belonged to her. That day, he had been sitting at his giant desk in his giant house, both of which usually gave him the impression of being an important man but which today left him looking deflated. The cleaner busily attended to her duties in the background while Sunny's older sister, Dove, lounged on a nearby sofa, and their grandfather's phone sat, silent and heavy, at his side. Although he appeared lonely and forlorn in that moment, his presence seemed always to be required at some sort of charity event, perhaps a dinner with semifamous people. It was a layer of her hometown Sunny had no interest in. She loved the earth, the mountains, the old trucks and tacos, and the way some of the women in town called her *mijita.* And most of all, she loved her best friend, Ricky, who had come up to her grandfather's house on the hill only once and had basically squirmed in his chair, melting under the chandelier lights and her grandfather's pitiless gaze, until they had left.

Though he was flawed, Sunny loved her grandfather: his cashmere sweaters with their elbow patches, the way he went from room to room calling for his dachshund, Teddy, and how much he adored a good strawberry shortcake. She especially loved the way he paced with a wrist clasped behind his back when he was excited about something. He was a career diplomat in hot spot regions mainly found in the Middle East, and once, when she was small, Sunny had seen him on the news, handling some sort of hostage crisis, and he had been pacing like that, back and forth, holding on to himself. That's how she had recognized him, though they didn't show his face.

"You've got to get out of this town," he said, holding her

acceptance letter in hand. "This is where one *retires*, not where one makes a life. This school will change everything. You won't be stuck here like your mother. The whole world will be open to you."

Sunny's mother had been to Taos with her father when she was a teenager, and she had come back as soon as she could, having fallen desperately in love with everything about it. This was a place where you could be whoever you wanted, a wonderland where you could build a castle or a cabin and be happy and accepted either way. She had waited tables. She had been a landscaper. She had worked at the gem shop and brought home hundreds of crystals and rocks. All this before she finally opened a small gallery that carried her favorite things. Sunny's mother did not seem to think she was a failure. She thought she was living her best life. But it was clear Sunny's grandfather did not concur.

"Your mother went to Georgetown," he said. "She could have done anything."

"*You* live here," Sunny offered. "Some of the time."

She looked around. It was true he didn't have houseplants.

"I've met my potential," he retorted, shaking the letter in Sunny's face.

Teddy clambered onto his lap and gifted Sunny an identical look of fury.

"But I don't want to go."

"Yes, you do. What are you going to do? Stay here for that *Ricky Gonzales?*"

Sunny did not like the sound of Ricky's name on her grandfather's tongue, like he was a corroded penny, worth less than the value of its materials. And she did not know how to explain to him that she wanted the four years she had left in Taos. She wanted the crazy high school. Four years of climbing mountains, of sitting on benches and staring into infinity, of hanging out with Dove and their howl-at-the-moon friends, and of knowing people in every nook and cranny of the place.

"It's settled. You will go to St. Anthony's, you will go to a wonderful university, and you will leave this place behind, thereby not repeating your mother's mistake of squandering her opportunities. It will be what's best for you," her grandfather had said, patting her on the hand gently, which was her Achilles' heel and her kryptonite, all wrapped in one palm-sized package. "You can come back to visit, of course," he added. "I'm proud of you."

Those four words sealed it. He had never said them before, and even though Sunny's mother said them all the time, they didn't carry as much weight, or any, really. The words from her grandfather had been hard earned.

"Ugh," Dove said from where she was lounging across a turn-of-the-century sofa. "Don't be a shill, Sun. You don't have to do everything he says."

"Young lady," their grandfather said.

Dove simply got up and left the room without looking back.

Sunny played that day over and over again. She knew the road had forked, and she kept waiting to understand why, waiting for the moment her grandfather had insisted would come, when her choice to attend the illustrious St. Anthony's School for Girls would feel good instead of bad.

It wasn't that the Spanish final was so hard, really. Sunny mostly knew the material. It was that Spanish was *painful* for her. Every time her teacher (or really anyone) spoke it, the scent of posole filled her nostrils. She had left just as roasting season kicked off, when the whole town of Taos filled with the smell of green chilies, and people came from all over to get their supply, buying them by the pound to be peeled and frozen. Gathering and preparing the supply of chilies was an annual tradition and one Sunny had spent with both her and Ricky's families since second grade, when she and Ricky had become friends.

She remembered the first time, when Ricky's family and hers had gathered in the kitchen and it had been her job to remove the seeds from the slimy innards. She had worked at the chilies for an hour before her hands started to burn, because she didn't know she was supposed to wear gloves and all the grown-ups had forgotten to tell her.

Avrora, Ricky's mom, had not been happy when they had decided not to talk once Sunny was at St. Anthony's.

"You don't turn up your nose at a friendship like the one you have," she had told them both. "You have been looking out for each other since you were little kids. Throwing that away is going to make your angels cry."

People in Taos were always talking about angels, so much so that Sunny imagined them all around, playing lutes and lyres, reading poetry to each other.

Sunny looked out the classroom window at the flat sky.

New Mexico gets three hundred days of sun annually, Georgia said, looking up from her painting.

Suddenly, passing Taos Mountain, Millicent added, *I felt I was a part of the earth, so that I felt the stars and the growth of the moon. Under me, rivers ran.*

Well, that's beautiful, Mabel said. *Did I ever tell you about the time D. H. Lawrence came to visit? Stayed four years.*

Mrs. Dale patted Sunny's shoulder and pointed to her blank exam, and Sunny surveyed her suspiciously. L.L.Bean all the way. Mrs. Dale was blond and had a pointy nose. She probably didn't know anything about green chilies.

And just look at her shoes, Millicent said. *Nobody has any style anymore.*

"Only thirty minutes left," Mrs. Dale reminded Sunny.

Sunny looked at her blankly.

Molly kicked the back of Sunny's chair.

Sunny blinked.

"Thirty minutes left to finish your exam." Mrs. Dale cleared her throat. "Or should I say, to *begin* your exam."

Molly kicked the back of her chair again.

Sunny threw her the finger as subtly as possible and turned back to her paper, but the words only swam on the page. She had to do this. She *had* to. Otherwise she would know that she had contributed to her grandfather's overall disappointment in the world.

"May I use the restroom?" Sunny asked.

Thank heavens, Mabel said. *Let's get the hell out of here.*

Before coming east, Sunny had watched every movie featuring kids in boarding schools with Dove while munching on huge bowls of popcorn slathered in butter and nutritional yeast. Whether it involved vampires, mean girls, or sadistic teachers, she and Dove had agreed she should anticipate a moral and psychic disaster, and to expect to have her head shoved in a toilet at least once a week. Dove had briefly attempted to teach Sunny krav maga, which she had recently taken up, but they had both quickly become exhausted and fallen asleep on the sofa.

As she drifted off, Sunny had stared at the tattoo on her sister's wrist, of a small black bird. Her mother had taken Dove to the tattoo place when Dove turned fifteen, muttering about how she was always to wear a long-sleeved shirt when they climbed the hill to their grandfather's vacation home. Their mother had realized that Dove would get the tattoo with or without her. No one expected Dove to do anything but be Dove, because who she was had never been open for discussion.

Sunny had boarded the plane in Albuquerque the following afternoon, and nothing had been the same since.

Anyway, Sunny and Dove had been wrong about the school. Instead of her head in a toilet, Sunny had found decent food, mostly caring teachers, and classmates who were kind of nice for rich, spoiled white people. In Taos, being white meant being in the minority, and it was like her eyes hadn't adjusted to the more recent, paler demographic. And the kids at this school weren't all rich, either. Just *most* of them. But they were friendly, even got over the fact that her name was Sunbow Rain without much fanfare. After all, there were famous people named Apple these days, and the students themselves had names like Staten and Apollo and Huckleberry.

And so Sunny would often think about how everything was okay, how nothing was actually wrong, how if she was going to be wandering the world away from home, this was probably the safest place for her to be. And yet.

And yet, she felt it.

Doom.

Or her own limitations.

She thought maybe she had gotten knocked out of place and that the universe hadn't noticed.

It wasn't clear to Sunny exactly how she got onto the bathroom floor, sopping wet, in the last shower stall back in the dorm. It would seem she had not returned to her class but instead had decided to take a shower while fully clothed. That hadn't gone well either, and now Miss Sam the dorm mother was standing above her.

She crouched so she and Sunny were eye to eye. The water pooled around Miss Sam and drained loudly. Miss Sam touched the side of Sunny's cheek. "Yes. I see you. You're here." She looked around. "Sally, she's okay!" she yelled. "You don't need to get the nurse!"

"I'm in New England?" Sunny said.

"Well, yeah, where the hell else would you be?"

Sunny began to cry.

"Oh, for Pete's sake, don't do that." Miss Sam leaned forward and placed an awkward arm around Sunny's shoulder. "Come here," she said with a thick Boston accent. "You're going to be okay. Shh, shh, shh."

Sunny almost felt like she could talk to Miss Sam, like if she told her what had been happening with the ghosts and about her feeling of doom, Miss Sam wouldn't freak out. *Almost.* The thing was, Sunny knew if a person was schizophrenic they might say the same things she would be saying right now, things that might land her in a padded room and in group circles, talking about her feelings and on heavy, complicated meds. But Sunny knew that wasn't it, not that her mental health was currently in peak condition. Either way, she decided to keep silent.

"Why did you leave your Spanish final?" Miss Sam asked.

"None of this seems real," she said before she could keep the words from tumbling forth. The statement missed the mark of what she was feeling. How to explain that there just wasn't *enough* of anything?

"Meaning?" Miss Sam prodded.

"Meaning I don't get it."

"What?"

"Any of it," Sunny said. "I don't get . . . chowder. Or how fast everything moves here."

"Well, you applied here. You got in."

"My mother went here. So did her mom. It's something we're supposed to do." Only her mom had messed it up and hadn't done what she was supposed to at all.

"I see," Miss Sam said. "Sunny, when was the last time you slept?"

"Uh," Sunny said.

Miss Sam scooted closer to Sunny and made herself comfortable. "I once went to New Mexico, to Taos, where you're from. It's a beautiful place. Those mountains. Maybe not enough opportunity, though? Seems a little sleepy."

"It's perfect. *It's* real." Sunny was unprepared for her own volcanic grief, and she began to hyperventilate. She held her face in her hands and pushed against her eyelids to stop the tears from flowing again.

"You're homesick. It's okay to be homesick." Miss Sam took a deep breath. "What do you want, Sunny?"

She shrugged. "I haven't thought about it."

"Okay," Miss Sam said. "Why don't you do that now?"

"What?"

"Think, Sunny. What do you want? *You.*"

Smart lady, Millicent said.

Sunny closed her eyes. This place meant every possibility was open to her, that she had access to every path so many other people would be grateful for. It meant Ivy League, probably, and a good job.

"Do you know what they call New Mexico?" Sunny said, suddenly smiling.

Land of Entrapment, all three ghosts said at once. New Mexico's state signs read, "Welcome to the land of enchantment," but this was something locals often said, because once you visited New Mexico, you could never fully leave with your whole heart.

One has to go back, Georgia said.

It's because of the magic, Mabel said.

The way I see it, Millicent added, swooping a fox stole over one shoulder, *being from Taos is like being a deep-sea fish. You can go up to the top and see the cute tropical fish, but then you have to drop right back down with the anglers and the treasure. You just can't survive up here, sweetheart. You have to know what you're made of.*

I have an idea, Mabel said. *Join an artist colony. That's the medicine.*

"It's okay," Miss Sam said. "It's okay to just go home."

"I can't," Sunny said.

"You can. No offense, but you're getting to be a liability . . . you know, in a nice way. I'd rather not have to document this.

And make sure you take all your candles and shit with you."
Miss Sam sighed dramatically. "I'm so lucky you didn't torch
the place."

Sunny took a deep breath and exhaled shakily. "I would like
my one phone call now."

Miss Sam cracked a smile. "I'm going to miss you, kid."

Things were still moving faster than Sunny could keep up with.
It took her mother only nine hours to get there. Sunny had not
wanted to see Molly or anyone else and had hidden in Miss
Sam's room, thinking, until everyone had gone to dinner. She
had packed surreptitiously and dragged her couple of boxes
down the hall.

Miss Sam had brought her some dinner of broth and a
grilled-cheese sandwich, but Sunny let it grow cold on its plastic tray while she curled up in a large chair. Even her ghosts
seemed tense now, not writing or painting or doing much of
anything except lounging or sitting in some fashion, waiting
just like Sunny was.

"Hold on, I'm still talking to you," she heard Miss Sam say
from the other side of the door.

Sunny and the ghosts sat at attention.

"One second," Miss Sam said. "I just want to—"

Sunny's mother burst through the door, wearing a black
beanie over her blond hair, swathed in alpaca wool and leggings,
finishing off the look with enormous Sorel boots that were still
wet from the snow outside.

"Baby," her mother said, and she swept Sunny into a huge
hug, then leaned back to look at her. "You know there was a

lunar eclipse yesterday. Those can be nasty." She surveyed the room with distaste. "Ugh, this place is so institutional."

Miss Sam made a disgruntled noise.

Sunny hurt everywhere, caught between shame and relief. All the things at once.

"I got a rental car," her mother went on. "The weather gods were on our side for the plane ride here, so I'm counting on them for the way back, too. It'll take us a few days, but—" She pulled a pink rock from her sweater pocket. "Just hang on to this rose quartz until we get in the car." She put the quartz in Sunny's hand and pressed it against her heart.

Sunny managed to nod and reluctantly admitted to herself that she did feel a little better. Before she could say anything, her mother had placed a few drops of something behind Sunny's ear. "Clary sage," she said. "And bergamot. Grounding."

"Uh, can I give you these?" Miss Sam handed Sunny's mom a couple of bags. "I'll help you with the rest." Miss Sam was looking at Sunny's mom the way people always did outside Taos: like she was an unidentifiable force that basically made no sense. She supposed it wouldn't help if she told Miss Sam that her mother had buried her placentas from both pregnancies under an aspen tree, which she regularly decorated with a shrine made up of various crystals and other rock formations.

"I have a surprise for you," Sunny's mom whispered in her ear. "Just wait."

Sunny rubbed the rose quartz against her skin. It had grown warm and seemed to soften.

* * *

Everyone in her dorm was getting ready for their nightly showers. They chatted pleasantly. Of course they gave Sunny's mom
a couple of solid stares, and at the end they crowded around
Sunny and offered her hugs. Molly cried a little, and the girls
stood in each other's arms for several minutes. Then Sunny
walked down the hallways, afraid that if she moved too quickly,
the doors of the old building would slam shut and prevent her
departure. Her mother looked around, and Sunny thought
maybe she felt the same way. As the giant oak doors closed
behind them, Sunny nearly swooned.

Her mother ticked her head to the side. "I thought we would
never get out of there. We're going to a hotel tonight, and we
can get on the road first thing in the morning."

Sleep is going to feel so good, Mabel said, yawning.

The ladies had wedged themselves into the backseat. Sunny
trilled with nerves.

"Here." Sunny's mother handed her something wrapped
in tinfoil. "I warmed it up at the University Market." Sunny
opened the package, and her nostrils filled with the smell of
green chile and beans and cheese. "I got one from Avrora before
I left. I . . ." She hesitated for a moment. "I know what it's like
to miss home."

"Thank you, Mom," Sunny said.

What? You're not going to share? Millicent pointed her chin
upward. *Well, that's rich.*

While Sunny had been putting food in her mouth at all
the appointed times since September, this was the first meal in
months she felt like she had actually eaten.

* * *

Sunny did not speak to her mother much, and her mother did not ask her to. Instead, in their room with the queen-size bed and the small window with the lace curtains, Sunny's mother rubbed the crown of Sunny's head, fingers bathed in lavender oil, so Sunny reached a semi-meditative state, as the ladies of Taos floated above her head. And though she did not truly sleep that night, things finally began to slow down.

When they crossed the border into New Mexico and passed the welcome sign, Sunny's eyes grew so heavy she knew sleep was finally coming to her.

"What does home even mean?" Sunny said. "Because some people thought that St. Anthony's was home."

Her mother shrugged. "Someone once asked a famous painter why she became an artist. She said it was because she liked the smell of paint. Your body always knows when you're in the right place, and if you're paying attention, it will tell you when you're in the wrong one until you listen." After a few minutes, she said, "It's a beautiful thing to make the contribution you're going to make where you want to make it. Not everyone has to leave and stay gone. And," she added, "it's okay to be fourteen and live at home and just be. It's all a dream anyway, kiddo. A beautiful dream you can either be awake in or sleep through."

Sunny thought of things that had come to seem like a dream, like mornings at the coffee shop with Ricky, the farmers' market on Saturdays, and concerts at the bar that seemed like something out of Star Wars and always had the best bands, and where they let kids dance until ten.

She couldn't wait to tell Ricky about her crazy boarding-school dream.

"Wake me up for it?" she said.

"Of course," her mother said.

And then, suddenly, Sunny was asleep.

Sunny's mother shook her. She didn't have to tell her what was happening or why. Sunny sat up straight. The entire canyon leading up to Taos was white with snow. The Rio Grande was on one side and a wall of rock jutted up the other. The road curved dangerously before her. Sunny had always thought this pass and its possible treachery were Taos Mountain's way of keeping all but the most daring out. You had to risk your life to get there.

I had a nervous breakdown, you know, Georgia said.

Me too, Millicent mused. *Clark Gable drove me to it. Broke my heart.*

My love and I wrote twenty-five thousand pages of letters to each other, Georgia said. *People ought to write more letters.*

There's nothing like it, Mabel said. *Coming over this pass.*

"Here we go," Sunny's mother said as they climbed over the lip of the curve.

Ever since Sunny could remember, her mother had done the same thing, taking her hands from the wheel and raising them momentarily above her head. "Wheee!" she would say. In just the right place, as the road curved and the cliff dropped, the earth opened up into a gorge, where the plateau had split in half, probably during some earthquake or another. The Rio Grande slid through the crack, and for just a second it looked as though you were going to leap off the road and into it.

People often died on these curves, and Sunny sometimes wondered if it was because they were too dazzled to pay attention to the road.

After a few moments, Sunny looked over. Her mother seemed shiny. "Mom," she said.

"Mmmm?"

"How did you deal with that school?"

"I smoked weed in the bathroom."

"Seriously?"

Her mother grinned. "No. I mean, maybe once." She looked over. "I cried. I pretended. But you know, my mom had died and there was no way my dad could take me all over with him. My brothers got to stay together, at least, but I had to go alone. And the thing is, it taught me something."

"What?"

"Well," she said, "I decided never to pretend again. Taos doesn't make you do that. It doesn't care about furniture or cars—"

"Or how you look or what clothes you have," Sunny continued. "Or how big your house is."

"No," her mother said. "It doesn't."

"Because no one is the same."

"No."

"There aren't even really subdivisions or anything."

"Nope," her mother said.

"But there's art," Sunny said, something electric climbing her insides. "There's all the food, and people know who you are and they just say okay."

"They do. They say okay."

They sat in silence a few minutes.

"I think maybe Grandfather is trying to keep us all from feeling pain."

Her mother looked over at her, brow furrowed.

"Like," Sunny went on, "if we just follow the road he's laid out for us, we will be safe all the time."

"Yes, I think that is what he's trying to do. Like he's the only one who should be allowed to take risks." Her mother's voice quavered. "No life is safe, honey, but this is *your* life to live and these are your choices to make. You understand?"

"That's why you didn't stop me from going."

Her mother gripped the steering wheel.

"Do you think Ricky missed me?"

"I don't know. We'll find out, won't we?"

Sunny nodded.

I can breathe, Georgia said.

Thank heavens, Millicent agreed. *Look at the sky.*

Sunny turned around and looked at the ghosts. Each of them patted her on the hand. This felt different from when Grandfather had done it. This felt like a blessing, a promise, and a reminder.

Georgia stroked her cheek.

Remember small things can add up to great things, Millicent said, *when paired with the right accessories.* She winked.

We'll see you, Sunny Rain Bronson, Mabel said.

And then they were gone.

"What are you looking at?" Sunny's mother asked.

Sunny thought a moment and took her mother's hand in her own. "We should go see Grandfather. Maybe take him a burrito or something. Thank him for bringing us to Taos in the first place."

"Good idea," Sunny's mom said, making the left into their driveway. She sighed. "Your sister has probably started a vegan-rock movement by now."

"I hope so," Sunny said. Then, with one foot out the door, "It'll be okay."

"What will?" her mother asked.

"If it's a long and winding road or whatever."

"Good, sweets," her mom said. "I'm glad that's how you feel. Because a long and winding road is what you're going to get."

AUTHOR'S NOTE: *The three women of Taos referenced in this story as ghosts are known within the town as leaders and pioneers. Although I took some liberties with their personalities, as I did not know them, some of their dialogue comes from their letters or from books about them. It is important to note that they all struggled with mental illness or depression in one way or another, and they all found some degree of peace in Taos, New Mexico. It is also important to note that they were all white. This was done purposefully. Although I wanted to represent Taos as accurately as possible, I can do so only through the lens of my own experience. In no way would I want its citizens to feel I had appropriated anything that was not mine, as I have enormous respect for all the cultures in Taos. There are many more brave and talented women, Native American and Hispanic, who were game changers and contributors to Taos and its rich history — Eva Mirabal (Eah Ha Wa), Benerisa Tafoya,*

and Josephine M. Cordova, just to name a few – and I
encourage anyone interested to take the time to get to
know them. A good place to start is womenoftaos.org.

My great-grandfather Welles Bosworth, who was an
architect and a world traveler, as well as a painter,
came to Taos in the 1920s and fell in love with it. He
told my grandfather William Eagleton all about it, and
he in turn came in the 1960s and bought land, vowing to
retire here. When I was a teenager, my mother brought
my little brother and me here, and within two months of
being in Taos, like the artist who knew she wanted to
be an artist because she loved the smell of paint, I knew
that I was a Taosena, and though I love to travel and
visit other places, my body knows where it most likes to
be. Taos is a place of mystery and wonder. It is a place
with a community so small and with so many layers, you
cannot help but get to the root of what it means to be
human: that life is about experience and expression and
truth, and possibly angels, but it is also always about a
winding road and embracing everything that goes along
with it. And though I spent a decade on the East Coast
and am grateful for that experience, and have a deep,
abiding love for New York City, I would never choose to
live anywhere but here, in Taos, New Mexico.

ABOUT THE CONTRIBUTORS

David Bowles

David Bowles is a Mexican American author from South Texas, where he teaches at the University of Texas Río Grande Valley. He has written several books, most notably *The Smoking Mirror* (a Pura Belpré Honor Book) and *They Call Me Güero* (a Pura Belpré Honor Book, a Walter Dean Myers Honor Book, and winner of a Tomás Rivera Mexican American Children's Book Award and a Claudia Lewis Award). His work has also been published in multiple anthologies, plus venues such as *Asymptote, Strange Horizons, Apex Magazine, Metamorphoses, Rattle, Translation Review*, and the *Journal of Children's Literature*. In 2017, he was inducted into the Texas Institute of Letters.

> *It was strange to grow up in a little border town, simultaneously rooted in my family's Mexican American culture, with its hundreds of years of tradition, and considered the weird one among my cousins and siblings, the liberal bookworm with bizarre dreams of college. I felt both part of something bigger and estranged from*

it, I longed for the cool, cutting-edge world I read about, but we were a decade behind the rest of the nation. At the same time, I didn't want to leave. I loved South Texas, loved my community (even as it rejected me more and more). It wasn't until I read the writings of Gloria Anzaldúa, a queer Chicana philosopher also from the Rio Grande Valley, that I understood I wasn't alone in feeling divided. Gloria called that in-between place I found myself in nepantla, an Aztec word that meant "the middle." I felt seen. It made the solitude easier to bear. I hope you have found something like that in these pages.

Joseph Bruchac

Joseph Bruchac lives in the Adirondack Mountain foothills town of Greenfield Center, New York, in the same house where his maternal grandparents raised him. He is an enrolled member of the Nulhegan Band of the Coosuk Abenaki Nation, and much of his writing draws on that land and his Native American ancestry. He holds a BA from Cornell University, an MA in literature and creative writing from Syracuse University, and a PhD in comparative literature from the Union Institute of Ohio. He has authored more than 160 books for adults and children, and his poems, articles, and stories have appeared in more than 500 publications, from *American Poetry Review*, *Cricket*, and *Aboriginal Voices* to *National Geographic*, *Parabola*, and *Smithsonian* magazine. His honors include a Rockefeller Foundation Humanities Fellowship, a National Endowment for the Arts Writing Fellowship for Poetry, the Cherokee Nation Prose Award, the Knickerbocker Award, the Hope S. Dean

Award for Notable Achievement in Children's Literature, and both the 1998 Writer of the Year Award and the 1998 Storyteller of the Year Award from the Wordcraft Circle of Native Writers and Storytellers.

When I was a kid, climbing trees, building tree houses in them, and just hanging out on branches forty feet off the ground reading a book was what I enjoyed most. The funny thing is that while it was building my vocabulary (and my interest in writing books of my own one day), it was also building my muscles. Although I didn't "get my growth" until the summer between my junior and senior years in high school – when I shot up six inches – I was strong for my size. I didn't realize that until one day in my junior year during recess, when a much bigger kid tried to bully me by grabbing me by the arm. I just stood there and didn't budge. Then he actually tried to break my arm by slamming it down across his knee. My arm didn't break, but he ended up limping away because he'd bruised his leg so badly. "Bruchac," another kid said, "maybe you should go out for sports." Hmm, I thought. Maybe I should. A year later I was the varsity heavyweight wrestler.

Veeda Bybee

Veeda Bybee grew up in a military household, collecting passport stamps and dreaming of castles in far-off places. She has been writing and drawing since she was seven years old. A former journalist, she has an MFA in creative writing from

Vermont College of Fine Arts. She lives with her family in the mountain west, where she reads, writes, and bakes.

Spending some of my early years in rural Idaho, I grew up loving potatoes. I still do. They are my not-so-secret guilty pleasure. Guilt, because my affection for potatoes and small-town American food had some people telling me I was whitewashed.

When I was a teen, people joked that because I didn't eat rice every day, I wasn't a real Asian. I heard this so much, I started to believe it. Over time I came to realize that I am not what I eat. My identity is much more complex. It's okay to have a soft spot for casseroles made from tater tots and cheddar cheese while also appreciating the time-consuming process of making a Shanghai soup dumpling.

I've lived in many cities and countries since my time in Idaho. While I thrive on the hustle of busy cities, with their late-night hours and possibilities, I also feel at home in a town with a population of barely five hundred. Where there are no streetlights, plenty of potatoes, and a single Thai restaurant at the edge of town.

Nora Shalaway Carpenter

Nora Shalaway Carpenter grew up on a mountain ridge deep in the West Virginia wilderness. A graduate of Vermont College of Fine Arts' MFA in Writing for Children and Young Adults program, she is the author of the YA novel *The Edge of Anything* and the picture book *Yoga Frog*. Before she wrote books, she worked as associate editor of *Wonderful West Virginia* magazine, and she has been a certified yoga teacher since 2012. She currently lives in Asheville, North Carolina, with her husband, three young children, and the world's most patient dog and cat.

I was about nine years old before I realized that most people don't need to drive to trick-or-treat on Halloween. But my closest neighbor was a mile away on a single-lane dirt road and all my friends also lived on mountain ridges, so until I noticed kids on TV walking to trick-or-treat, the concept never even occurred to me.

There are certainly drawbacks to living so far out – clothes shopping, cinemas, and doctor's appointments were all about an hour away. But rural life gave me gifts my urban family members couldn't imagine – the freedom to roam for hours in a ninety-acre forest; a connection to wildlife, which I saw daily, and a passion for its conservation; and ample places to retreat and daydream.

I know my friends and family from large cities felt sorry for me, growing up where I did. But I've always considered myself pretty darn lucky.

Shae Carys

Shae Carys has been writing for as long as she can remember (probably longer, since time can get a little fuzzy around the edges). She holds an MFA from Vermont College of Fine Arts and is a regular contributor to *HorrorHound* magazine. She can usually be found at her laptop, guarding the space from her jealous Jack Chi and doing all manner of things (some of which actually constitute writing). She takes pride in being a member of both the rural and disabled writing communities and in bringing awareness to both.

> The prevailing view on small towns seems to be that if you're rural, you can't be intelligent or cultured or unique. Totally wrong. A good deal of the kids I grew up with were smart, kind, and singular people. My town was better known for its arts and academics than sports, though the one time we did win sectional, it was a much bigger deal than our academic teams conquering state yet again. The prejudice I faced growing up wasn't because I was smart but because I was different, which I eventually embraced and learned to love. Growing up, I didn't appreciate my hometown as much as I do now. I've also learned that prejudice isn't an exclusively small-town thing. It's an ignorance thing, and ignorance doesn't have a zip code.

S. A. Cosby

S. A. Cosby is an award-nominated writer from southeastern Virginia whose short fiction has appeared in numerous anthologies and magazines. His story "Slant-Six" was selected as a Distinguished Story in *The Best American Mystery Stories 2017.* His crime novel *My Darkest Prayer* was published in 2019.

His writing has been called "gritty and heartbreaking" and "dark, thrilling, and tragic." His style and tone are influenced by his varied life experiences, which include but are not limited to being a bouncer, a construction worker, a retail manager, and, for six hours, a mascot for a major fast-food chain inside the world's hottest costume. He resides in Gloucester County, Virginia.

> *Growing up poor in the country is different than growing up poor in the city. If you are poor in the country and your car breaks down, there are no stores within walking distance. There is no city water, so you might not have indoor plumbing. There are no soup kitchens to feed you, and few shelters to house you. Poverty in the country is more complex, more implacable than in the city.*
>
> *But by the very nature of its desolation, poverty in the hills and in the mountains makes you grow up with an unshakable strength born of desperation. Once you have to slaughter a deer to salt the meat for the winter, dealing with the office jerk in the next cubicle is a breeze.*

Rob Costello

Rob Costello (he/him) writes fiction for and about queer youth. He holds an MFA from the Writing for Children and Young Adults program at Vermont College of Fine Arts. He is an alumnus of the Millay Colony for the Arts and the New York State Summer Writers Institute, and his short fiction has appeared in numerous literary journals, including *Hunger Mountain, Stone Canoe, Eclectica,* and *Narrative.* He recently completed his debut young-adult novel, and he lives with his husband and their menagerie of four-legged pals in Enfield, New York.

When I was growing up fat and queer in the 1980s, the woods provided the only sanctuary I had outside the seclusion of my bedroom walls. And what a sanctuary! Everything felt possible in the magical woodland that stretched just beyond my backyard, or in the vast, untrammeled forests of the Adirondack Mountains, where I often spent my summers. Safe among the trees, I could become a superhero, a warlock, an explorer. Or, better still, I could simply be myself, unafraid and unashamed, a genuine luxury at a time when an average day at school presented far greater peril than a night alone in the backcountry. Sure, the wilderness can be a dangerous and unforgiving place, but unlike with fellow humans, you always know where you stand with it. That's a lesson I learned young and have always carried with me.

Randy DuBurke

Born in Washington, Georgia, Randy DuBurke has been a professional illustrator for more than twenty years. He's done artwork for DC Comics, Marvel Comics, the *New York Times*, MTV Animation, and many additional entertainment companies and publishing houses. He is the creator of the picture book *The Moon Ring*, which earned him a John Steptoe New Talent Award. He illustrated the graphic novels *Yummy: The Last Days of a Southside Shorty*, which received a Once Upon a World Children's Book Award from the Museum of Tolerance, *Malcom X: A Graphic Biography*, and *Emanon*, a companion to Wayne Shorter's Grammy-winning jazz album of the same name. His illustrations for *The Best Shot in the West*, a Junior Library Guild Selection, earned him a silver medal from the Society of Illustrators of Los Angeles. He has six reproductions of fully painted comic pages concerning civil rights across the globe on permanent display at the Birmingham Civil Rights Institute.

> *I was born in the South and was surrounded by love from my grandfather and grandmother. I had a wonderful upbringing, playing with friends, reading books (I did not always understand!), watching television, and acting out in the woods behind the house, where I could let my imagination run wild.*
>
> *It was truly a great time. Those deep southern woods helped and still nurture my love for art and writing to this day.*

David Macinnis Gill

David Macinnis Gill is an associate professor of English education at UNC Wilmington, specializing in young-adult literature, and a faculty member at the MFA in Writing for Children and Young Adults program at Vermont College of Fine Arts. His novel *Soul Enchilada* was an American Library Association Best Book for Young Adults, a *Kirkus Reviews* Best Young Adult Book of the Year, a Bank Street College Best Children's Book of the Year, and a New York Public Library Stuff for the Teen Age selection. He is also the author of *Uncanny* and the award-winning Black Hole Sun series, and his work has appeared on a dozen state "best" lists.

When I was in third grade, my father drove me and my older sister and brother to school every day in the termite truck, a beat-up Chevy pickup that started when it felt like it and stopped when we didn't. One morning when the fall skies had opened at dawn and still hadn't closed in time for us to leave, Daddy drove through a road that was more like a river. The high water flooded out the termite truck, and we had to walk the rest of the way to school. When I got there an hour late, muddy and soaked to the bone, the teacher marched me to the back of the room. There, she made me wipe my arms and face and told me that the next time I showed up late or dirty, I would be sent to the principal. Then she demanded an explanation, and I knew there was no way to explain a busted-down termite truck, a mama who worked nights at a yarn mill, a daddy who sobered up on Mondays, and how hard it was to walk to school when you couldn't afford luxuries like a raincoat or an umbrella. So I gave her no answer, just a long silent stare that she only ended when she muttered "white trash" and sent me to my seat. I always knew that we were poor, even among country people, but until that moment, I didn't know how much it mattered to others, even the people we were supposed to trust.

Nasuġraq Rainey Hopson

Born and raised in the rural expanse of the North Slope of Alaska, Nasuġraq Rainey Hopson grew up on fantastic tales from her unique and rich indigenous Inupiaq culture. When she is not writing or creating art inspired by these stories, she is studying how to grow food in the arctic and working at preserving traditional Inupiaq knowledge. She has a degree in studio art and has taught all levels of art from kindergarten to college. She lives with her husband and daughter, three dogs, and a small flock of arctic chickens in Anaktuvuk Pass, Alaska, where she lives off the land and the amazing bounty it provides as her ancestors did for thousands of years.

Most of the people I have met in the "Lower Forty-eight" believe that my people, the Inupiaq people, do not exist. That we are a fictional culture of smiling round fur-clad cartoons, pretty much at the same level as Cyclops and Amazonian tribal women. Even now when ordering goods online, we are told that they don't "ship to foreign countries" or are met with silent disbelief over the phone that someone . . . anyone . . . actually lives so far up north. Isn't it just ice and snow and polar bears? I guess it's not surprising that as a "mythical" being, I would gravitate toward writing. It's as if putting my words on paper proves our existence, every sentence and paragraph a string of evidence.

Estelle Laure

Estelle Laure is the author of books for young adults, including the *City of Villains* Disney series, *Mayhem*, and *This Raging Light*, an Indie Next List selection and a BookExpo Buzz

Book. Her books have been translated into twelve languages. She holds an MFA from Vermont College of Fine Arts and is obsessed with music, the color black, and true crime. She is a proud resident of Taos, New Mexico, for which she thanks her stars every day.

When I moved to Taos from the Bay Area in California after middle school, my yearbook was filled with things like "Have fun in Mexico!" and "Hope you can speak Spanish!" Even my teachers had trouble understanding that New Mexico and Mexico were not the same thing. When we reached our new home and found that the house was full of strange bugs (the first night was all screams when my mom found a centipede in her bathtub), that we had to chop wood for warmth, and that sometimes it would snow so much there was no leaving the house for days, I had a full-on meltdown. There was no shopping. No public transportation. No . . . city. But within weeks I had found the tradeoff in the warmth of the people, the beauty all around me, and the magic that seemed to be everywhere and in every moment. I felt free. The fact that people outside New Mexico seemed not to understand it was even a real location, while occasionally annoying, has come to feel right to me, because it should be a secret wonder. Now when the odd postal worker in a far corner of the country tries to charge me internationally for sending a package home (no, New Mexico, New) or squints at me questioningly and tells me I speak great English for someone living in Mexico, I just say thank you and move on.

Yamile Saied Méndez

Yamile (sha-MEE-lay) Saied Méndez is a fútbol-obsessed
Argentine American author who loves meteor showers, summer, astrology, and pizza. She lives in Utah with her Puerto
Rican husband and their five kids, two adorable dogs, and one
majestic cat. An inaugural Walter Dean Myers Grant recipient,
she's also a graduate of VONA and the Vermont College of Fine
Arts MFA in Writing for Children and Young Adult program.
She's also a founding member of Las Musas, a marketing collective of Latinx women and non-binary authors.

*Every year on July 24, Utah celebrates Pioneer Day to
honor its ancestors — mostly of European ancestry — who
crossed the plains in search of a place where they could
live free of persecution and their children could grow
up to reach their potential. The modern-day pioneers
who arrive in our state from every country now share
the same dreams as those of long ago. Utah is rich
in its cultural, ethnic, and religious diversity. When I
first arrived in a small town nestled in the Wasatch
mountains more than twenty years ago, other immigrants
like me took me in and became my family. Before food
trucks became a gastronomical sensation, every Saturday
morning my friends and I eagerly waited at a gas station
for Argentine pastries or Puerto Rican delicacies. The
taste of home helped shorten the distance and time away
from our loved ones. In my family, food and sports became
the ways in which our cultures fused and evolved into
something unique to us. Empanadas go great with fry*

sauce, and barbecues are much better with a side of arroz con gandules and chimichurri before we head out to cheer for our favorite athletes at the town rodeo grounds or before a fútbol game at Rio Tinto Stadium.

Ashley Hope Pérez

Ashley Hope Pérez grew up in the Piney Woods of East Texas and is the author of three novels. Her most recent, *Out of Darkness*, was described by the *New York Times* as a "layered tale of color lines, love and struggle" and was named one of *Booklist*'s 50 Best YA Books of All Time. It also won a 2016 Tomás Rivera Book Award, a 2016 Américas Award, and a 2016 Michael L. Printz Honor from the American Library Association. When she's not writing or hanging out with her two beautiful sons, Liam Miguel and Ethan Andrés, she works as an assistant professor of world literature at The Ohio State University.

By the time I went to college, I knew how to put my accent away, and I avoided mentioning where I was from. I was ashamed. Once, a professor told me, "There's no way East Texas produced a mind like yours."

Then I found the lovely, lyrical novel House of Breath by William Goyen, which is essentially a love song to the particular part of the Piney Woods where I grew up. That book was beautiful—and so very full of the world of my childhood. It showed me that where I was from could matter in literature.

East Texas did produce my mind; it filled me with

the music of flattened vowels and sultry summers; it taught me longing and loss. I may not ever move back in East Texas, but it's where I'm from, and it's part of why I'm the writer I am today.

Tirzah Price

Tirzah (TEER-zuh) Price grew up on a farm in Michigan, where she read every book she could get her hands on and never outgrew her love for YA fiction. She holds an MFA in writing for children and young adults from Vermont College of Fine Arts and has worked as a bookseller and library assistant. She is currently a contributing editor for *Book Riot*, where she writes about YA books and cohosts the *Read Harder* podcast. When she's not writing or reading, she splits her time between experimenting in the kitchen and knitting enough socks to last the fierce Michigan winters.

I was attending a book club meeting in my hometown library when another member said, "I feel bad for anyone who is gay and lives here. They have to move away in order to have a life." I was dumbfounded—not only that she said it, but that she truly believed it. I couldn't resist speaking up, telling her that I am queer, that I am happy where I am, and that my partner is also from our hometown and this is where we fell in love. I think she was equally surprised to hear this. The narrative that queer people must leave their small towns in order to find happiness is an old, tired story that I see reflected in so much of the media we consume, but it has never been *my lived experience. Instead, I've found myself at turns anxious, joyful, and defensive, but ultimately proud to be someone whose existence defies the common stereotypes of queer people in small towns. There are more of us than you think.*

Monica Roe

Monica Roe was born and raised in a small dairy farming community at the northern end of Appalachia and is a proud first-generation university graduate. While she was studying at Vermont College of Fine Arts, her thesis, entitled "Taking Out the Trash—Confronting Stereotypes of Rural and Blue-Collar Culture in Young Adult Literature and the MFA Academy," was awarded VCFA's critical thesis prize. Her first novel, *Thaw*, was published in 2008. She is also a physical therapist and divides her time between Alaska, where she clinically practices in several northwestern bush communities, and rural South Carolina, where she and her family own a small apiary.

"You don't seem like you're from a rural place!"

I hear it all the time, and I'm still not sure what it means. I suppose there is a societal value placed upon places — a sense that bigger is better, a default assumption that small towns must only breed small minds.

Nonsense.

Small minds exist in all sorts of spaces. As do minds that hunger to be fed, to seek, to expand.

I'm weary of the idea that the only guiding star a kid

from the "middle of nowhere" needs – or should want – is one leading somewhere that really matters. I'd challenge anyone who truly believes this to consider whether their own mind might have a few narrow spaces in need of a bit of expansion.

ACKNOWLEDGMENTS

Sometimes, no matter how long an idea has (secretly) been in your heart, you don't have the courage to breathe life into it without the nudge of someone else. This project might not exist if not for the offhand comment my friend Mary Winn Heider made while she, Rachel Hylton, and I sat writing at a small café near my home. I was lamenting the fact that, while so many wonderful and diverse YA anthologies were emerging, none of them featured rural people. "I keep waiting," I told her. "But no one is making one."

"So why don't you do it?" Mary Winn said, like it was the most obvious thing ever.

I remember the catch in my chest at her words. I admit the idea had crossed my mind before. "But I'm nobody," I said. "My debut isn't even out yet. Who would sign up?"

Rachel shrugged. "Ask Victoria [my agent]. See what she says."

So I did. I also texted my good friend Tirzah Price, with whom I'd had many conversations about rural stereotypes and the lack of authentic rural stories in the market, and asked if she'd write a story for the collection. Her response was instant and full of enthusiasm. (Thank you, Tirzah!) I texted some other authors I knew might be interested, and they were all on board, too. We brainstormed some other names. A short while later, Victoria emailed back that she loved the idea and had already floated it to an editor she was lunching with, who also thought it was great. She gave me advice for next steps and what I'd need for a proposal, like the project was a given.

"Oh my gosh," I told Mary Winn and Rachel. "I think it's happening."

From that moment on, things never seemed to slow down. My deepest gratitude for all the contributors who signed on, committed to helping destroy the myth of a rural monolith that's so pervasive in our culture: David Bowles, Joseph Bruchac, Veeda Bybee, Shae Carys, S. A. Cosby, Rob Costello, Randy DuBurke, David Macinnis Gill, Nasuġraq Rainey Hopson, Estelle Laure, Yamile Saied Méndez, Ashley Hope Pérez, Tirzah Price, and Monica Roe. All of you are such gifted writers, and I'm so honored and grateful you gave your gifts to this book.

Huge thanks to my agent, Victoria Wells Arms, for embarking on this monumental project with such love and encouragement. You are truly the best, and I am one lucky writer.

Special thanks to Cynthia Leitich Smith for offering support and guidance along the way and introducing me to potential contributors.

Thank you to Anna Drury Secino, Tirzah Price, and Meg Cook for their valuable feedback on early drafts of "Close Enough."

Massive thanks to editor Kaylan Adair—also rural!—for immediately seeing the need for this book and its potential to spark critical new conversations about rural America. Thank you also for pushing my writing and this anthology as a whole to make it the strongest version of itself and for being so dang easy to work with. I have loved every moment of the process.

Thanks to the entire Candlewick team, in particular Stephanie Pando for marketing, Jackie Shepherd for the amazing interior design, and Matt Roeser for a beautiful cover.

Thanks to my Marshall University (go Herd!) professor from many years ago, Dr. Shirley Lumpkin, for your course on Appalachian literature. I confess I really didn't want to take it at the time, but it turned into one of my favorite courses ever. Thank you for introducing me to a body of work I didn't know existed and for showing me the importance of non-canon literature, specifically when it comes from a segment of the population often regarded as a cultural joke.

Thank you to my Vermont College of Fine Arts community, without which I never would have met so many brilliant rural authors! Special shout out to my VCFA class, the Secret Gardeners. You guys are the greatest.

And of course, thank you to Mary Winn Heider and Rachel Hylton for that initial nudge that got the whole ball rolling. I suppose there's a lesson here, to never underestimate oneself, which seems to be an all too common trait among writers of all experience levels and perhaps people in general. If you have an idea, readers, I hope you pursue it with your whole heart. This is me, giving you the nudge.

Thank you to my children, Garek, Zander, and Lyra.

And last but never least, thank you to my rock of stability and my biggest supporter, my husband, Josh.